Monstrous Tales

Haunting Encounters with Britain's Mythical Beasts

RAVEN BOOKS
LONDON · OXFORD · NEW YORK · NEW DELHI · SYDNEY

RAVEN BOOKS
Bloomsbury Publishing Plc
50 Bedford Square, London, WC1B 3DP, UK
Bloomsbury Publishing Ireland Limited,
29 Earlsfort Terrace, Dublin 2, D02 AY28, Ireland

BLOOMSBURY, RAVEN BOOKS and the Raven Books logo are trademarks
of Bloomsbury Publishing Plc

First published in Great Britain 2025

Copyright © Rosie Andrews, Jenn Ashworth, Sunyi Dean, Janice Hallett, Jane Johnson,
Dan Jones, Abir Mukherjee, Rebecca Netley and Stuart Turton, 2025
Illustrations © Joe McLaren, 2025

Rosie Andrews, Jenn Ashworth, Sunyi Dean, Janice Hallett, Jane Johnson, Dan Jones,
Abir Mukherjee, Rebecca Netley and Stuart Turton are identified as the authors of this
work in accordance with the Copyright, Designs and Patents Act 1988

Every reasonable effort has been made to trace copyright holders of material
reproduced in this book, but if any have been inadvertently overlooked the
publishers would be glad to hear from them

This is a work of fiction. Names and characters are the product of the author's imagination
and any resemblance to actual persons, living or dead, is entirely coincidental

All rights reserved. No part of this publication may be: i) reproduced or transmitted in any form, electronic
or mechanical, including photocopying, recording or by means of any information
storage or retrieval system without prior permission in writing from the publishers; or
ii) used or reproduced in any way for the training, development or operation of artificial
intelligence (AI) technologies, including generative AI technologies. The rights holders
expressly reserve this publication from the text and data mining exception as per
Article 4(3) of the Digital Single Market Directive (EU) 2019/790

A catalogue record for this book is available from the British Library

ISBN: HB: 978-1-5266-9232-0; EBOOK: 978-1-5266-9248-1

2 4 6 8 10 9 7 5 3 1

Commissioning editor: Therese Keating
Project editors: Emily Jones and Faye Robinson

Typeset by Six Red Marbles India
Printed and bound in Great Britain by Clays Ltd, Elcograf S.p.A

MIX
Paper | Supporting
responsible forestry
FSC® C018072

To find out more about our authors and books visit www.bloomsbury.com
and sign up for our newsletters
For product-safety-related questions contact productsafety@bloomsbury.com

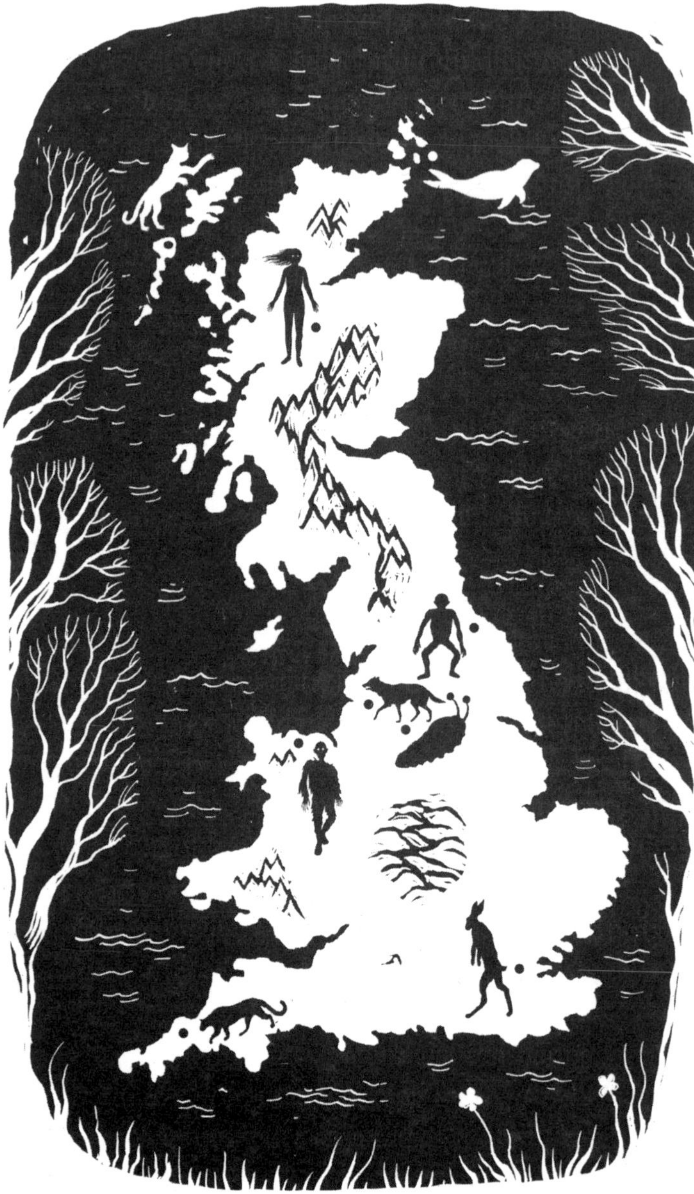

CONTENTS

The Yellow Death Rosie Andrews	1
Old Trash Jenn Ashworth	21
Eynhallow Free Sunyi Dean	49
Boneless Janice Hallett	71
The Beast of Bodmin Jane Johnson	109
These Things Happen Dan Jones	133
The Doctor's Wife Abir Mukherjee	165
Mr Mischief Rebecca Netley	209
Deaths in the Family Stuart Turton	235
A Note on the Authors	264

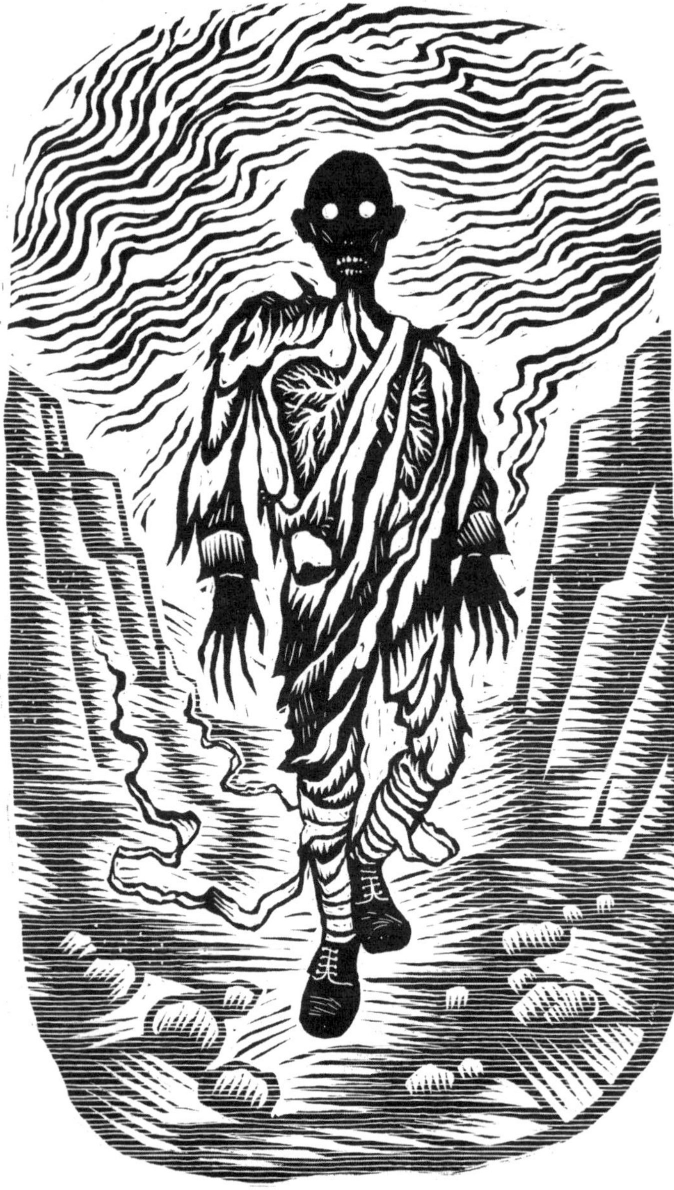

The Yellow Death

ROSIE ANDREWS

Mae'r hen delynau genid gynt,
Ynghrog ar gangau'r helyg draw,
A gwaedd y bechgyn lond y gwynt,
A'u gwaed yn gymysg efo'r glaw
— Hedd Wyn, 'Rhyfel'

Christmas Eve, 1918

'You're lucky, you know. With your father.'

They are walking in the old quarries above Creuddyn. Rhonda wheezes from the climb, but it doesn't stop her talking as she and Elen ford a stream, swollen after the downpours of the last fortnight. The girls balance each careful step on the stones breaching the misted surface, but the water is choppy and their boots are wet to the ankle.

'At least he came back,' Rhonda says. 'You've got that.' She hesitates before pressing the point. 'You can hold on to that. So many can't.'

Elen, concentrating, doesn't answer.

Undeterred, Rhonda says again, 'At least he came back. And after all, although it's not exactly the same because ...' She lets the thought fall away. 'Well, anyway, if my father had come back, everything would be different. Mam and I wouldn't be moving. I'd be going into the Third with you and the others next year. Not to Cardiff,' she adds glumly, observing her socks as more water sloshes over them. 'So you see, you are lucky, in some ways. You shouldn't talk it down, that's all.'

By now Elen has reached the other side of the ford, where she studies the map. 'West, then up round the quarry, then back down towards the church. A fog later,' she reminds herself. This warning, issued by her mother before Elen left at first light, is hard to believe. It's crisp and cold. The sky ribbons white and blue above the hills; a strong breeze the only hint of rougher weather drifting over Anglesey towards Conwy Bay.

'I can hold that,' offers Rhonda, nodding to the map.

'It's all right,' says Elen quietly.

'I don't mind.'

'I know,' Elen says. 'Let's get round the quarry, and maybe ...' But, having no actual intention of giving up the map, she leaves the sentence unfinished.

Rhonda has moved on. 'Mam wants to visit with your mother. Everybody does. Do you think she'll be up to it soon?' She comes to the final stone, obviously not paying attention because she slips and wobbles a moment, giving her companion time to offer a hand.

As she puts her arm out, Elen gains a sudden insight into what she really wants: to see Rhonda land, together with her questions, in the cold, shallow stream. She thinks on this feeling as Rhonda says, 'We could come on Sunday, after church.'

Elen tells herself she doesn't want Rhonda to get hurt. She only wants her to stop talking, for that unbearable look, with its needling combination of envy and martyrdom, to be dispelled.

No more than that.

She helps her friend to the bank, avoiding her eyes.

When both are on dry ground, Elen peels back the leather of her right glove, exposing her wristwatch. The gloves are her mother's: good capeskin, but not completely suitable for a walk, being a bit too fancy, with deep yellow cowslip embroidery. Still, they're warm. That's all that matters.

She worries about time. It's nearly two o'clock. Only a couple of hours of light left. It should be plenty of time to round the quarry and get down to St Hilary's, but if the weather rolls in it will get dark early, and then Rhonda will begin to insist they turn back. Elen, quite determined to reach the church today, knows she will refuse. She's not going to tell Rhonda, but she has a spare map in her knapsack, as well as a handheld mirror for signalling, a mess tin containing sandwiches and apples, a compass and, right at the bottom, two pairs of rolled-up socks.

She also knows, because she saw them when trying to find some space for a mackintosh, that Rhonda packed toffee, a Bible and a photograph of her father. Poor dead Tomi. No spare map, though, and no spare socks either.

Sighing, Elen rummages in her knapsack. She takes out several items before finding a pair of socks and passing them to Rhonda, who accepts with a sheepish thanks. The two girls sit on the ground to unlace their boots.

Elen remembers Rhonda's father in fragments. To her, he is Sunday mornings in church and afternoons at the Jones's table drinking the stodgy farmhouse milk. She recalls how he would swing Rhonda up on his shoulders each day when the children finished at the schoolhouse, and hand out bits of treacle toffee on Christmas morning every year. She hoards these memories – which seem to come from a time when things made sense – but despite her efforts, the time before 1914 is slipping away, pulled under a strong current.

Tomi is why Rhonda keeps calling Elen lucky. Because of his death, Rhonda, her mother and her three little brothers – sweet little chaps in the space between four and nine, with identical cowlicks and pointed chins – are leaving the village, going back to their people in Cardiff. Elen doesn't expect she will see Rhonda much after that.

Having closed up her pack, she realises she has left the mirror on the ground. Unwilling to lose the time, she stuffs it in her pocket. 'We're getting behind,' she says, standing. 'Let's get to the church.'

Rhonda nods amiably, still tying her laces, giving no sign of having noticed her friend's thoughtfulness. With nothing to do, Elen notices how Rhonda's head is haloed by the afternoon light, a trick that has the unfortunate effect of turning her scalp and the thin strands of hair around her crown the same dull yellow. Convinced there should be more contrast in a person – more colour, light and shadow – she is suddenly repelled; yet even a year ago, she recognises, this wouldn't have occurred to her. She has changed. It happened without her noticing, but now she is almost painfully aware of a new contempt for her friend's underdeveloped nature.

She finds herself saying idly, 'There's a ghost story about St Hilary's, or sort of. Do you know it?'

Rhonda shakes her head. 'I don't know any ghost stories. My dad wouldn't hear them in the house. He said he didn't want us scared, and Father Padrig wouldn't like it.'

That sounds right enough. Tomi had been pious, always worried what the rector might say. He was the sort of man to straighten the Bible on its stand every night and dust it as lovingly as his own dead mother's portrait. Of course he banished ghosts. Ghosts were untidy, unmanageable, the real world screaming across his threshold.

Elen's father had told the story a few Christmases ago. He was a big man, Ellis Evans. He had sat at the piano, his broad frame making the instrument look small, and called his daughter to him. She had felt like a doll when he swung her up to his knee like that, although she thinks she was eight or even nine. She can still summon up his breath, pungent with rum, and see her mother by the hearth, a flowering of woad-coloured bruises just beginning at her temple, staring down at her Christmas crochet.

Jiggling his daughter up and down, her father began to play '*Rhyfedd, rhyfedd gan angylion*'. When finished, he asked, 'Shall I tell you a tale?' This mood was rare even before the war and, warming in the glow of his approval, Elen put her head close to his heart to listen to its regular rhythm, and the hypnotic voice above. As he reached the middle of the tale, she put her thumb in her mouth. Seeing this, his expression changed and he shoved her from his knee. 'You're not a baby,' he said roughly.

He never finished the story. She never found out how it ended. From time to time she had begged him, but the mood had not come over him again.

She clings to the memory, but says vaguely, 'It's not that scary.'

'I don't like ghost stories,' says Rhonda. Elen wishes she would say it laconically, or sceptically, with the sort of cynicism that would stake out a claim to being an equal, but Rhonda's voice contains only a childish whine.

Elen says, 'This is a good one. And not exactly a ghost story.' She is being cruel, and knows it.

'Don't,' says Rhonda stubbornly. 'I don't want you to.'

The ground starts to rise sharply. Walking takes more effort, so Elen puts talking aside for a while. To the right and below lies the quarry. Their path traverses its crescent-shaped edge all the way up the ridge, where clouds sidle across to meet the hilltops, smudging their usually sharp relief. As they climb, the wind swells and the sky darkens. A thin layer of snow dusts the ground.

'Lord,' says Rhonda after a while. Turning, Elen sees a shadow beneath her friend's left nostril. Holding the back of her hand to her nose, then taking it away and seeing a daub of blood, Rhonda stumbles.

Fighting not to roll her eyes, Elen searches through her pack again. This time she hands over some tissue paper, saying, 'Sit down. Put your head forward and open your mouth.' Rhonda pales at her friend's unsympathetic tone.

Eyeing the sullen sky, fretting about lateness and still eager to get to the church, Elen fumbles in her pocket for the mirror and gives her friend that, too. 'You can see when it stops,' she says, and Rhonda takes it with a pathetic smile, as if it's a peace offering.

Rhonda gets nosebleeds. She is known for it at school: a bleeder, a bone-breaker, the girl whose fountain pen explodes, one of those unfortunate people who gathers up calamity like knitting needles tugging on wool. Elen, who never gets so much as a cold, is used to it. But as she waits, listening to Rhonda's breathing and stamping her own feet to keep some warmth in her lower body, she finds herself returning to the impulse that began with wishing Rhonda would fall into the water. She wants to scare her. She wants Rhonda to know what Elen has never allowed her to know, that her friend is not only older and fitter, and better at nearly everything, but cleverer. This, she decides, will serve Rhonda right for what she said: that Elen is *lucky*.

She speaks over Rhonda's head, letting the wind carry her words. 'There have always been demons. You don't see them; they're secretive. You come across their leavings – the echo of their footprints, their breath, carrying disease in the water or on the air. A plague is a demon. So is a wave that breaks down a city wall. A war is a hundred thousand of them fighting, invisible in a mist all around us, enticing men to do deranged things.'

Rhonda's reply is muffled by the wind and her hand over her nose. 'My father said superstitious rubbish about monsters only makes us more sinful. It gives excuses for the bad. When the bad is just us,' she finishes doggedly.

Although, however hard she tries, Elen can't remember if it was in her father's version or not, she likes the idea of the mist. Its sinuousness, its opacity, its gift of concealment – they appeal to her. She wants to finish the story, so she continues. 'Hundreds of years ago, a mist just like that came down. Like the breath of a dragon that ravages whatever it touches, it spread over whole villages and countries, but they couldn't tell if it rolled in from the sea, or if it was exhaled by the land itself. They just knew it carried grief with it. They called it *Y Fad Felen*. The Yellow Death.'

It's mostly nonsense, formed only in part from her father's tale, but even so, her own words have begun to exert a chill, causing the intrusion of unwelcome images: sallow skin, an incessant, hacking cough, a smell like something rotting from the inside out.

'The mist could take any shape. For some it appeared as a dragon, letting out a putrid fire. Anyone who breathed it died writhing in agony. Or it came to them as a wandering crone, a hag with burning yellow eyes, spreading its pestilence house to house. They say the children died first,' she added.

It was like a spring welling up inside her. She couldn't stop. 'Died spluttering, coughing as if even the air couldn't bear to be drawn inside them.' She hesitates, remembering something else her father had said between knee bumps, her mother looking on, just a pair of tapping needles and a wan expression. 'It took Maelgwn Gwynedd.'

'The King?' Rhonda sounds sharper, as if she had understood little until Elen mentioned the long-dead ruler of North Wales. 'King in olden times, Miss Bowen said. Didn't she?' she asks, seeming suddenly unsure as she recalls the teacher they had shared when they were small.

'High King of the Brythonic Kingdoms,' says Elen confidently. This is too easy. She was always quicker at her studies than Rhonda. 'The Dragon of the Island, they said he was. The *Fad Felen* decided Maelgwn was a usurper and unnatural lord. To take him, it took the shape of a basilisk. But the King was cunning. He thought he would hide here, in old St Hilary's church, safe on holy soil. Yet when he looked out through the keyhole of the ancient oak door, there it was: the *Fad Felen*, disguised as a gigantic pillar of flame, waiting for him, swimming in a poisonous yellow mist.'

'Don't.' Rhonda's voice wavers. She sends apprehensive glances at the rocks like she expects the *Fad Felen* to slither out and sink its fangs into her ankle.

Elen carries on, 'The King swore then and there never to come out. He would have his servants bring him food and drink, and eventually the *Fad Felen* would give up, and seek out some other victim. But the *Fad Felen* was cunning, too. It tricked him. It returned to its mist form and seeped beneath the sill. As it rose up, it became a snake again, and ate him up, every bit.' She gives the last words a malicious emphasis.

'Don't,' says Rhonda again, getting to her feet, her eyes bulging. Her nose has stopped bleeding but a murky blot stains her upper lip. 'If you're going to be such a beast ...'

'Don't be a baby,' says Elen with a brittle laugh. 'It's just a story.' But it isn't. Part of her is enjoying Rhonda's fear; another part, deeper down, tells her to stop, that she is going too far, but she doesn't.

'... then I'll find my own way back,' Rhonda finishes.

'Don't be so stupid—'

'Stop it!' comes a cry, raking, quite unlike her friend's usual bovine voice. 'Don't call me that! I know you think I *am*. Well, I'm not, that's all. You think we don't know ... that people haven't worked it out. Well, we have. The whole village is talking about it.'

'About what?'

Rhonda has worked herself up to a fever pitch and doesn't notice how the inflection in Elen's voice has changed. 'That your father was getting better, not dying at all. That you and your mother did something—'

'Shut up.'

'It's true. My mother said so. He was strong, wasn't he? I bet—'

Taking a step forward, Elen shoves her.

She doesn't mean to push so hard. She isn't thinking about the narrow path, or the drop. As Rhonda skids, clawing the air, Elen reaches for her – or means to – but it's too late. Rhonda totters, vanishing with a yell down the slippery scree.

After a few moments, Elen scrapes together the courage to walk to the edge. Swaying in the sough, she calls out, 'Rhonda?'

The quarry is sheer, dirty, deeper than she remembers. It peels away like a pitted skin, its bottom a distant chalky crater silvered with smog. Even if she fell all that way, Elen should still be able to see her, but she can only make out rock, and mist settling the quarry floor.

The silence stretches. Elen fills it with catastrophe. What if Rhonda has broken something? She might have hit her head, lost consciousness. Is there time to go for help? In fifteen minutes of hard walking she might reach the saddle over the hill and get down to the village, but not without leaving Rhonda alone in the dark.

How thick the mist has become already. A fog later, she reminds herself, bringing her gloved hands before her face. As she turns her palms outwards, she can barely see the cowslip pattern.

At least he came back, Rhonda had said.

Not all of him. For his sins, Ellis Evans had been vital, with a booming voice, big limbs and oversized hands and feet. Rhonda wasn't wrong about that. But when shipped back, trussed up like a parcel and dragged out of the army van on a stretcher, he had been as shrunken as the mummies in Elen's history books. Muscle and fat had fallen off him, leaving shredded ribs rising like mountains against the crater of his chest. His tongue had blistered so thick from the gas he could hardly form words, so there was only his breath, foetid, rattling in wet and bloody exhalations from his tormented mouth.

He had occupied that bed, heart ticking away, no more her father than a glove was a hand. His skin had seemed moulded to his face instead of *being* his face. Still, that hadn't been the worst thing. The worst was Liliwen, her mother, undressing him – *help, Elen, roll him, do it, bloody hell, girl* – and the lumps under his armpits oozing pus. Elen had scrubbed herself with wire wool after, but in certain lights, even now, her hands seemed to shine yellow with it.

Elen had dreamed of yellow for months, of the mustard gas, a baleful cloud clinging to the feet of gasping men, waiting, flickering tiny tongues upwards to receive them. Every night the dream came, and still, she and her mother had worked. They had trekked up and down the stairs, exhausted, carrying sheets, towels and flannels, changing them so often they couldn't dry them fast enough. Sometimes Liliwen would mumble as they worked, asking why it was so much easier to keep someone on the front line than in a hospital bed, or asking, without answer from Elen, what they were to live on now, but mostly she kept on in silence, scouring and squeezing.

Soon people wanted to visit. To help, they said, and pray with the family. *They can all bugger off*, Liliwen had said fiercely. *Ghouls. I'll give them something to gossip about.* It was the most spirited thing Elen had ever heard her mother say.

Elen had heard that word – lucky – in the village. Lucky to have him back home. Lucky she didn't have to move away, Rhonda had insisted, the offending word descending like a hammer until Elen was happy to see her friend tumble in the stream, happy to see her scared, to see her fall ...

No. Not that. You didn't want that, not really.

But she knows this for a lie, a last line of defence.

Any course of action seems better than this confrontation with her own spitefulness. She puts her pack on the ground, turns about and shins down the first four or five feet of the slope to a jutting ledge. With her long, strong limbs, she is confident she will be able to clamber back up. She will just look, and hopefully see Rhonda waving back at her from the quarry floor, and then they will go home.

The earth is soaked from the rain. As she rests her weight on it, the platform disintegrates and she falls away down the slope, banging her head at the bottom of the beetling quarry wall.

She stands uneasily, her ears ringing, the swales and mounds rising up in dim shapes around her. There is a rank, familiar smell on the air, that she cannot account for. Her right temple burns, and when she puts her gloved hand to it, the leather comes away wet with blood.

Away from the wind, it's quiet and still. The day's light falters, turning her surroundings a dreamy grey. Off to the east, she remembers, the snow-flecked ground gives way to a belt of trees, but any view of this is lost in the thick pall of the weather.

What is that? Something small and dark peeps from the marshy grass.

The signalling mirror. She takes a few steps and retrieves it, realising Rhonda must have dropped it, then immediately wishes she had not. Even those few yards away from the wall, she feels deeper in the mist, set adrift.

'Rhonda?' Her voice sounds different – hollow, very young. 'Rhonda?'

Something answers from a little way off. Her teeth chatter as she stares into the fug, each breath stitched loudly in her ears.

But— That can't be right. She is near-frozen, hardly breathing at all. What was that?

It comes again, a deep, mangled rattle, a brief shudder of footsteps.

A sudden craving to be near what she knows takes over – she wants to see the village lights twinkling at the bottom of the hill, or hear Rhonda's prosaic tread.

She is half-turned towards the quarry wall, deciding whether she will go for help, when the sound, like footsteps, but not at all like the comforting *clap-clap* of Rhonda's hiking boots, comes again. It seems to move around her. Her next thought is unwelcome: the word is *circling*. It's circling you. This idea is so horrible that she has to dismiss it as fanciful, but still, the thought of moving towards the sound is intolerable. She can't bring herself to look, much less move.

But she has the mirror. She can look without looking. She flubs the opening at first. As she unfolds it, it takes a few moments to calm the effect of the whirling fog and her shaking limbs, and see.

Her right eye and cheek fill the frame. Beads of rain or sweat roll down the stark bones of her face. Her voice had sounded young, but in this light she looks old, her skin almost leathered. She draws the mirror away, enlarging its field. The mist has gathered thicker even in the time she has been stood here. She can see nothing.

But she can hear.

She listens, overtaken by a realisation both gradual and horrible, that the noise, making her want to burrow into the ground like an animal, is her own name, repeated over and over – *Elen*.

It crawls over her. She gives way to fright, screwing her eyes shut.

Somehow, her sight cut off like this, she sees more. She sees that she envied Rhonda. It was a soul-scratching thing, that envy, a bitter coveting of her friend's devout father and simple truisms handed down from her mother. Rhonda had called her lucky, but Rhonda was the lucky one. Tomi had never come back. They had sent his body home. He had been buried in the churchyard, decent, mourned by a family that never knew how much worse it could have been.

She had behaved as if her experiences made her better than Rhonda. But she understands now, they didn't. They took something instead, leaving a space quickly filled by the common malice that so easily moves into an empty heart.

Elen.

Its voice is half-drowned, like it breathes the mist.

She will not open her eyes; she will not see.

That last day, around dusk, she had carried a posset up the stairs to the back bedroom. The milk and rum sometimes settled his wild outbreaks of coughing. He was too weak to clear his lungs, so the milk and mucus would run back down his airway, then they would be faced with the task of turning him until everything was out. With this done, he would cry and curse unintelligibly at them, flailing with tobacco-stained yellow fingers.

But that night, at the top of the stairs, her mother had taken the posset out of her hands. 'I'll do it,' Elen said quietly.

'Go downstairs. I'll be there in a minute.' Liliwen's tone was sharp.

Elen had knelt in front of the pittering fire between the thickest walls of the cottage. Through the tiny quartered window she could see a single star, as silver-bright as the one that led the Magi to Our Lord. She warmed her hands and hummed '*Rhyfedd, rhyfedd gan angylion*', letting the melody swell until the tabby lying prostrate by the hearth stalked away, mewing resentfully. When she finally stopped, alert for her mother's reassuring tread on the ceiling, she couldn't make it out. All was silent.

After a while, kept from returning her attention to the fire by the sense that something was wrong, she crept barefoot up the stone stairs. Three from the top, she knelt and peeped down the long landing.

Liliwen occupied her usual stool between the door and the bed. The posset bowl was in her lap, balanced on a pillow, but the stillness of the bundled shape beyond told Elen the bowl was empty. Something new had crept into her mother's posture. Liliwen watched over the wracked shape in the bed as she always did, but her usual manner of fussing was absent. Only her profile was visible, and that was grave, almost puzzled, as if she did not understand how she had come to be there. Putting the bowl on the table, Liliwen clutched the pillow in her left hand, meaning, Elen assumed, to place it under her father's head.

Instead, Liliwen brought the pillow down hard on his face and leant on it. As Elen watched, bewildered, her mother locked her elbows, sealing the fabric between man and woman. Her father must have been asleep, but, as the imperative to breathe resurged, he began to struggle – even in his weakened state, he was so much stronger. His arms found her mother's shoulders. He was moving her back, pushing the pillow away.

Liliwen turned her head, seeing Elen on the stair. The colour fled her face. Caught in her daughter's gaze, she seemed to sag, her will wavering.

He was nearly free.

Elen scrambled up and staggered down the landing. Reaching the doorway, she flew to the other side of the bed. She didn't know what she was going to do until she did it.

She added her weight to her mother's. Liliwen, understanding, lurched as if to push Elen away, but up close, her eyes were wild and desperate; her instinctive rejection of her daughter's silent aid was short-lived. Elen pushed down. Now the pillow was held by the strength of two. As powerful as he was, he could not overcome it.

She hardly heard her mother's whisper – 'He died. We say he died.' – as her father thrashed and kicked, but his fight was bleeding away. Elen kept her eyes screwed tight, breathing in his stench. She would not see. Not, not, not ...

Now, swaddled in the mist, snatching every breath, the past and the present run together. Something is down here with her. Something that exhales rum, and running sores the colour of visceral fat ...

She bolts for the cliff path. Between witless sobs, her awareness anchors to a single idea: escape. She can hide in the church. The thought of its great stones, heavy, impassable, seems to pull her heavenward, and although somewhere deep down a voice whispers her betrayal – *Rhonda is still here, somewhere* – her fright is a great, booming thing, and her slower friend is soon forgotten.

She claws at the base of the slope, nails tearing on limestone. She has to get away, far away from the halting, gasping noise that follows, a noise so like a human being trying to breathe that it is a few moments before she understands she is making the sound, and a few more before she begins to know in her marrow that she won't find the path, that she was never supposed to, that the ending to the story is happening, here, now.

The mist encircles her. Its touch is anticipatory, slight. Icy tendrils follow the lines of her neck and shoulders, the air vibrating with strains of familiar music. All around the smell is sulphurous, mustard-caustic ... yellow.

She bends and seizes on something heavy, her nails scratching and bleeding against rock. Grunting, she prises the stone from the browning grass, and lifts it over her head.

A hand encircles her raised forearm. Enveloped in rotting flesh, she turns, bringing the rock down with all her might on what she cannot see. There is a sickening crunch, then, much quieter, a reedy gasp, before the fiend drops to the turf.

Elen stares.

The mist is thinning, clearing.

Rhonda lies on the ground. Her face is the colour of filthy sheets. The angles of her body are jarring. From somewhere in the colourless thatch of her hair seeps an obscene darkness and, as Elen watches, numb, its shadow spreads like wings over the deadened ground, and mingles with the rain-soaked earth.

Elen is beginning to fathom the sight when, from just behind, the hand takes her wrist again in a grip like iron. As she looks down on long, tobacco-stained fingers, pianist's fingers, the reek of sulphur floods her nostrils. She glimpses a maw of yellowed teeth, then her first scream echoes off the quarry walls.

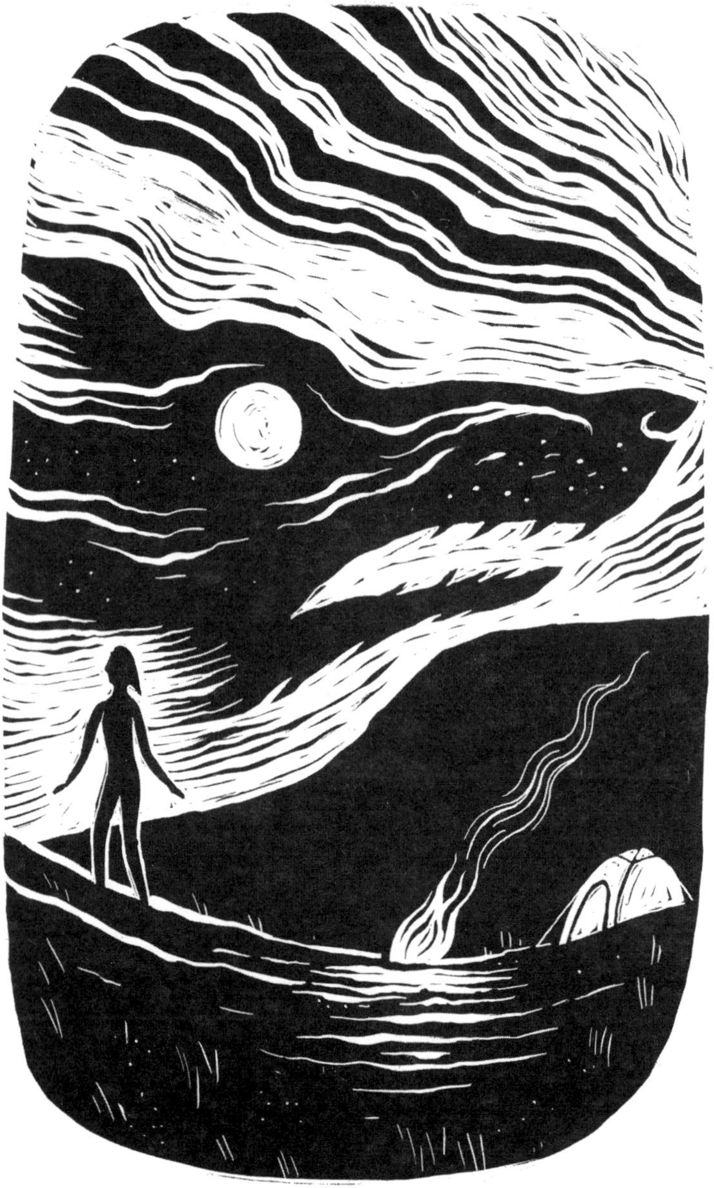

Old Trash

JENN ASHWORTH

'I remembered certain of Bessie's tales, wherein
figured a North-of-England spirit called a "Gytrash",
which, in the form of horse, mule, or large dog,
haunted solitary ways, and sometimes came upon
belated travellers'
— Charlotte Brontë, *Jane Eyre*

'… a frequent visitor to Lancashire […] this sprite is
considered a certain death-sign, and has obtained the
local names of "Trash" and "Skriker". He generally
appears to one of the family from which death is
about to select his victim. […] On most occasions,
"Trash" is described as having the appearance of
a large dog, with very broad feet, shaggy hair,
drooping ears, and eyes "as large as saucers". When
walking, his feet make a loud splashing noise, like old
shoes on a miry road'
— *Transactions of the Historical Society of Lancashire
and Cheshire*, Vol. 12 (1860)

'[Old Trash] shrieked at times and was said to be about the width of a lane and the size of a woolsack; flames came from his mouth, and his eyes were as big as dinner plates. Although it might be seen, the hound could not be struck because it had no substance'
— Terrence W. Whitaker, *Lancashire's Ghosts and Legends*, 1980

The day of the trip was hot, the sky clear and nearly cloudless. There'd been a train from Manchester, then a local bus service called the Witch Hopper, which took them on a circuitous route through the little towns and villages around Pendle before finally dropping them within a mile of the lower Ogden Reservoir, beside which they planned to camp. It wasn't an official site, but there was a pub nearby where they could use the toilet, and it was only going to be overnight.

Rachael struggled with the tent pole, trying to push it into the fabric socket where it, apparently, was supposed to fit. Mae was sitting in the long grass nearby, leaning against her rucksack and swiping furiously at her mobile phone, resolutely not helping. The pole escaped Rachael's grasp and sprung onto the grass. She silently counted to five, then bent to retrieve it.

'At least we've got nice weather,' she called, feeling the sweat on her hairline. There were midges, but there was no point in complaining about them. The pole whipped backwards and forwards, a thing possessed, and Rachael sweated and swore under her breath until – nipping the skin between her thumb and finger in the process – she managed to force it into place. There. She stood back and admired the tent: bright against the sun-baked grass and the dark, hazy rise of the wooded hill behind them. *Ta-da.*

'Shall we unpack? Make a cup of tea?' She winced at the sound of her own voice – eager and high-pitched. Mae grunted and Rachael risked a glance at her. Her face still tilted phone-wards, her bare legs bent at the knee and gaping wide like a puppet whose strings had been cut. Just beyond her, the grey square lip of the lower reservoir; behind them, Fell Wood.

'Or we could just dump the stuff in the tent and go down to the pub? Cold drinks? Some chips?'

Mae huffed and tucked the phone into the front pocket of her shorts. She'd made them herself, cut down from a brand-new pair of jeans with a pair of kitchen scissors.

'Do you want to get changed?'

'No. It's too hot.'

She must not stare. It irritated Mae and was likely to provoke an argument. Instead, Rachael heaved her own rucksack up from the grass and put it inside the tent. Threw the sleeping bags, still bundled up tight, in after it. Mae slapped at a midge on her bare thigh. What she was wearing didn't matter, Rachael told herself. What Mae wore fell into the category of things over which she was no longer willing to pick a battle.

'Mae? Mae, love? What do you reckon?'

'Will they have Wi-Fi in the pub? I can't get any signal up here.'

'They might,' Rachael said. 'But I thought we could …'

'Are we going then?'

Mae had already set off, striding along the footpath that hugged the concrete edge of the reservoir. There was no guardrail. It would be possible to sit on it and touch the water with the toe of an outstretched foot. Maybe they would do that later. Rachael looked at the still, grey-indigo surface and knew that no matter how long this rare summer's succession of hot days lasted, the water down there would be very, very cold. Then she retrieved her purse from the tent and hurried to catch up. The air was still and hot and thick with insects: she walked quickly through a cloud of them, feeling them in her hair.

But things were going well. The trip had been a good idea. Rachael had not allowed herself to hope that this would be a time – just twenty-four hours was all that Mae would agree to – in which they would build bridges. If she handled it carefully, and if everything went without a hitch (she'd checked the weather forecast hourly the day before they were due to leave), it would simply be a period of time when hostilities would cease. And, yes: she knew it was unlikely Mae would be able to get signal on her phone and that's why she'd chosen Pendle Hill, the shadow of it falling onto the reservoir, the steep bank of its foreside supervising Newchurch and Sabden and Barley. She had no interest in the tiny old villages and their little pubs with brooms over the door and post offices with adverts from crystal healers pinned to their notice boards and racks of cheap postcards with pictures of comedic, friendly witches on them: she cared only about the hill, and its special property of cutting off the signal that her daughter relied on.

The footpath met the road: Mae vaulted over the stile, her boots slapping the pavement as she landed.

'This is nice, isn't it?' Rachael clambered after her.

'It's boring,' Mae said.

'How can you be bored?' Rachael knew what she sounded like but couldn't stop herself. 'There's all this scenery, and the birds – I think I saw a kite earlier – and this is a lovely walk, and,' she paused, panting, 'we've got each other for company.'

'That's what I'm talking about,' Mae said. Then, in one of her turn-on-a-sixpence mood changes, smiled – a smile as flimsy as a trick of the light – and waited for Rachael to catch up. 'We're going to eat at the pub?'

'We can if you want,' Rachael said. 'Or we can make a fire and do some potatoes in tin foil. Would you like that?'

Mae put her hand over her face to shield her eyes from the sun. 'Pub. Pub tea, definitely.' She looped her arm through Rachael's, and they walked alongside each other like that for a while, along the centre of the road, flanked by hedges.

When Mae stopped to pick cow parsley and thread it into her hair, Rachael waited for her, saying nothing, and hoping that she'd take her arm again when she was finished. And she did. It made Rachael feel grateful, absurdly chosen. She stroked Mae's arm, smelled her sweat and the bruised cow parsley, ignored the reek of cigarettes from her hair and walked onwards, the pub, according to the map, just around the crook in the road.

Was this how Mae's boyfriend felt? The one she snuck out to meet, late at night? The one who drove her around in his car? Chosen, like that? Or was it the other way around? Was it Mae herself who felt chosen? Was it about feeling special? They trudged on in a silence that was not quite companionable, and the pub appeared.

'Come on,' Rachael said, 'let's go inside.'

'Mum,' Mae said gently. She wanted something. They hesitated in the doorway, the light picking out the fine hair on her arms and turning the rest of her into a silhouette. 'Can I have something to drink as well? A proper drink. Seeing as we're on holiday?'

Delay. That was the advice from the keyworker. Don't get drawn into an argument; don't fall into the trap of conflict.

'Let's look at the menu, shall we? See what they've got? Come on, love. I'm starving. Aren't you?' Rachael held her breath.

'They'd better have something vegetarian,' Mae said.

'I'm sure they will. And you can order the drinks for both of us,' Rachael said. 'I'll give you the money.'

They went inside.

*

He wasn't a boy, though – the one Mae had chosen, or who had chosen her. He was a man. Rachael had been able to do what was needed with a keylogger on her daughter's laptop. She was still paying for that laptop, which meant that she still owned it. It was a household possession and not quite Mae's private property, not in the same way an email account was. Though Rachael had got into that too – and the second mobile phone tucked inside a slit in the side of her daughter's mattress. She had seen the messages. The photographs Mae had been sending. The presents too: trainers still in their shoeboxes under her bed, drawers full of perfume bottles and make-up sets, mainly untouched. Vodka bottles, half-empty.

Rachael watched her daughter's back as she stood at the bar: the way the soles of her boots were worn unevenly, the coltish length of her legs. She looked around the pub. No danger – by which she meant, no men. A young woman reading a newspaper and thoughtfully eating chips with her fingers. No threat at all. A couple of female hikers sitting in a nook beside the unlit fireplace – probably an actual couple, judging by the way they sat together, sharing a plate of sandwiches in a kind of unfocused intimacy she felt guilty observing – but there was no one else. The pub was safe.

*

Mae came back from the bar. Plonked two bottles of Perrier, two ice-filled glasses, on the table. Flung herself onto the seat.

'She wanted ID,' she said sullenly. 'Stupid bitch.'

'Never mind,' Rachael said mildly, 'maybe next year. You do look …' Mae was distracted, already fiddling with her phone, and Rachael caught herself in time and let the sentence tiptoe away into the shadows, unspoken.

You do look underage …

You do look like you need a hair wash …

You do look – lovely.

'Mum? Mum? You hear me? No Wi-Fi. Nothing. Can you believe it?'

Mae sat fidgeting on the stool, then stood up again. Always so restless. 'I'm going to the toilet,' she said. 'Order some food for me, will you? I'm starving.'

*

The woman behind the bar – gloriously fat, with smudged black eyeliner and dyed red hair – caught Rachael's eye as she leafed through the menu.

'I can't serve her alcohol,' she said, 'not even a shandy. They'd hold me personally responsible.' She smiled apologetically. 'Sorry.'

'I'm actually rather glad that you didn't,' Rachael said, and laughed, as if she was making a joke she was relying on the woman to understand.

'Soup is lentil and tomato,' the red-haired woman said, 'but there's not much left. You camping?'

Rachael blushed. Camping – and not even in a proper campsite. It was probably against the law.

'Just for the night. My friend said ... well, it was a bit impromptu. If you could tell us who owns the land ... ?'

'I don't care about that,' the woman said, and laughed. 'You'll want to be careful going back, though.'

'Really?'

Rachael wanted her to wait – to save her stories of the pixies and haunted wells and boggarts and ghosts of witches from times past – until Mae came back. 'Tell my daughter,' she wanted to say. She'd enjoy that. But perhaps she wouldn't. Maybe Mae was too old for ghost stories now.

'No streetlamps on the lane. You've not seen proper dark till you've been out here at night,' the woman said. Rachael ordered sandwiches and chips and returned to her seat.

*

Did he know, this man, that Mae was only fourteen? That was probably part of the attraction. The time for delicacy had long since passed. She'd said as much to the school: 'My daughter's boyfriend is twenty-eight years old. He is raping her and I believe his friends are too,' and then again, to social services, who were overstretched – and anyway, Mae came from a nice home in a nice part of town and her schoolwork wasn't suffering, not that much, not really, and she was a good weight. Rachael said it again, to the police, who weren't able to do anything without proof, and proof was what Mae would not provide – not a word against her boyfriend who had been banned from the house, from the street, but who would park up by the swings and to whose car she would flit in the night, out of a locked window, through a locked door. Mae had threatened, in fact, to set the house on fire if the locks were used again, and Rachael believed her.

It might be worse, though, she thought, watching her daughter come back from the toilet, wiping her wet hands on the front of her shorts. It might be worse if she felt herself a victim. Felt that a terrible wrong had been done to her – as it had. Perhaps better for her to feel she was part of a great romance and have Rachael around to gather the pieces when they fell?

Mae sat down and started impatiently flicking through an abandoned newspaper, thrumming with boredom. Was it better to wait for this man to lose interest in her? Wait for Mae to grow up? The two were the same thing, most probably. She was on the pill. At least there was that: the GP had prescribed it without turning a hair. And could all broken things be mended? The keyworker had been silent on this matter. Had only advised that home should be – above all – a place of peace and calm and safety. A refuge to which Mae could always return.

*

'We can walk tomorrow. Right up the hill if you want to. Or just ... chill out? Near the tent. Did you bring a book?'

Mae snorted. The table they were sitting at was next to a rack of leaflets on tourist attractions that were no good unless you had a car, and hikes, which were no good if you didn't want to do them – and Mae abandoned the newspaper and started to rake through them.

'We don't have to decide right now. We could just play it by ear?'

The woman with the red hair appeared with their sandwiches, smiling.

'There's a lot that camp up there,' she said, 'you won't get into any trouble about it. Don't fret.'

'We weren't planning to light a fire,' Rachael lied. Mae glanced at her meaningfully and rolled her eyes, which the woman noticed, and giggled at.

'You can have a fire if you like. You'll probably want one.'

'The dark. Yes, you said. It gets very dark here at night,' Rachael said stiffly.

'And Old Trash, he don't like the fire,' the woman said, and winked.

Rachael knew she was supposed to ask who Old Trash was – some local legend, no doubt, a flasher or a hobgoblin or a sprite – the hills were soaked in these types of fictions, their walking guide packed with them, as if you could follow a public footpath right to the site of a haunting and call up the ghost to arrive for inspection, just for your own pleasure. But she'd changed her mind about the potential for these stories to entertain Mae. The woman was being entirely too familiar, and Rachael wasn't going to play along.

'What's Old Trash?' Mae asked, delighted, and Rachael hated her. She should make her mind up. If she wanted the bedtime ghost stories and the petting and admiration from strangers, she couldn't have the phone and the boyfriend and the bottles of vodka. It was one or the other. She was either a child, or she wasn't. Rachael sipped at her water, the fizz burning the roof of her mouth – and kept silent.

*

Peace. Calm. Safety. Rachael had flushed with shame when the keyworker had mentioned this, and the woman had handed her a tissue.

'I do try to keep things as calm as possible,' she'd said. But Rachael had not mentioned the most recent scuffle over the mobile phone. Had not outlined the way she and her daughter had actually come to blows over the thing. Rachael had tried to prise it out of Mae's hands; Mae had kicked her, hard, and before Rachael had time to think about it – before she'd consciously decided what she was doing to do – Mae had thrown the phone onto the floor and Rachael had her hands full of Mae's hair and was pulling at it, shaking her around like a doll. Mae had hit her in the face and the two of them had stepped apart from each other in the hallway, panting, Rachael nursing a red mark on her cheekbone that a day later would come up in a bruise. Even as it happened, she realised the whack to the face could be some kind of comfort to her because it was proof Mae was stronger than she looked and could defend herself from this man if she ever felt the need to. But Mae only screamed – so loudly the neighbours both sides and beyond could hear.

'You've hurt me! You bitch! You bitch!'

Rachael, still panting, saw the hair that was clinging to her fingers, hair she'd ripped from her daughter's scalp. She dropped to her knees, scrabbling for the phone, which Mae reached first, scooped up and ran out of the front door with, slipping away like water down a plughole. She didn't come home for three days.

Rachael had not told the keyworker about any of that. She'd only taken the tissue and dabbed at her eyes. There was a poster taped to the wall – something to do with drugs. There was a helpline number. The poster was crooked and Rachael felt a sudden overwhelming desire to get up from her chair and straighten it. She turned her gaze down to her sensible lace-up shoes and her second-best pair of tights. She'd thought carefully about what to wear for this meeting: wanting to look professional and neat, but also motherly. There was no man of the house, but there was no need to look as if she had resigned herself to being left on the shelf permanently, now was there?

'Yes. Peace and calm. Of course. She does know she can always come home. I never lock the door on her. I'd never do that.'

*

One of the books she'd read over the last year had advised 'love-bombing' a wayward child, which was a technique that cults used on the damaged and down-at-heel to get new recruits, but which was also supposed to repair a splintering bond between parent and offspring. The gist of it was to let the child get their own way for well-defined periods of time each week – to reverse the normal order of things – to cherish them and meet their every demand, as you did with a newborn baby. Accordingly, Rachael had let Mae order two different types of dessert and play as many games of pool with the red-haired woman behind the bar as she wanted. She'd watched her daughter and this woman bond – Mae laughing at all of her jokes and being entertained by her tall tales about the Pendle witches and their familiars: cats and goats and even, according to local lore, a dog called Old Trash that still roamed Fell Wood, baying at the moon, chewing up sheep and generally making a nuisance of himself. He was, according to the woman (*Triana* – and what kind of name was that?), the devil himself in canine form.

'What's so scary about meeting the devil?' Mae asked.

That was the thing about children: they weren't fearless because they were brave, they were fearless because they didn't yet know how terrible the world could be.

The woman behind the bar dried her hands on a towel, slung it over her shoulder and smiled mysteriously.

'I couldn't tell you. Never had the pleasure myself. If Old Trash comes to you, you'll hear him before you see him. He always sounds like he's running through water, even if you're in the middle of a cow field. Only a witch could see him and live.'

'And yet everyone seems to know what he looks like,' Rachael chipped in, having exhausted all the leaflets, the newspaper and as much of an abandoned Catherine Cookson novel as she could stand. She went on, 'His dark shaggy coat. His eyes as wide as saucers, glowing with the fires of hell. Feet as big as church Bibles. Sounds like plenty of people have had a good look at him and survived to tell the tale.'

This, right now, what she was doing, was why Mae didn't want to spend time with her anymore. Rachael knew this and was helpless to stop herself.

'Right you are,' Triana said, and laughed.

'We'd better get going. Can I pay the tab?' Rachael asked, annoyed with all of this.

'Already?' Mae's expression darkened.

'The light's going,' Rachael began, and Triana interrupted.

'Your mother's right, sweetheart. You want to get back early enough to make your fire. Get yourself tucked in. But come back tomorrow if you like. We'll do you a cooked breakfast. Real coffee. How about that?'

Mae, mollified, headed towards the door and Rachael followed her. Her daughter was in one of her rare talkative moods. It was all Triana this, and Triana that, and Rachael trudged behind her, nodding – not that Mae was paying any attention to her.

*

The light went suddenly: probably because of the hill. With it, the heat. As they found the footpath where it cut into the lane and clambered over the stile, Mae started to shiver.

'Maybe we should have that fire,' Rachael said. 'We could make tea?'

'We should definitely have a fire. Triana says ...'

'Old Trash doesn't like a fire. Yes, I heard.'

Mae laughed. 'I'd love to see him. A great big slavering dog.' She lifted her phone. 'I'd take a picture of him, then leg it.'

'Would you?' Rachael imagined her tone was mild, faintly interested.

'There's a group, apparently, that goes out at night looking for him. Triana says you can pay the guide and go out on a walk with them. We should have done that.'

'Maybe next time?' Rachael said hopefully.

'Definitely.'

Definitely! She wanted to come again. It was like being in love, this – hopelessly, horribly in love – then finding a note in your school bag from the boy you'd had your eye on, and realising that he'd had his eye on you too, all along. Rachael's head fizzed with plans: they would come back soon. Maybe in a fortnight or so. As soon as Mae wanted to. And this time, they'd avoid the bloody pub.

'Apparently, he sends you nuts if you see him. Barmy. Triana says there's people who have been up on the hill at night,' she gestured vaguely, 'and ended up walking miles without knowing where they were. They come down in the morning and they've gone fucking mental. He gets into your head and Triana says …'

'Triana says a lot. I wonder if she's part of the business that runs the walks,' Rachael began, and Mae laughed and swatted her on the arm – a little too hard to be playful.

'Triana says,' she went on, 'he comes to let you know someone in your family is going to die. Rather you than me.'

'Charming,' Rachael replied, feeling absurdly hurt. But yes, rather her than Mae.

'It makes sense,' Mae said. 'All those witches must have been on to something …' She flicked her hair away from her face: Rachael saw it move in the dark – a ripple – and smelled cigarettes again. Where was she getting them from? Rachael had turned her room upside down.

'Well, we're here now. Old Trash or not, I'd like a fire.'

'I'm going to go through the woods,' Mae said. Informing, not asking. That was her way now. There was barely enough light to see by – the reservoir to their right, the steep bank of Fell Woods sloping upwards to their left. 'Triana says if you go up to the top, where the trees clear a bit, you can get a good signal. She says it'll only take five minutes. You boil water if you want, I'll be back before it's ready.'

They were in sight of the tent now: brash and orange and oddly shaped, as if built to withstand a terrible storm – the type that never happened in England. The man in the shop had said it was a good tent. Easy to put up and take down on your own. But looking at it now, it seemed flimsy and cramped and Rachael wondered if they'd get any sleep at all, or if they'd lie awake all night, elbowing each other and shivering.

'I'm not sure you want to go crashing around in the dark, do you?' she said, as mildly as she could muster. They were there now and Mae knelt, unzipped the tent, crawled in and emerged with a sweater.

'I'll bring you back some sticks for your fire,' she said indulgently. As if she were the one doing the love bombing, not Rachael, and she were the one delaying answering difficult questions in order to avoid the nonsense of a silly confrontation.

'There's nothing so important on your phone that it can't wait until tomorrow, can it?'

'Don't ... *start*.'

'Mae?'

She was already off, striding up the bank that swiftly became wooded. Rachael heard her, the twigs and leaves crackling underfoot, and then – when she turned on the torch setting on her phone – saw her, the cool bright light swinging around through the branches of the trees. It wasn't a big hill. And it wasn't a heavy wood: nothing like the woods in fairy tales. It was just a rise – a little rise with some trees on it. And at the top, there would be signal, or there wouldn't, and Mae would answer her text messages and post a picture of herself posing against the deepening dusk on Instagram, pretending to look scared because she'd seen the witches' dog. Then she'd Snap-talk or whatever with the man she was seeing – and there could be no real harm in that, not when she was here, and he was – well, wherever he was, doing whatever he did. Rachael didn't want to think about him. And anyway, as Mae had so often reminded her, what exactly was she going to do about it?

'Don't be long ...' she called, and her voice spooled away across the surface of the reservoir and echoed back to her, and there was no answering call from the trees. She walked along the edge of the woods, gathering fallen sticks.

*

After half an hour, it was full dark and Rachael had the fire going and the water boiling. She made tea. She set the two metal cups – brand new from the camping shop where she'd bought the tent (love bombing was *expensive*) – on a stone and poured water from the pan into them. She watched the steam rise and waited. Mae was always a little elastic around time: could get caught up easily in her online life. She was probably safer alone up at the top of that hill – probably less than a quarter of a mile away – than she was at school, or wherever it was she went when she was supposed to be at school. Rachael walked to the edge of the woods and called up to her. Once, twice. And of course there was no answer. She held her breath and listened. Was that Mae's voice she heard? Or perhaps a thin stream of water running through the concrete channel down the hill and into the reservoir? Or birds, settling in for the night? Birds, most likely.

She sat on her rucksack in front of the tent, the ground quite cold now – and, beyond the light of the fire, found herself unable to pick out the edge of the reservoir, the shape of the hill against the sky, or much of anything else. The fire crackled and popped – loud in the wide silence she waited in – and she drank her tea. Suppose Mae didn't come back? What should she do then? Should she wait an hour? More? Mae could easily sit up there and chat for an hour, and she'd be furious if Rachael over-reacted, and then the whole trip would be spoiled. They still had tomorrow. Tomorrow they'd wake up together in the tent, and it would be light and quiet, and they wouldn't go back to the pub for a cooked breakfast, they'd have another fire and boil eggs and eat bananas slit open and stuffed with chocolate and warmed inside tin foil. Rachael listened again. There were sheep – or a sheep, perhaps – nearby. She heard its baby-voiced bleat. And nothing else except the crackling fire.

She could go up the hill herself. Go and retrieve her daughter and risk the fight. She was talking to that man. The man who had a car. Who was perhaps even now in it, picking up Mae's location from her Find Your Friend or whatever it was – the app he used to supervise her – and coming to collect her. The road they came in on curved around the back end of Fell Wood: the bus had dropped them off there and all they'd needed to do was carry their packs downhill to the water's edge. He could just as easily ... Rachael stood up. But it would be foolish and perhaps unsafe to leave the fire, and not be here when Mae came back, wanting her tea and her bed.

Another fifteen minutes passed. She could walk down to the pub if it came to it. Would Triana be there? Cleaning, perhaps, after the serving hours were over? Or maybe even sleeping there, in a room upstairs? Rachael could wake her up and use the telephone and call someone – who? Mountain Rescue? This was hardly a mountain. And what would they do? Laugh at her, probably. Triana would make her a coffee and try to have a woman-to-woman chat about raising teenagers, about giving them their freedom, about making sure home was always a place of peace and calm. 'You've got to let her come to you,' she'd say, and Rachael would have no option but to nod, humbly, and take the blame. Even imagining this speculative kindness sent her into a rage. She stood, gathered more sticks, and built up the fire. It would be quite visible now, in the dark. Would help Mae to get back if she'd got muddled in the woods and come down the hill too far along the path.

*

Mae loved bananas with chocolate. For a while, when she'd been a toddler, it had been the only thing she'd reliably eat. Bananas, mashed up and warmed in the microwave with a piece of chocolate mixed into them. Not melted, only softened. Rachael had consulted the doctor about this, who had listened, and examined little Mae, fat and happy and grabbing at his tie with her pudgy fists, and had only made a speech about how impossible it was to force a child to do anything.

'You can't make them sleep,' he'd said sympathetically, 'you can't make them eat. You can't make them do much of anything, not really. Don't believe anyone who says you can. Bananas and chocolate are fine. She'll grow out of it.'

Rachael had protested; he'd asked her how she was sleeping and eating (*her*, not Mae!) and, in the end, had offered her anti-depressants. 'Lots of mothers take them,' he'd said, pen poised above the prescription he had already printed. Rachael had been furious and felt forced to change surgery.

But Mae had always loved chocolate and warm bananas, and now Rachael retrieved them from her rucksack. It was supposed to be a surprise: a little treat for breakfast. Part of the love bombing. But when she came back – she'd be back any minute, surely this man would have other girls to turn to while Mae was away and would not bother making the drive to Pendle? – they could have them tonight. An extra dessert. The sugar would keep her awake but it didn't matter. Mae could eat as much as she wanted tonight, and tomorrow Rachael would find a place to buy some more, if she wanted them again.

*

An hour and a half later, both cups of tea drunk and the water boiled again and set aside in the pan to get cold. The bananas still waiting in their tin-foil packaging. Rachael furious – so furious that when she heard the commotion at the edge of the woods, some way along the path from the tent, she stood up and strode through the dark.

'You get back here this minute,' she shouted. 'All that messing about! We're supposed to be here spending time with each other, you ungrateful little …'

No answer, but still the commotion continued. A breaking of sticks and – growing nearer, but strangely constant – a sound as if someone were rolling down the hill, rather than walking down it.

'Mae? Are you all right? Have you hurt yourself?'

Rachael paused. There was no answer – just the sound of something coming nearer – a crashing through the undergrowth. She squinted into the darkness.

'Mae? Answer me?'

There was a torch in the tent. She'd run back there – it was only a few paces away – and get it then shine it into the woods. The light would help Mae, who was probably a little tired and disorientated (had she smuggled in some vodka in her bag? Was that what was going on here?), find her way back down the hill.

'Mae? If this is some kind of joke …'

Rachael turned, and the sound behind her continued – and seemed to deepen somehow – as if whatever was trying and failing to find its way out of the woods had broken free of whatever tethered it, and was tumbling and trundling closer. Perhaps it wasn't Mae. Perhaps it was some drunken hiker or an animal – a sheep, perhaps?

Did sheep growl? Because now, as Rachael walked slowly away from the edge of the woods and towards the light of the fire, which seemed much further away than it should be, she heard a kind of breathing behind her – a guttural, heaving type of breathing. Far away, further away than seemed possible, twin lights glowed through the trees: Mae's phone, perhaps? Or the women hikers they'd seen in the pub, weaving their way through the woods to their own secret camping spot? Rachael watched and tried to prevent the thought that what she was looking at was a pair of eyes – eyes shining with their own light – from forming in her mind.

'Mum?'

Mae's voice came thinly, as if from a very long way away. Rachael looked away from the eyes – not glowing eyes, but *burning* – and back to the tent. There she was – sitting beside the fire. She must have come out of the woods at the top of the hill and walked down the lane. They'd missed each other. She'd brought a massive armful of sticks and was building up the fire. Thank God. And look – Mae had spotted the tin-foil parcels and she was pleased about them. She waved and Rachael smiled.

'I'm over here, love! Where did you get to?'

Her voice sounded loud and quiet at the same time. It was strange to shout at night, but there was nobody else here to disturb, so she tried it anyway, and could muster only a whisper. The fire was so small – really, just a glowing red speck in the dark – and so far away – impossibly far away – and there was this – this something behind her – and surely Rachael should be leading it away from the tent and away from her daughter?

'Stay where you are, Mae. I'm coming!'

But Rachael stood still and felt the presence of the something behind her move. She could smell it, even – the stink of a packet of sausages gone bad – rotten meat, sweet and cloying. Her mouth filled with bile and she spat, and retched, and tried to take a few more steps, and surely – this was like a dream – she should be at the tent now?

'Mum? Where are you?'

Rachael tried to call but didn't. She felt held – somehow. Held by the air itself, which had solidified around her, like the way everything turns to treacle in nightmares, and the thing that was behind her was moving quite slowly, padding through the grass on four feet – she could hear that now. She shouldn't be able to hear it: the grass between the edge of the wood and the reservoir was soft and springy – but whatever was coming sounded like it was trotting – galloping now – through shallow water. The sore place on her hand – the bit of flesh she'd nipped with the tent pole – started to burn and throb. Rachael raised it to her face – wiggled her fingers – and could see nothing. How strange that was, she thought dimly.

'Muuuum? Bananas? You brought bananas? You nutter. I *hate* bananas.'

Mae's tone was amused – friendly. Whatever she'd been wanting to do on her phone, she'd been able to do it. Talk to that man, probably. Make some kind of arrangement with him? Was he on his way? Was this friendliness a distraction – meant to lull Rachael into sleep so Mae could sneak out later?

'Just hang on, Mae ...' she called, her tongue feeling strange and swollen in her mouth – there, and not there – and she couldn't be sure this time that she'd made any sound at all. Rachael hurled herself against the air and the stillness holding her broke suddenly. She ran towards her daughter, misjudging the distance. When the ground gave way beneath her, she had just a second to realise she'd tripped over the side of the path before her head hit the concrete edge of the reservoir, too hard to hurt – and one more second to taste blood in her mouth and wonder who would take care of Mae now. Her face was turned upwards as she fell and, finally, she saw the dark shape leering down from above her. She saw its broad and heavy shoulders, its wild and tangled pelt, and its perfectly round eyes, glowing with their own hot light – before the dark water closed over her head.

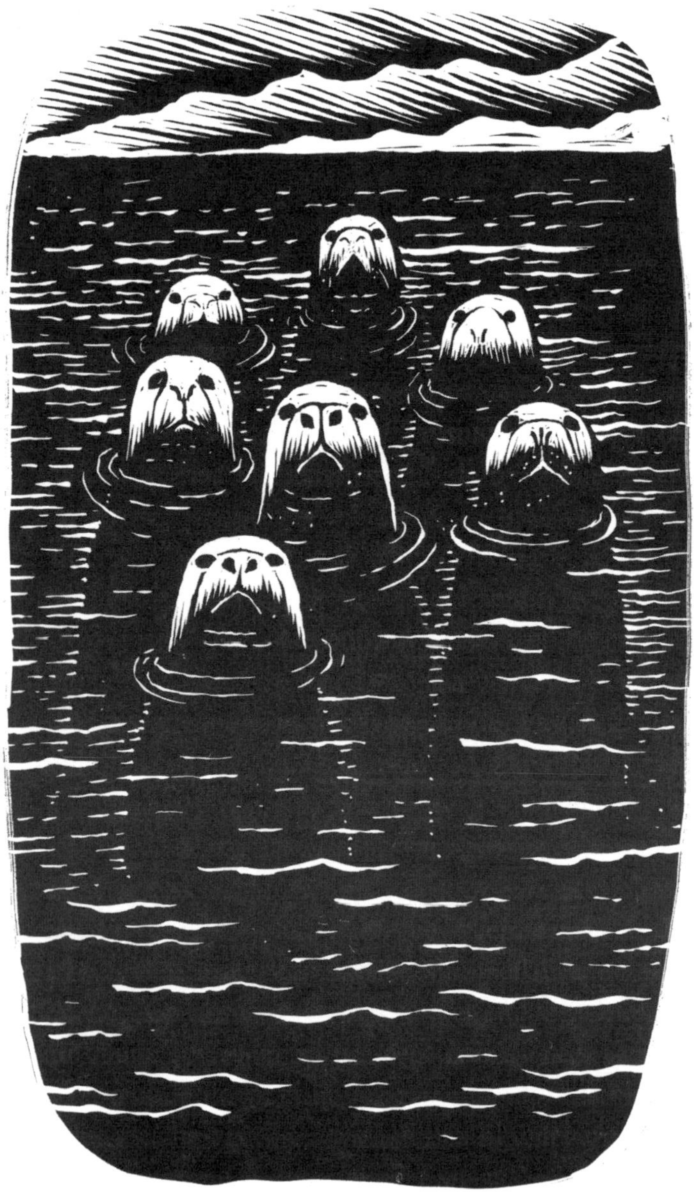

Eynhallow Free

SUNYI DEAN

Eynhallow frank, Eynhallow free
Eynhallow stands in the middle of the sea
a roaring roost on every side
Eynhallow stands in the middle of the tide.
— an old Orkney rhyme

You are cold and can't get warm.

It's supposedly summer in these northern isles, yet the air remains stubbornly damp and chill. Hunch your shoulders as you walk along Eynhallow's shore, wrap both arms around yourself. It doesn't help.

The morning is heavy with congealing mist, clouds rolling low across waves and beach and the treeless landscape. A shaggy terrier trots at your heels, muddy and cheerful. His name is Magellan, though he never answers to it and only does as he pleases. Currently, that means following you around.

You're glad of the company. There is plenty of life on Eynhallow, but none of it is human aside from you and your husband. There are the birds, so many of them: kittiwakes and puffins, oystercatchers and terns. The seals who wail mournfully at sunset.

Those seals are out there now, lurking in the shallows with their heads just above water. Their crooning noises are unsettling; you didn't know they sang like that. Most people find them cute, but honestly, you find them a little frightening.

Maybe it's the solid dark orbs of their eyes, the unblinking gaze, the eerie way they disappear if you get too close. Maybe it's the fact that, against all reason or common sense, they seem to stare at you, wherever you go along this shore.

In Norway lands there lived a maid ...

For a moment, you could swear there is somebody singing, the words half-hidden under all the seal-howling. But that's nonsense, the mind playing tricks. There is only discordant animal noise.

You shake your head, stomping determinedly back towards camp.

The seals watch you leave, and I watch with them.

Tom Henderson faces the camera, peering through large spectacles. Behind him is a smear of grey sky above hills covered in wiry grass; in the distance, a crashing grey ocean.

'On this episode of *Travels with Tom*, I've taken myself to Eynhallow, a remote Orkney island in northernmost

Scotland. According to legend, Eynhallow is a place of intense mystery, steeped in folklore and ancient magic, even in the present day. It is a place where – according to locals – animals refuse to live, bad luck befalls inhabitants, tourists go missing, and ghosts can be found.

'Some might call these stories coincidence or rumour. But after nearly a thousand years of folk tradition, Eynhallow's mysteries are deeply entrenched. In this mini-series, we'll be diving into the history of this wonderful little corner of the world, and all that it contains.'

The camera fades to black.

Human thoughts spill out from their skulls like water, and I can read you all like a printed page.

Your name is Libby Henderson. A biographer might note that you are a thirty-four-year-old from Bristol, formerly a nursery teacher. Currently married to one Tom Henderson, a history lecturer with a popular video blog. Parent to one child, now deceased.

But I am not a biographer. So I will say, instead, that you are nervous and slight, a worn doormat of a woman with lacklustre brown hair and more freckles than courage. Nobody listens to you, not even the nursery toddlers you used to look after.

And instead of saying *one child, now deceased*, I will say *one child, killed by negligence*. His death was your fault and you know it, Tom knows it, everybody knows it. Even I, who never leave this island, know it. Guilt hangs over you the way mist hangs over the waters of the Sound on an autumn morning.

It is that guilt, along with a dose of shame and loneliness, that brought you here in the first place. The alternative is staying in Bristol, trapped in that empty house with nothing to do and nowhere to go. The walls are bare after you pulled down every picture of Finlay, his small bedroom a blank space.

The marriage is over, though you're the last one to recognise that. In fairness, it was over long before Finlay was born, let alone after he died; those events just made it harder for Tom to hide his contempt.

The truth is, he soured on you about a year after the wedding and you're not sure why.

Perhaps it was inevitable that you should start drinking after Finlay was born, as much to pass the time as to dull the loneliness. There was no one around to stop you from sliding into that abyss, and Tom certainly didn't care. Not until that tepid March afternoon, when three-year-old Finlay wandered out of the house while you lay oblivious on the living-room floor. One car accident later, and the rest is cliché history.

And so, here you are on Eynhallow: a timid wreck of a housewife, reduced now to a silent shadow who drifts along empty beaches while her husband directs all his words to a video blog. A tiny part of you still hopes to bridge the gulf in this marriage, but deep down, I think you know the truth: your husband would rather talk to a camera lens than to you.

Tom gestures expansively to the landscape behind him, shirt ruffling in the sea wind. In the background is a rocky shoreline, dotted with placid seals.

'Our story begins in the twelfth century. In those days, Eynhallow was known as a bridge to Hildaland, the realm of the Finfolk. They were a race of shapeshifting undersea sorcerers, who could make the island appear or disappear at their will. Sometimes, they kidnapped humans, who were never seen again.

'One such victim was the wife of a farmer, known as the Goodman of Thorodale. While walking by the shore, she was stolen by the Finfolk and dragged down to live in their realm forever.'

Soon enough, you arrive back at the little campsite that Tom set up yesterday, on the island's western side. It is sparse because the trip is short. In the morning, he will load up the kayak and head back to Rousay if the tides are calm enough.

Your husband is exactly where you left him: seated in front of video equipment, shooting yet another retake. His videos aren't very long, but they're carefully made. He's surprisingly popular, given the niche content matter. It'd be rude to interfere in his shot, so you hover nearby but keep out of the camera line. Magellan knows the drill and stays curled quietly at your feet.

When the clip ends, Tom presses Stop on his tripod remote. The brightness and verve which made him so engaging on camera seem to dim instantly, like a switch has been flicked off. His shoulders and spine sag in unison.

'Not my best, but could have been worse,' he mutters, and leans forward to fiddle with his video recorder. 'Suppose I'll keep it.'

'I thought it was good.' Your attempt to sound sincere falls flat.

Tom pokes the touchscreen and says in a melancholy tone that is barely audible, 'God, it's quiet in this place. Finlay would have loved it here.'

'That's not true,' you say, floored by his nonsense. Tom played at fatherhood the way he played at marriage: showing up for the fun, disappearing during anything tough. The only thing more selective than his attention was his memory. 'Finlay would have hated it here, and you'd know that if you knew him at all!'

Half of you is terrified, because you've never pushed back like this before. It's far from the conversation starter you had planned in your head; uncontrolled, emotional, unfocused.

And yet the other half of you is elated, for precisely the same reasons. And seriously, Finlay had been three years old, for God's sake. What three-year-old would like this trip?

Magellan starts barking at you. He always hates it when his humans argue.

'Christ, give it a rest.' Tom sets down the camera and starts rifling through his bag.

'Don't ignore me,' you snap. 'If you don't want me here, then why did you let me come along?'

You feel a twinge of unease. Why *had* he let you come along? It's a very small thing but, oddly, you can't remember discussing it.

He pulls out a sandwich, unwrapping it tiredly.

'Tom? Tom, look at me!' And you grab his shoulder, trying to shake him.

He doesn't budge. Doesn't feel you, doesn't react. Keeps chewing like a dumb farm animal, oblivious to your presence.

Shock cascades through you. You're not a strong person but touching him was like trying to shove a mountain. There was texture beneath your fingers, the fabric and rustle of his clothes, yet you exerted no force.

The cold seems to press in closer, and something like blind panic descends. You shove him again, frantic, with all your strength. When that does nothing, you slap him.

The slap doesn't hurt. Your hand doesn't sting. Neither does it move your husband; the wind affects him more than you do.

Your husband gulps in another mouthful of food and says to Magellan, 'I think we can get in a little more filming tonight. I've nearly got enough content for the whole episode.'

He isn't ignoring you. This isn't the silent treatment. *He just doesn't know you're here.* When he speaks, he is talking only to the dog.

Yes, the dog. Magellan stares at you, ears cocked. You stare back. Fingers trembling, you reach down and stroke the furry head, since he seems anxious. As with your husband, the textures of wiry fur brush your skin, or seem to, but when you try to pick him up, he doesn't move.

Interesting. You should be afraid, panicked, maybe sobbing in a corner. But now that the surprise is fading, all you can feel is a sense of disconnection. After all, what is there to be afraid of now? Dead women have nothing to fear from life.

The only question that remains is *how* you died, because you can't remember that and it frustrates you.

In Norway lands there lived a maid ...

The voice of a young boy, warbly and sweet, interweaves with the incessant wailing of the seals. It is coming from somewhere further along the shore, away from the camp.

... 'Baloo, my babe,' this maid began ...

A tight pain spears your chest. You know those words, that voice. 'The Great Silkie of Sule Skerry' is a very old Scottish song, one you picked up during your days as a nursery teacher. Later, you taught it to Finlay. It was one of the few songs that always seemed to get him to sleep.

... 'I know not where your father is ...'

Tom has nearly finished his sandwich and is already setting up for another take. There is no way to reach or speak to him.

Even if you could, would he help you? Maybe that question is better left unanswered.

... 'Or if land or sea he travels in ...'

You turn and walk towards the sound while an oblivious Tom begins to record again.

Tom gestures energetically, his eyes bright and focused.

'Heartbroken, the Goodman searched the ocean high and low, desperate to find her. Yet he could not even see the island, let alone land on it. Eventually, with the help of a local witch, he performed a ritual and could now see the island with mortal eyes. He set off from Rousay in a boat, accompanied by his three grown sons, carrying a good supply of salt and crosses.'

The sound of seals rises loud and eerie. They stare at the camera, heads tilted, while the birds flutter and shriek. Tom keeps speaking, doesn't seem to notice.

'The Goodman of Thorodale battled sirens and monsters and waves to reach the island, never once looking away lest it disappear from view. Once they were upon it, a great Finfolk warrior appeared, mighty and tall with hatred in his eyes. He roared out, "Flee this place, human filth! You are not welcome in this secret land. Be gone at once, or I shall spill thy blood upon the shore, and wear thy skin as a cape!"'

Grey water thrashes the rocky shore, rain clouds gathering overhead as you walk towards the sound of singing.
   ... Then in came a good grey selkie ...
   Mist gathers, cloying and moist. The birds have faded to silence, Magellan has not come with you, and Tom's endless droning can no longer be heard. Nothing but fog and water and the echoes of a familiar melody.

... Who sat down at her bed's feet ...

Clamber over a small outcropping of rocks, face damped by sea spray, and pause. The figure of a young boy sits facing away from you, cross-legged with hands on his knees. Singing in an all-too-familiar lilt.

*... Saying, 'Awake, awake, my pretty fair maid
For, oh, how soundest thou dost sleep ...'*

Clear your throat and call back in sing-song: '"And I'll tell thee where thy baby's father is/He is sitting close, at thy bed's feet."'

I turn to look at you.

At first glance, I am the very image of your child on the day he died. The same dark hair, slightly shaggy and curled at the ends. The same nose and the same tidy, upturned chin. Dressed in Finlay's favourite Pac-Man shirt, which you buried him in.

For a moment, wild hope kindles.

Then you meet my gaze and recoil as if struck. My eyes are round as stones and dark as night; there is nothing human about them. They are the eyes of a seal, wet and glimmering.

'Libby Henderson.' When I speak, there is a flash of pointed teeth. Made for tearing fish. 'Be welcome on Eynhallow.'

'You're ... not my son.'

'No.' My smile is slow and liquid. 'I am neither him, nor his ghost.'

'Then why ... how ...'

I pre-empt the question. 'He seeps from your thoughts and gives shape to my form. Humans call us shapeshifters, but often it is they who shape us into what they wish to see. Be that a beautiful maiden or a demonic warrior.'

'That isn't possible,' you say shakily. 'Finfolk aren't real.'

I drop my blade of grass. 'Neither are ghosts, Libby Henderson. Which is why you and I can speak as equals, for we are both unreal things.'

Again, there is no despair, no sense of devastation. What I say to you is merely a confirmation of a truth you have already begun to accept, and it cannot shock you anymore.

'I don't remember dying,' you say numbly. 'That's the thing I don't understand. I remember the journey up here—'

'Are you sure about that?' I stick out my tongue like a child, like an animal, tasting the air out of habit. It smells of northerly winds and unsettled currents. 'Give me one detail, then, of the trip you took to reach this place.'

Open your mouth to answer. The confident assertion dies on your lips.

There should have been a long train journey, from Bristol to Scotland. Maybe even a flight. But as you search through every memory, nothing turns up. No plane, no airport, no train station, no driving. How you got here is a blank, one your mind has happily skipped over till now.

'I thought so.' My form shivers and twists, skin briefly going grey and body rounding out, then reasserts once more into Finlay's constricting shape. I must be disciplined and maintain this form, no matter how cold and weak it feels, or you will cease to trust me. 'What is the first thing you remember?'

'The beach,' you say, after a long moment. 'Standing on the sand, feeling chilly.'

Look down at yourself and realise with a jolt that you are wearing only thin cotton pyjamas.

You are cold and can't get warm, and now you know why.

I step closer; it takes all your resolve not to step back. Bending down, I reach a small childish hand into the sand. It parts easily before my touch, as I will it to. Lying there, chipped yet intact, is a grit-covered glass tumbler.

Your breath catches. 'That's mine. It belonged to my father.' To your deep frustration, trying to pick it up ends in failure. You're intangible, and it slips through ghostly fingers like water. 'How did this get here?'

'That husband of yours threw it in the sea while kayaking to the island. But the ocean in these parts belongs to us, and nothing is lost unless we wish it to be.' I pick up the whisky glass and hold it to your lips. 'Here, Libby. Have a drink.'

Here, Libby. Have a drink. Tom's face hovers in your memory, blending with mine. You can recall it, now: the smell of alcohol rising up.

'You deserve it.' My tone is mocking, but my touch is gentle.

You deserve it. Tom's touch had been gentle, too. Proffering you that sip of Laphroaig.

Press the tumbler to your lips, in memory and in truth. A powdery residue stains your tongue; that's not right.

'What's in this?'

What's in this?

'Just something for the pain.'

Just something for the pain.

Tom's angular face is framed against the light – the last thing you see, before dying.

There is a frenzied quality to Tom's voice as he speaks; his eyes are wild, his face drawn. The story pours out of him, compulsively.

'The Finfolk could not fight the Goodman, for he was armed with crosses and salt, and had the might of his three sons. Together, they defeated the warrior and threw him down. And then the humans walked back and forth across the island, scattering salt wherever they went, driving forth the remaining Finfolk. The Finmen roared and the mermaids screamed, shifting their forms to that of seals as they plunged into safer water.

'But the Goodman did not stop there! He brought forth a knife and strode across the land. Therein he carved nine crosses in the earth, scoring deep. Onto his knees he fell, declaring before God above that this place was made sacred, and belonged only to the Christian realm.'

'What was that?' You jerk away hard, scrabbling on hands and knees to escape me. 'What did you do?'

A living woman would be covered in filth and grime, but death has rendered you permanently clean. No sand or grit can mar those pristine white pyjamas, and no rocks can cut into the flesh of your hands.

That brings you no relief, though, only despair. It is a terrible feeling to know you are invisible and intangible. You have never been strong in life, but in death you are utterly powerless.

'I helped you remember.' The tumbler rests, still, on my open palm. I keep my hand level, holding it out. 'Do you remember now what happened?'

Your shoulders sagging. 'He killed me. Spiked my drink.'

Something for the pain. Paracetamol? Codeine? You had both of those in the house.

'Yes.'

'He made it look like a suicide,' you say in a low voice.

And who wouldn't believe it? Everyone knew how miserable and sad poor Libby Henderson had been. Her history of mental health problems, her penchant for alcohol. You wonder, bitterly, how hard they bothered to investigate.

It occurs to you then, with a rising sense of indignation, that Tom is going to get away with it. Has already got away with it, in fact.

You twist around, clutching limply at my arm. 'Finlay, or whatever your name is—'

'My name cannot be spoken in human tongues. Finlay will do, for now.'

'Finlay,' you agree, and take an irrational comfort in those familiar syllables. 'Can you help me? Please.'

'I understand. You wish to touch the world again.' I sidle closer, resting a pudgy little face against your shoulder. 'Let us help each other, Libby. For we also have been unjustly treated.'

You flinch at my touch, but don't pull back. 'What do you mean?'

'This island was made sacred by the Goodman of Thorodale. We have power, but it is limited and we cannot free it ourselves. We have tried. *We have tried.*'

The seals howl in unison, slapping their flanks and baring their teeth.

'We cannot touch the crosses that mar this island, for we are not human.' I lean closer as I speak, my lips almost against your ear. 'You cannot touch the husband who killed you, for you are dead. Let us trade, Libby. Look.'

And I put the tumbler in your palms, pressing my hands around yours. My touch burns hot against your ghostly skin, yet you hardly notice because your attention is on the glass. The tumbler is cold and hard and *real*, the surface smeared with grains of sand. It is the first thing you have *felt* since awakening as a spirit, and for once, it does not slip like vapour through your fingers.

'I can be corporeal?!'

'We can give you form, little ghost. For a short time.'

'And then?' You cradle the tumbler, enamoured by that simple sensation. 'What do you want me to do with my … form?'

'It is simple. We ask you to mar the crosses that cover this island. We can show you where they are. *Break the sanctity forced upon us.* Then Eynhallow will be free, and so shall we.'

'I see.' A frown crosses your lips. 'Why don't you ask someone living?'

'What, like Tom?' My laughter sounds like an animal's bark. 'You are dead, Libby. The angry spirits of murdered women are not sacred, and it is your unholy touch that we need. Nothing less will desecrate this ground.'

'Yeah? And what happens to me, once your unholy island is free?'

'All that is on the island, will go down with the island.' I cock my head. 'Spirits can dwell beneath the waves in Finfolkaheem, if that is what you wish to do.'

'That's nice, but not what I meant.' Your fingers curl and uncurl. 'I'm talking about my husband.'

'As I said, whatever is on the island, will go down with the island.'

The seals chitter and burble, slapping their own flanks with broad flippers. You hear it for what it is: cruel laughter and harsh delight. Against your better judgement, you are also smiling. The thought of Tom drowning does not horrify you at all.

'What do you think?' I ask, in Finlay's sweet little voice. 'Will you walk with me, and set all of us free?'

A long, drawn-out moment as you hesitate, trying to think. We wait; the seals anxious, me holding my breath. We hope that you will do as we ask, but we can never know for sure. It has been a long time since a spirit walked this place, and we do not know how long it may be before another arrives.

'Save the dog and I'll do it,' you say, at last. 'Magellan deserves better.'

The seals cluster closer, grey flesh piled on grey flesh, bristly whiskers twitching. Their confusion mirrors my own, because none of us can understand why you should care so much for so lowly a creature.

Still, we are not complaining. Not if that is your only demand.

'Unexpected, I admit, but we have no objection. Do you have conditions for how we save it?'

'Him, not it,' you say, holding my gaze levelly. 'Tom came here on a kayak. Put Magellan onboard and let the boat go safe to shore. Then, yes, we have a deal.'

Relief and savage joy cascade through me. My control ebbs and my form flickers, briefly revealing a hulking four-armed creature with ridged fins and teeth like needles. The moment passes, though. In the blink of an eye, I am again a small, helpless-looking child.

The seals bay like hounds as I extend my hand, grinning like a shark. 'Very well, mortal girl. It is agreed.'

I take your ghostly hand in mine, feeding your spirit a fraction of the power that roils within me. For the first time since awakening on the beach, you grip back forcefully and match my smile with your own.

From all across Eynhallow, the birds begin screaming.

Tom clutches the camera, sweating and wild-eyed, nose almost mashed to the lens. He never seems to blink and cannot seem to stem the tide of words which flows from his mouth.

'A great booming noise rose from the ground. Hildaland was no more, for it had been made holy, and was conquered from the Finfolk. There came then a screaming and a weeping, for all Finfolk nearby were torn away, too: trapped in animal form, doomed to swim the waters of their lost summer home, forever caught between tides.'

Eynhallow truly is tiny. It does not take long to walk the length and breadth of the island, my hand in yours. I am not your son, yet I can sense the comfort it brings you, to hold the hand of something which takes his form. As long as you don't meet my gaze, you can pretend, and that is enough.

The salt that the Goodman poured on our soil was long since washed away by tide and time. But the salt was only ever a way of keeping us off the land while he wreaked his damage. What truly matters are the crosses.

Nine of them, carved into the earth with a priest-blessed blade. To the naked eye, they are long invisible, yet in my vision they burn the retinas, shining up from beneath the earth.

I lead you to each and every one, pointing them out since you cannot see them. Lending you my power and strength so that you are tangible enough to dig in the earth with human touch, and deface each cross with your dead, murdered hands.

When that first cross crumbles, the world around me seems to glow with deeper, brighter colours. There is a strong salt tinge to the air, and the wind picks up speed.

'Is everything alright?' Your arm encircles my shoulders, anxious and tender.

'Perfect. Wonderful. Please, let's keep going!' I throw childish arms around your waist in a hug. You soften noticeably. Even knowing it is an illusion.

Humans are simple things, truly.

On we go, step by step. As each cross falls, the island shudders, its tether to the mortal world loosening. My power grows, and your spirit strengthens.

By the time we reach the final cross, I no longer need to hold your hand. You bend down, scoring the earth furiously, pleased to see how the soil parts from your efforts, thrilled once again to make your mark on the world.

'Thank you.' I gift you with a final hug, because it costs me nothing but will mean a great deal to you. 'We thank you greatly, Libby!'

I feel your arms tremble as you put them around me; I sense, too, your deep reluctance as I pull away. But you cannot hold me forever, and we both know that.

'How long will it last?' you ask, brushing dirt from your knees. How amazing it is, to feel muddy and solid, humanly clumsy. 'This corporeality, I mean.'

'How long do you need?'

'Not long,' you say, musing. 'But I want to see my husband.'

I giggle like a child. 'Take all the time you wish, Libby Henderson. I shall come with you ... and watch.'

He is, after all, the last human ever to set foot on this place. When the waves swallow Eynhallow, and it becomes Hildaland once more, we will not make the mistake of returning to your dangerous little realm.

We arrive at Tom's camp just in time. One of my kind has already lured Magellan into the kayak. It did not take much, only a scrap of food, carefully placed. Then a lead tied tight, so he can't flee. The rest we can take care of later. The Finfolk keep their bargains.

Meanwhile, Eynhallow groans and grinds, as if its very foundations are breaking, because they are. There is an earth-shattering sound, as if the gods have broken an entire forest's worth of trees at once, and the whole place trembles. It is the sound of this place untethering from the mortal world.

All along the shore, the water recedes further and further and further, building into a tidal wave that surrounds Eynhallow on all sides. At any moment, it will come crashing down, to sink this land once more. Forever.

'Li-Libby?'

You turn away from watching Magellan, slow and ethereal.

Tom Henderson crouches on the ground, clutching at his tent for support as the ground judders and trembles. He has stopped recording; the camera lies smashed at his feet. Whatever obsession gripped him before, is gone.

I step back, keeping myself hidden, and watch with avid interest.

'Tom.' You speak his name like a curse.

'It *is* you!' He stares at you in shock. 'But how are you here? You're ... you're ...'

'Dead? Yes, I am.'

'Libby, I ...' For the first time since you've known him, Tom is so terrified he's shaking. 'I'm sorry, I didn't mean—'

'Shh,' you tell him, catching hold of his jaw with your free hand. 'Everything will be just fine.'

He gawks at you, too overwhelmed to argue back.

'You must be thirsty, my love. Why don't you have a drink?' you whisper, then raise the grime-smeared whisky tumbler and ram it forcefully between his teeth. 'Yes, have a drink, Tom. I think you deserve it!'

He is still screaming through a mouthful of broken glass when the tidal waves come crashing down, to swallow Eynhallow forever.

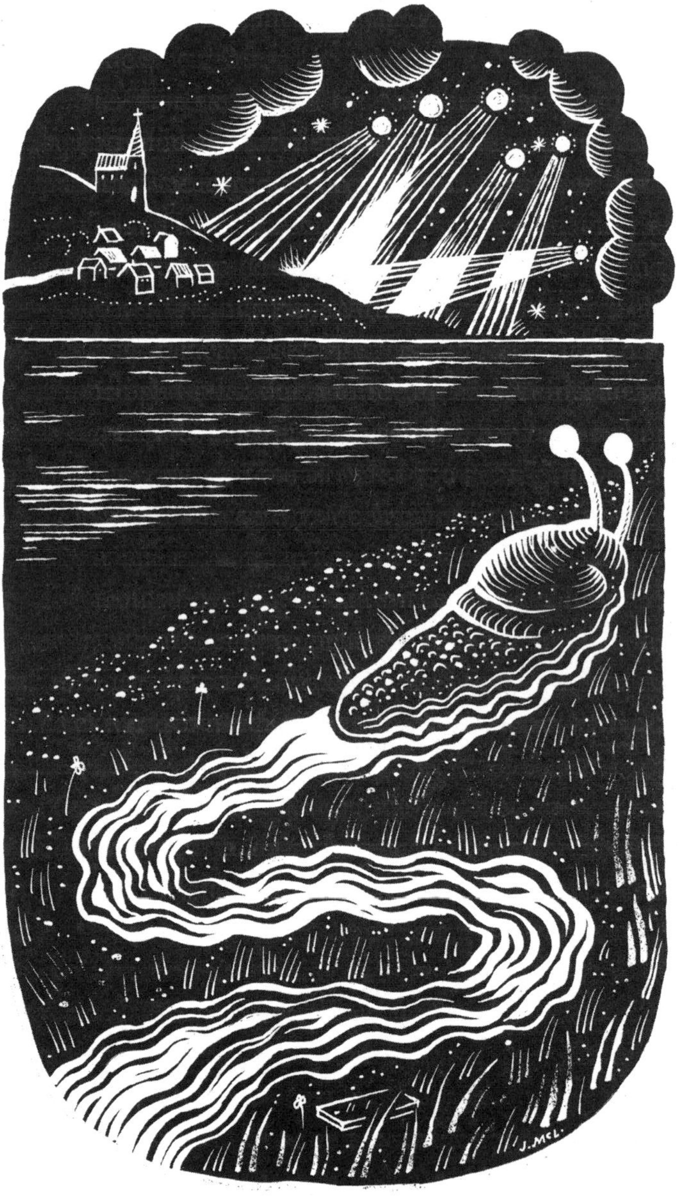
J.McL.

Boneless

JANICE HALLETT

Not long ago, I received an unexpected package through the post. There was no record of the sender and all it contained was a battered smartphone wrapped in a sheet of grubby lined paper torn from a cheap notebook. On it, six numbers were written in a neat, deliberate hand. I did what anyone else would and charged it up. When asked for a passcode, I tried those six numbers.

On the phone I found various documents: notes, drafts, emails, texts, photographs and a voice-note diary, all made by a young man called Rowan Quinn ... I transcribed the audio files, printed everything relevant and placed it in chronological order.

The process reminded me eerily of the way I present 'found footage' in my novels. Perhaps that's why whoever discovered the phone sent it to me. I don't know quite what to make of it. Do you?

Janice Hallett, 2025

Boneless feature for Beastopia.com - first draft

Boneless

My Hunt for the Beast of Snake Pass
by
Rowan Quinn

I arrived at Ashbower Basin the week before finals. My cohort were feverishly revising, studying, panicking, day drinking and night eating, intent on earning a good degree and making their families proud. Not me. I wasn't worrying about grades or even the embarrassment of a 2:2 drinker's degree ... I'd dropped out at the end of April.

I don't care anymore about having a BSc after my name. A lot happens between the ages of eighteen and twenty-one. It did to me, anyway, because over those three years I realised *what* you know is way less important than *who* you know. That's how people start their careers in the right places, at a decent level. I'm the first in my family to reach university. I know *no one* in big pharma or even at any smaller R&D departments. Literally no one. So, I'll need either a stunning First (no chance), a whole bunch of money (forget it), a decade flattering the right people (fuck that) *and* a massive dose of luck (not happening based on prior stats) to get where some of these dudes will be in six weeks' time.

Haven't got round to telling the fam yet. I mention lectures, tutorials, nights out with housemates, how hard I'm working for finals, but the truth is I've already moved out of halls to a studio flat across town.

Can't lie, I'm as passionate about biological science as ever, just tired of learning about known things. Think about that, because it's all education is: learning what other people know. For a start, it's impossible to cram everything in, and while you're desperately *trying* to, your own life, and every chance to make something of it, drains away.

So, give me the unknown any day. Forget what other people learned – discover something *new*, something no one else knows, *that's* when you make a name for yourself. That's when the big people come looking for *you*.

*

To: hello@beastopia.com
From: Rowan Quinn
Subject: Boneless

Dear Beastopia.com,
Firstly, thanks a million for starting this site – I'm a *huge* fan. I'm also a biology undergrad with a professional interest in cryptozoology. Attached are two features I've written: 'The Black Cat of Nan Clark's Lane', a story set in my home town, and 'The Visit', about an encounter the mother of a friend of a friend had at Loch

Ness in the 1970s. Neither story has been published, so if you like them, we can talk. You'll see I have a strong scientific approach and can look objectively at primary and secondary evidence.

I also propose to write a feature specially for you, about a UK cryptid known colloquially as *Boneless*, whose most significant sighting was in the Peak District National Park in Derbyshire, central England.

Eyewitnesses describe Boneless as 'a giant black slug, the height of a small horse'. Which may sound unlikely, but when you consider all the evidence, as I have, then you'll see how the singular ecology of this area *vastly increases* the probability such a creature has evolved. In fact, conditions there are *so* ideal for its evolution, it would be more surprising if Boneless did not exist.

What's more, Derbyshire's Boneless is not the only slug-like cryptid rumoured to have been sighted in the United Kingdom. Yorkshire has Sludgeback, in Scotland they call a similar creature the Nightmire, in Wales it's Mwythwr and in East Anglia I found legends about a 'shell-less snail' called either Fogcrawler or Fencrawler. All are 'giant, slug-like' creatures, slow yet terrifying, and the sound they make as they move is enough to freeze any onlooker in their shoes.

If you commission me to write a piece about Boneless, I can use the advance to stay at Ashbower Basin, the reservoir where the creature was reportedly seen, spend some time with local people and gather primary evidence. It would be a coup for Beastopia.com!

Happy to discuss further and look forward to hearing from you,
Rowan Quinn

*

To: Rowan Quinn
From: Nancy D
Subject: Re: Boneless

Hey Rowan,
Thanks for reaching out. We love your writing so much! Boneless sounds cool, for sure. We'll schedule all three features for the site.

Now for the money thing. Beastopia.com is so new we can't afford to pay anyone yet. An advance won't work for us either. But it's in our business plan to be inclusive and collective, so once we make healthy profits, everyone who works for us now will be at a higher level of pay. It's a great opportunity for you to get in at the start of something big and grow your career with us.

If that's cool, then we can run Black Cat and Loch Ness next week. There's no hurry for the Boneless article. Send it when you're ready.

Best,
Nancy
CEO Beastopia.com

*

To: Nancy D
From: Rowan Quinn
Subject: Boneless

Hey Nancy,
Great news! In that case I'll have to camp rather than stay somewhere, but I guess it's cool.

I'll look out for my byline on the site and will send 'Boneless' by the end of next week.

Rowan

*

Messages between Sheila and Rowan Quinn

Mum
Sorry to disturb your studying, but are you coming home for Dad's birthday? I want to make it extra nice this year.

Rowan
On a revision retreat. Finals in a week.

Mum
Please can you call him? It'll make his day.

Mum
Next Wednesday.

Rowan
OK. Busy rn

Mum
I know, love. Good luck!

*

Messages between Bill and Rowan Quinn

Dad
Has Mum texted about next week?

Rowan
Yes

Dad
She's not good after this new drug. Recovery takes longer and longer after each session. They said it might happen.

Dad
She didn't want to mention it. Worrying you with this as your finals are looming is the last thing we want, but I think you should be prepared.

Dad

Just so you know, when you come back, she might not be strong enough to cook. But I'll get a delivery on an app I downloaded. Let's make it extra nice for her, you know what I mean.

*

The following documents were in a folder called 'Primary evidence for the existence of Boneless'. I understand 'primary evidence' to mean: sightings, first-person accounts, published material and physical samples.

[Screenshot from Wikicrypt]

Boneless: On the night of 25 December 1959, farm hand Gerard Briggs was making his way home around Ashbower Basin, a Victorian reservoir in the Derwent Valley of Derbyshire. The night was dark but mild and it had been raining heavily, on and off, for a week, relatively unusual for the time of year. I need to demon: that certain meteorological condits are necessary for Boneless.

Gerard Briggs lived in a shepherd's cottage on the north shore of the water and had been drinking at the Drowned Oak public house, a Christmas outing he made alone that year as his wife had a cold. On his way home, on foot, at about 11.30 p.m., he took the trail beside the water that would lead him there more directly than the road. Called Snake Pass, it was a well-established footpath and he had with him a small torch, as he had anticipated how dark it would be.

He claims he stepped out firmly and quickly, and that he had not consumed enough alcohol to make him unsteady or slower on his feet than normal. Although he had taken this route many times before, Gerard felt uneasy. More than once he thought he heard a sound and spun round. The suspicion someone was following him squirmed like a dying fly in his mind. But no one was there.

He rounded the curve of the reservoir, crossed a small bridge over a tributary, but found his pace slowing, despite his increased desire to get home. He describes being unable to breathe or quicken his steps, as if the very air had become treacle, his feet stuck to the ground, every step a monumental effort. *Explain microclimate role in evol.

Finally, he sank to his knees; the torch dropped from his hand and rolled away, its beam suddenly static, illuminating the path ahead at an obscure angle.

It was around that time, he said, that he became aware of a different sound. It was the muffled noise of something wet and heavy being dragged, or possibly dragging itself, across dry land. It pulsed, as if the entity was heaving its own bulk forward with each breath but stopping to exhale. Whatever it might be, he said, he knew it was alive.

Gerard felt panic rise in his chest, but escape eluded him. His hands had landed flat on the ground. As he lifted them, he realised what was making his feet feel so heavy ... the thickest, most sticky and noxious slime he had ever encountered covered his palms. He yanked himself up, great strings of the stuff tethering his hands, knees and feet to the path, only snapping and freeing him when he was fully standing. He tried to shake away the slime, but ... as he wiped it away on his overcoat, he described the torch beam as suddenly growing larger, illuminating more of the path ahead, where, between the water and the undergrowth, was a creature of a sort Gerard had never set eyes on before.

As black as jet and just as shiny, its front part – he stopped short of saying 'face' – bore two swivelling eyes and on its head it had a pulsating blowhole ... like a whale, and yet not. Its body was black and jelly-like under a bulbous front section that tapered into a tail at the back, with no arms or legs. It moved on its belly, but not crisply or silently like a snake. The grating sound came as it hauled itself across the ground, on a carpet of slime, churning over stones and grit, its muscles creaking and groaning as they worked, punctuated by the hiss of its exhalations as the blowhole opened and closed.

He'd witnessed nothing like it in his life, and the best description Gerard could give was that this creature resembled a giant slug – a slug the size of a small horse. And he wasn't the first or the last to speak of it: a cryptid the locals call Old Boneless.

*

Rowan Quinn, Biological Science Year 3, DeVere University, Rochester

Secondary evidence for the existence of Boneless:

This comprises the scientific *likelihood* of such a creature as a giant slug evolving, thriving and reproducing in the natural history and current conditions of the surrounding area.

- ✦ Slug is simply the common name for any terrestrial gastropod, distinct from snails in that they lack a shell into which the body retracts. Different species of slug are not as closely related as might be assumed from their physical similarities. Several different evolutionary lineages account for the variety in slug species observed today. They likely all evolved convergently due to the prevalence of similar external conditions.
- ✦ To thrive, all species of terrestrial 'slug' require food, moisture, shade, shelter in undisturbed damp places, absence of frost, and ground conditions conducive to their method of movement (the contraction of a muscular 'foot' facilitates forward motion by gliding over the mucus it secretes).

Therefore, the genealogy of species that led to the evolution of several different lines of slug increases the likelihood of a cryptid line.

Given their slow rate of movement, they need to eat any organic matter they encounter and their diet is limited only to the size of the edibles they find. They are, for the most part, omnivorous and detritivorous. This ability to eat anything is key to the success of the genus.

Meteorological conditions in central England:

Derbyshire is situated at an elevation of 129.27 metres above sea level, with an average yearly temperature of 10.2 degrees centigrade. Annual rainfall is at an average of 28.22 mm over 84.55 rainy days.

The effects of climate change on the area, which over a 12-year period has seen a 2% reduction in the number of days with sub-zero temperatures, may be playing into the improvement of conditions for large gastropods to survive.

Ashbower Basin is a reservoir of 11.5 square kilometres, created in 1848. Its north shore is semi-isolated from the surrounding eco-system by steep hillsides and two small tributaries at either end. The result is a microcosm, rich in plant and animal life, that enjoys higher temperatures and heavier precipitation over fewer rainy days. In short, ideal conditions for gastropods.

Conditions that lead to 'giant' species:

Absence of predators
Isolation
Abundant resources
Spontaneous genetic mutations that extend natural lifespan and/or growth phases
Unnatural genetic mutation following chemical or other man-made interference, either deliberate, ambient or accidental

Climate change: role? As CC negatively affects resources, animals and plants are observed to be shrinking, not growing. Yet, mathematical perfection does not exist. Fundamental imbalances created by these changes, e.g. the decline of one species, can lead to another species gaining disproportionately _more_ resources and therefore displaying an _increase_ in size.

My theory

The curved north shore of Ashbower Basin creates a wet microclimate super-conducive to the distinct evolution of a large gastropod rarely seen by humans. Such a creature might potentially secrete a mucus/slime that discourages predation. Additionally, my theory will look at the possibility that Boneless is essentially a water slug that exists in the shallows, using its blowhole to breathe and feeding on rotting aquatic matter. It ventures onto land only rarely, when it perceives conditions are right.

*

Rowan's earlier diary entries are discursive and relaxed. He recorded them in a Word document, probably created on his laptop while writing in his tent, and also a Notes app on his phone, most likely while out and about. They are presented here unedited.

A Diary of my field visit to Ashbower Basin by Rowan Quinn

Friday 21 June, 10 p.m.

I hauled my backpack through the double doors of the Drowned Oak after a miserable nine-hour journey that, at every step, seemed to place obstacles between me and the reservoir – not least the heavy rainfall this area has experienced over the last two weeks.

I was ready to eat a good meal, drink a cold beer and sleep in a soft bed, but my banking app had other ideas, so there were energy bars and water for three days in my backpack – underneath an old tent and ground sheet.

Silence fell in the bar as the door swung shut behind me. The barman was inscrutable, but curiosity always gets the better of hostility, doesn't it?

"Can I get yer?"

Not a big bar bill, thanks.

'Local brew. Half.'

I watched the golden liquid hit the bottom of the glass, then found my eyes caught by a single fly stuck fast on a hanging flypaper, its legs slowly waving as the paper turned out of my sight. Flies feed in a unique way. With no mouth parts, they regurgitate digestive enzymes that break down organic matter externally, ready for them to drink it through their straw-like proboscis. Flies can feed on organisms of any size. This vastly expands their larder of available resources and therefore chances of survival. Good for them.

My stomach rumbled, a long way from lunch.

'OK to camp near the water here?'

'People do. Just stay off the pass.'

The card reader glowered at me. If I didn't have at least a couple of drinks I'd never get talking to the locals, but having to explain why my credit card was declined would be getting off on the wrong foot. Blood pulsed in my ears as the screen buffered. *Ding.* Phew.

'Why?' I searched the barman's eyes, remembering the sighting of Boneless was on the path beside the water: Snake Pass. But there wasn't a hint of mystery to be found in his answer.

'Tractors use the route before dawn,' he shrugged, 'sometimes. What you over for, fish or birds?'

'Gastropods. I'm writing a piece for an American website. Rowan Quinn.' The barman's eyebrows shot up – his first facial expression since I stepped through the door. At last, a connection!

'Then you've come to the right place, Rowan! I'm Ted, welcome to the Drowned Oak.'

'You're famous for your gastropods round here.'

'I know, and I'll show you why!'

Ding ding ding.

He tapped a glass for quiet. I felt my face flush red. The clientele, who had only just returned to murmuring among themselves, fell silent again ...

'This is Rowan. He's reviewing the Drowned Oak for a foodie website.'

Gastropubs ... He thought I said 'gastropubs'.

'Come sit over here, Rowan! Here's our menu ...'

Sure enough, I spent the evening accepting free drinks, burger and fries, and engaging in pleasant convo with a sheep farmer called Rory, a couple called Maggie and Tim whose wedding venue had just flooded, and a man who introduced himself as John, but later I heard someone call him Colin. John or Colin had just moved his sheep and cows 'uphill' for midsummer. I asked why and he gave me a look that made me feel like the townie I am.

'To stop 'em going, that's why.'

They were all too young. Did anyone drink here who'd known Gerard Briggs in the late fifties, or at least remembered the story of his encounter with Boneless?

Later on, I spotted a likely candidate across the room and used my new identity as an international restaurant critic to introduce myself.

'Mind if I sit here? I'm Rowan.'

'Sally.'

She was at a corner table on her own, nursing half a Guinness and the same inscrutable expression as Ted.

'Lived here long, Sally?'

'Seventy-seven.'

She'd lived here seventy-seven years? Or was she seventy-seven? Or had she lived here since 1977? Did it matter, whichever it was? The Gerard Briggs story was from 1959. How many years ago was that? How long ago was 1977? I tried, but after four pints, the local ale didn't want any of that maths shit in my head.

'I read a funny story from back in the day. You might remember it. Dude saw a giant slug on the path beside the water.'

Nope. Still inscrutable.

'Lots of funny stories round here. People like to laugh.'

That expressionless face again. But whatever shuts off the numbers after four pints, lets loose the words …

'Maybe, but actually the steep sides between both branches of the reservoir creates an isolated microclimate where cloud forms quickly and rainfall comes in heavy bursts. Temperatures are higher and there's kilometres of protection from predators. Ideal conditions for a giant species to evolve, and if it's a creature that can use the water to hide in, which given its blowhole is quite …'

The next word – 'possible' – froze in my throat. The whole pub had fallen silent again and was listening.

'Giant slugs?' It was Ted, back to dour and unsmiling behind the bar. 'Folk round here used to eat 'em back in the day. Thought the slime kept 'em young and fought off plague. But there's a price to pay.' He nodded knowingly into the silence. What did he mean? I had to hear this.

'What? What's the price?'

'What d'yer think? You have to eat a giant slug!' The room erupted into laughter, of a kind. Is it possible to laugh without smiling?

The moment over, faces turned away, back to their drinks. *Tick tick tick*. Sally was tapping my pint glass with a beer mat.

'There you have it.' She pointed at the logo on the glass. I peered closer and for the first time noticed the name of the local lager: Mystery Lights. *Lots of funny stories round here*.

After that fourth pint my head was craving a pillow. I needed to get my tent up quickly. Ted gave me another penetrating stare as I handed back my glass.

'You know, if you're afraid, you can stay here,' he whispered, 'there's a couch in the hallway.'

Afraid? Why would I be afraid? Boneless might sound alarming, but if you saw a giraffe or a turtle with no prior knowledge or context, they would be terrifying too. Cryptozoology isn't about monsters or ghosts or parallel universes or the supernatural. It's about knowledge.

'Thanks, but no. Looking forward to camping by the water. Got a torch, got a groundsheet …'

'OK. Well, remember what I said. Steer clear of Snake Pass at night.'

'Tractors.'

'Aye. Tractors.'

*

The following are transcripts of recorded voice notes, compiled in chronological order and with punctuation and speaker names inserted for clarity.

Voice note # 1: Saturday 22 June

6 a.m. Slept well. Woke up to a headache and a chorus of coots and geese. Sat outside the tent, ate an energy bar and watched the dawn light change over the water. Mist swirled and rose. I'm spending today exploring the shores. Looking for places Boneless might live, and especially where it could find its way onto land. Being a reservoir, Ashbower's ecosystem hasn't evolved naturally over millennia the way a river's or lake's has. When the river was dammed, nature's hand was forced. Could a large species of slug have become trapped here while its predators were excluded? Throw in a genetic mutation and the conditions for Boneless to exist are ideal — I'll be the first to document and register it.

Voice note # 2: Saturday 22 June

12 p.m. I trekked up the west branch of the water, crossed at a wooden bridge and made my way along the north shore.

Whispering because this is the first person I've bumped into. He looks local so I'm ... getting a bit nearer.

Hi. Morning.

[In an undertone] *He's fishing from the entrance to his tent, his rod perfectly straight and low over the water. Can he not see or hear me? I'll get closer ... I'm practically standing in his bait box ...*

[Loudly] *HELLO!*

Fisherman: *Holy Mary! Thought you were the devil come to snatch me away!*
Rowan: *Not today! Mind if I sit down? I'm Rowan.*
Fisherman: *Rod.*
Rowan: *Caught much yet?*
Rod: *Much, no.* [Long pause]
Rowan: *Lived round here long?*
Rod: *Here? Born here.*
Rowan: *Amazing.* [Long pause] *Have you heard the story of Boneless, the giant slug? It was last seen in 1959 by ...*
Rod: *Gerard Briggs. Aye. I were fourteen. Big mystery. They said he fell in the water, drunk as a lord, accident, but my old pa always said there was more to it than that.*
Rowan: *Really? Like what?*
Rod: *Said he got into a row at the pub and never made it home.*

Rowan: [Long pause] *Gerard Briggs died? None of the reports mention that.*
Rod: *Dunno 'bout died ... no one saw him again.*
Rowan: *But how could he have told anyone about Boneless if he never made it home?*
Rod: *Ask at the old church on Crook Hill. Up thereabouts.*
Rowan: *OK ... have you ever seen any strange creatures around here?*
Rod: *I've seen the lights and that's enough.*
Rowan: *Lights? When? What happened?*
Rod: *You be quick. They lock up at one.*

Voice note #3: Saturday 22 June
This is a whole new angle on the Boneless story and not a good one for me. If Briggs had never actually told anyone, first-hand, about what happened on Christmas night 1959, then the story could have grown up entirely devoid of any actual cryptid sighting. Briggs could have left his wife that night, not gone home, run off with another woman. He might have fallen by accident into the water and his body never found. He might have been murdered. But if so, then how did the legend of Boneless become connected to him? If he didn't give that detailed description of a large black slug with its dragging gait and noxious slime, then who did?

Voice note #4: Saturday 22 June
OK. Here we are. Out of breath! [Long pause]

St Sebaldus is a tiny, ancient building of grey stone clinging to Crook Hill, a steep incline overlooking the water. The sign boasts regular services thanks to a church restoration charity and the parish padre, a Reverend Mitchell Enson. Two doors are set side by side, one marked 'In' and one 'Out'. Let's enter through the 'Out' door.

[Brief pause]

Rowan: *I'm standing in a stone-walled room with oak pews that would be full with a congregation of twenty. I can see the vicar busy at the back by the old font. HELLO? Father Enson?*

Vicar: *What do you want with him?*

Rowan: *I'm a biologist, looking into the cryptozoology of the area ...*

Vicar: *Ah, so you're the fellow looking for Boneless.*

Rowan: *Wow. That's the first time anyone has mentioned its name unprompted.*

Vicar: *We're a small community here and news travels fast. Cryptozoology, eh?*

Rowan: *The study of animals not known to science – and those considered extinct. There's a notional overlap with supernatural, paranormal or mythical creatures, but ... basically, I want to discover something no one else knows about.*

Vicar: *How can I help?*

Rowan: *A man called Gerard Briggs reportedly saw a giant slug here on Christmas night in 1959, yet I spoke to a fisherman by the water, just now, who said Briggs disappeared after leaving the pub that night.*

Vicar: *That's right. He was never seen again.*

[Brief pause]

Rowan: *It's one or the other, surely? He either saw the creature and told his story, or he disappeared and no one knew why. Rod the fisherman said to ask here, at the old church.*

Vicar: *Rod the fisherman? I think someone's having a joke with you.*

Rowan: *Fishing rod ... Oh. Right.* [Brief pause] *Well, if he didn't tell me his real name, I can't trust anything he said. He's probably sent me up here on a wild goose chase. If so, then I apologise, Father Enson.*

Vicar: *No, he was right to direct you here. I'll show you what he meant, come with me ... But I should tell you, I'm not Father Enson. He left the area soon after becoming parish priest. There's never been money enough to change the sign. I'm Father Nick.*

[Brief pause]

Rowan: *Father Nick unlocks a small cupboard door in the wall behind the font.*

Father Nick: *What's that you said?*

Rowan: *Just making a verbal note in my voice diary. I'm recording this on my phone. I'm writing a feature for an ...*

Father Nick: *Switch it off. I don't want to be recorded.*

Rowan: *Oh, OK. Sure.*

Voice note #5: Saturday 22 June

I'm back outside the church. So, Father Nick brought out a scuffed and faded old leather album. Ancient photographs fell out and fluttered to the floor. I picked up what I could. Black-and-white snaps of people standing outside the church holding flower arrangements and, in one case, a baby goat.

He said they used to have regular fêtes three, four times a year. Local people walked miles for Sunday service. But those days are long gone.

What he wanted to show me was an old sheet of paper, yellowed, frayed – glued into the album. The handwriting was large and wobbly and the ink faded brown. Still kicking myself for telling him I was recording our convo, I slipped my phone out and took a photo while his back was turned.

I found this photograph on Rowan's phone

On path big slug. Tall as a pony and black as dog. Gasping. Stuck the ground. Dropped torch light bigger blinding. Tell Bella sorry, love you
Gerry.

[Continued]
Apparently, it was found in reeds between the path and the water by villagers who were on their way to church on Boxing Day, 1959. They handed it to the priest and it's stayed at St Sebaldus ever since. Father Nick said Gerry Briggs himself was never seen again. But that note is where the Boneless legend comes from.

BONELESS

I sat on an old, damp pew and studied it. Tried to read between the lines, the words, the letters even. What had Gerry seen that night? Of course, he was a farm hand in the late 1950s, how well did he read and write? My eyes focused on three words: light bigger blinding. *I remembered the local brew. Mystery Lights.*

I asked Father Nick what was special about the lights in this area?

He lifted the album off my knee and hurried it back into the hole in the wall, turning a large key to lock it in.

Oh, strange lights are seen here from time to time, he told me. It's no doubt a natural phenomenon, or an optical illusion. In the darkness, a light in the window of a cottage can be seen for miles, even when the cottage itself isn't visible in daylight. Every so often a ... stranger sighting happens.

I asked him outright if he'd seen them himself. His eyelids flickered. Would he, a man of the cloth, stand there in a church, under a statue of Jesus and a stained-glass window of the Crucifixion, and tell a lie?

BANG! The 'Out' door slammed closed before he could answer. He hurried to open it and I took the opportunity to pick something up off the floor that I'd had my eye on since he'd stashed that album back in the wall.

I've got it here with me now. A photograph of three young girls standing in a row outside this church. They are in late-Edwardian dress, flower garlands in their hair and around their necks. Each carries a doll. What might be an ordinary scene is made extraordinary by the fact not one of them is smiling.

Voice note #6: Saturday 22 Jun

5 p.m. I stopped off at the Drowned Oak on my way back. The reservoir looks, to me, like the ideal microclimate for Boneless, yet my heart is sinking. I've been studying the picture of Gerry Briggs's letter on my phone. 'Slug' can mean a heavy blow. 'Tall as a pony' a colloquial way to describe a tall person? 'Black as dog' a blackout. 'Stuck the ground' or did he mean 'struck the ground'? Was my eyewitness the victim of an assault that night? Did he struggle to write that note before his lanky attacker returned, finished him off and threw his body in the water? If so, then the 'giant slug' story was a good cover for his murderer.

Or did he mean the 'black dog' of depression? Is this a barely literate man's suicide note, addled by alcohol and his own clouded psyche? The ink is faded to brown ... or was it written in blood?

I'm going to drag my sore feet to the pub, hoping they still want a good review enough to give me something to eat and a drink. Or three.

Voice note #7: Saturday 22 June

11 p.m. Back in the tent. Getting torch batteries. Spoke to Sally again. I think she's seventy-seven. Showed her flower girls pic. It's the midsummer Ashbower festival and one of them is her mother!! She married the vicar of St Sebaldus's,

Sally's father. Anyway, Sally was at the church with her parents the night Gerry saw Boneless. They were 'waiting for the lights to pass' because 'when the lights come, something goes. A sheep, a cow or a poor soul'.

'They disappear?' I asked.

'They're never seen again,' was the reply.

It took a minute before the difference between my question and her answer filtered through the Mystery Lights in my bloodstream.

John or Colin, the farmer I spoke to yesterday. He moved his cows and sheep uphill: 'to stop 'em going'.

Mysterious lights have fuelled myth and legend around the world, but in all cases the cause is most likely natural, from atmospheric light refraction to escaping fossil gasses to biological luminescence.

Why don't these people just choose knowledge? Boneless is an animal, its behaviour dictated by its environment. Whatever atmospheric conditions cause the lights also trigger Boneless to head for land to feed. That slime is key to its success. Potentially poisonous or hallucinogenic secretions, like tree frogs'? Or perhaps it has solvent properties that break down the fibres of its prey, like the fly. Whatever ... that slime allows Boneless to feed on whatever organic matter it comes across.

Farm animals would be in danger for sure, but also unsuspecting humans out at night on the path, especially if they were passed out drunk. If Gerard Briggs was caught in the slime, couldn't get up, couldn't escape, the connective tissues in his body would break down ready for the giant slug to move in and feed ... if you stay awake when the lights are due, you will likely avoid that fate.

'What happened to your father?' I asked. 'Where did he go?'

But by then Sally had received too many warning stares across tables crowded with empty glasses. She did not answer me.

As I hurried out of the Drowned Oak, Ted whispered from behind the bar, 'Be careful, now.'

Gonna pack up my tent and ground sheet and hike up to the church. I'll stay there tonight, speak to Father Nick again in the morning.

Voice note #8: Sunday 23 June

Stopped to get my bearings. Taking too long. So dark. Shoes wet from the grass. Path so twisty can't stay on it. Steer clear of Snake Pass at night. Lost all track of time and space. Where's the water? Stick to the path, it runs alongside all the way round. Ahead there's a big dark shape. A cracking noise like fabric snapping in the wind. Heart nearly stopped. It's just darkness! Fear's so illogical. I want evidence of Boneless, don't I? So why am I fighting this terror? There are no monsters, just gaps in our knowledge. Whatever this is, it's fine. I just need to take one step forward and it's perfectly ... no. There's something there, ahead of me, between the path and the water. But what? What the fuck is that?

Voice note #9: Sunday 23 June
Rod! Rod! Shit, that's not his name, is it. Wish I'd kicked his fat face into the reservoir! There, I've kicked the tent. If Rod is on the other side of the canvas it would be a happy accident but it's empty, just a stool and a rod holder. I could stay here. I don't have to go up to the church, but I will. I don't have to kick the stool and rod holder into the water, but I do. I'm just having a laugh! And another one!
[Long pause]
I'm back on Snake Pass. It's darker than anywhere I've ever been, not a star in the sky. But am I looking up or down? How long ago did I see the tent ... ?
The land seems to rise beneath my feet. This must be the lower slope of Crook Hill. This darkness feels solid.
Ding
What's that? There's no signal here.

Printed from Rowan's text app:

Mum
This is Dad. I left my phone at home in the panic. Sorry to disturb your revision but it's urgent. Please call.

[Continued]
Fuck, yeah. I should be at a study retreat. No, I should be at home but I'm here on a dark hillside chasing a myth. I should be feasting on other people's knowledge, feeling desperate about finals, research projects, grades, interviews.

It's ... it's 1.33 a.m. I don't need to call to know what Dad's going to say. I don't want to hear it.
The time! I want to get up to the church where they've known Boneless for generations. You're never seen again.
[A long interlude of heavy breathing and footsteps]
There's a light in the sky.
[A shorter interval of heavy breathing and footsteps]
Is that the sky though? It's high above me, but where am I? Walking up Crook Hill. Of course the light will be above me! It's the church. A night light above the 'In' door. Locked. Doesn't matter. I'll camp outside and see Father Nick tomorrow. He's got some explaining to do.

*

There are no more voice notes, but the following material is reproduced from a series of photographs all taken on 28 June. They show notes written on different paper. Each page is thin, like the paper of a Bible or hymn book. The ink is a strange shade of brown.

Pulsing sound. Blue light, blinding but no shadows. Ran towards the water, running, running, but it never came. Legs wouldn't move. Slime. Got on my knees to look at it. Careful. Don't touch. Thick, like drying glue but stronger by the minute. Weird metallic smell. Weird. Need to save some, but can't breathe, lungs too small. I'm still, like the eye of the storm, while the world around me changes.

BONELESS

So much to find out, but no time. Tried to take picture but phone too big. It grew 'til I couldn't even hold it. The torch was huge too and lit up the whole area. *Light bigger blinding.* Surely someone will see all this light? Alice in Wonderland, hold my beer. My pint of Mystery Lights. Told myself this is just a trip. I inhaled. The slime messes with your visual perspective. This isn't real, isn't happening. I laughed because I'm here to prove Boneless IS real! *People like to laugh.*

I was stuck to the ground, the water a mile away, the hill a mountain. Everything is bigger and *more* somehow. My senses are heightened, magnified. Water lapping, insects flying, plants growing, worms moving in the earth beneath my feet. Then a rasping, yawning sound or something dragging itself across the ground towards me. The sound a slug might make as it moves.

*

Boneless is a gastropod of unknown genus. The highest point of its back is level with my eye. Glossy black, shorter tentacles and larger breathing hole than known species. It seemed to grow as I watched it, or was it just getting nearer? How can it move that quickly? I struggle to move out of its way. Its eye swivels on its eye stalk, but I'm still fighting to breathe – there's no space in my lungs anymore. I close my eyes and decide to sleep off the effects of the drug. I can have the slime analysed at uni. I'll apologise, ask if I can repeat the year and graduate next summer. When I tell them about what I saw, they'll organise a field trip here for the department. Just need to sleep that feeling off – that feeling of being so small – so overwhelmed by the landscape.

*

I woke, stuck fast in the slime, like the fly on the flypaper at the Drowned Oak. My arms, legs paralysed as it reared above me, its wet jaws closed around my leg ...

*

'Rowan. Rowan.' Father Nick's voice, louder and deeper than I remembered. I'm lying in the church but still tripping.

What happened out there? I'm wet. Father Nick ... but wait, his hand is enormous. Terrifying! It holds a giant cloth ... 'Tricky to get off, but it's all gone now.' He moves away. This place is cavernous. I can see my things strewn on the floor around me, papers, the torch, my phone, the photograph, but all of them huge, like film props.

That photo of the young girls is beside me. They're so serious. Surrounded by garlands of flowers. I know they're only images on a small card, yet they're the same height I am. I look closer, see something I didn't notice before. They aren't holding dolls, like I thought. I feel my chest lurch with that sensation again, a sensation as if my lungs have shrunk, because for me it's literally the cold light of day.

I sit up. I'm not lying on the floor, but on the altar. And I'm tiny.

*

I'm not drunk or drugged and I finally know ... there are no *giant* slugs, just tiny people. And now I'm one of them.

Father Nick loomed above me. He extended his hand, an unspoken invitation for me to step onto it.

'I'll take you to the others,' he said, 'Father Enson will help you adjust. He's one hundred and fourteen and has been their leader for seventy years.' *Sally's father*. 'The shrinking process seems to extend life considerably. With your scientific background, you can help explain to them why. You'll be an asset to the small community. You want to discover something no one else knows? This is your chance.'

'But what happened?'

'After the lights, come the slugs ... their slime shrinks and incapacitates any animal or human unfortunate enough to inhale or touch it and, once they're small enough, the slugs come back to eat them. Very few escape. You're one of the lucky ones. Beyond that, we're not sure. Perhaps you can help us find out?'

He smiled at me. Finally.

*

I liken it to ants, living in nests far beneath the ground. The young queens know instinctively when conditions in the upper atmosphere are conducive to their mating rituals and that's when they swarm.

It's this basin, this landscape. The lights suggest a gaseous or electric element to the microclimate, or a meteorological change that renders the lights visible at certain times. Boneless responds to that same trigger as a signal to venture onto land. I wondered if this was part of its reproductive cycle. But given the evidence, I now suspect something else. The shrinking phenomenon is the clue.

This is my theory: I suspect decaying sludge in this man-made body of water lacks a natural variety of protein, so the slug must periodically seek meat on land. For similar reasons, wild chimpanzees hunt and eat smaller monkeys on occasion, not as part of their regular vegetarian diet.

This line of gastropods has a unique way of feeding. It faces danger on land, so nature limits the amount of time it spends there and has made its feeding process super-efficient. The slime means it can eat any creature, regardless of how big. It simply shrinks them to a suitable size for the slug to feed upon.

Nature. Evolution. Purely and simply, Boneless is a result of nature's survival imperative.

People who, like me, survive the slime, must be studied and the chemical event deconstructed. It may be key to humanity's survival. It may be a cure-all. If the slime's cell-reducing power can be harnessed, then this could shrink cancer cells, tumours, viral molecules, disease: the possibilities are endless.

I need to tell people. Get this message out. But Father Nick and the Ashbower community won't help me. Why do they want this area and its extraordinary properties to remain a secret? There are scientists, experts, people I need to tell, things I need to say – but my voice is so small now. It can't be heard.

*

How long have I been in this tiny village beneath the church? Time is different here. Each day like a season. I'm with the others. People who disappeared. Some in a cloud of rumour and mystery, some with not a word of speculation as to where they'd gone. Sheep and calves were eaten regularly, but how many humans became slug food and no one ever knew what happened to them? We, the survivors here, are the lucky ones. That's what the big people tell us.

Gerard Briggs died three years ago. His tiny grave is outside. His name written on a lolly stick to mark it.

Father Enson told me his own story. The lights were due, but his daughter hadn't come home. He went out to find her and when he woke up, he was being carried into the church in a shoebox. He keeps saying his daughter Sally had been at home all the time, that she'd been hiding as a joke. He babbles a lot. I don't know what's true. They're all damaged here, all raging. None of them are like me. This is such a small world and if I don't escape, I'll simply adapt and become like them.

So if you're reading this, please, please contact

The last word is smeared as if he had to stop writing very abruptly.

*

I looked up the following:

Article posted by Derbyonline.co.uk on 29 June:

Hope fades for missing camper

Hope of finding missing student Rowan Quinn alive is fading, police say. Quinn (21) went on a camping trip, alone, to Ashbower Basin on 21 June. His father said yesterday, 'Rowan's mother very sadly passed away at the weekend. I didn't get the chance to tell him. We're afraid the stress of her illness and the fact he hadn't told us he'd dropped out of his course mean he's done something rash and irreversible. If anyone out there is struggling, please, please ask for help.'

Rowan Quinn was last seen on Saturday evening (22 June) at the Drowned Oak pub on the reservoir's south shore in a state of 'agitation', according to locals. His tent and other personal items were found at the bottom of Crook Hill. Police have asked anyone with information to contact them.

*

I've looked closely at Rowan's last messages, written by hand on thin, almost transparent paper. The ink is brown. It looks natural, like something made from clay and water. I thought it might be scratched onto the page as if by a quill or other sharp implement, but now I can see it's more rounded and less even than that. Smudged, blurred, as if each letter was smeared there ... by two tiny, determined hands.

Who sent me this phone? Father Nick? Sally? Ted, landlord of the Drowned Oak? There's no doubt residents of the Basin know what's going on there. Perhaps Rowan convinced one of them that science will benefit from the extraordinary properties of the local slugs' slime, but they're too scared to expose these dark secrets themselves.

Mystery lights. Giant slugs. Slime that shrinks people. Anyone going public with such a fantastical story would face scepticism and humiliation at the very least. Then, what if I tell the police and they investigate, but the residents of Ashbower – realising an outsider knows everything – cover their tracks, hide the evidence? I'd be in trouble for wasting police time ... No, it's best I stick with fiction and leave paranormal exposés to the journalists. It's such a good story though, perhaps I'll save it. It's ideal for a collection of short stories – say, a dark, folk horror anthology ... the sort of publication in which no one expects to believe what they read.

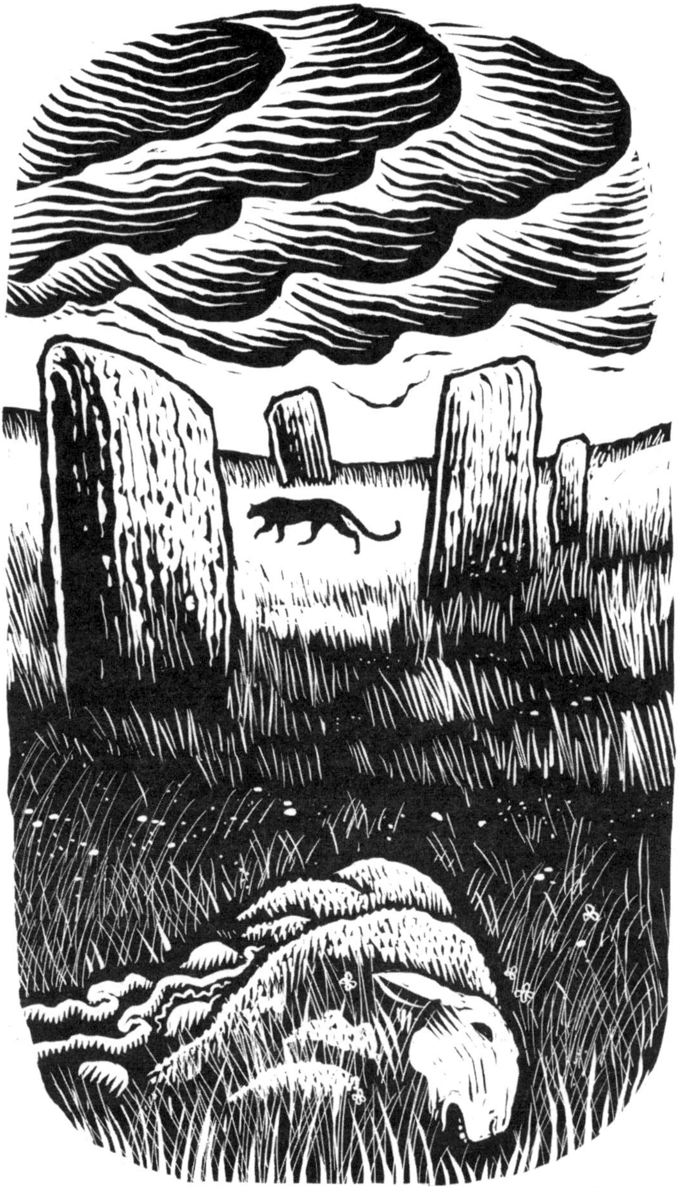

The Beast of Bodmin

JANE JOHNSON

Gina had always dreamed of living in Cornwall. She had never felt as if she fitted in anywhere else; or rather, that wherever else she had lived was missing some vital component. On summer holidays as a kid she had poked around in Cornish rockpools to induce tiny otherworldly creatures to dart out of the cloaking seaweed, and searched the storm wrack for treasures thrown up by retreating tides. She had found mermaids' purses (though, disappointingly, no mermaids) and cuttlefish bones, sea glass rendered smooth and opaque by the waves, and once, memorably, a tiny, stoppered bottle on which thrillingly foreign letters from some unrecognisable alphabet were barely visible in the glass, all reminders of the unknowability of the ocean. These talisman objects were so freighted with memory that she had kept them ever since. They had accompanied her to college in Peckham, to flat shares around the less salubrious areas of London, to the heart of Bristol, and then to her rented home with Daniel in Clevedon. A corner of every bathroom was forever Cornwall, a reminder of a time before life became fully explicable and prosaic. Even so, Dan hated them, referring to her collection as 'a heap of junk'. Eventually she stowed them away in a dusty box. And almost forgot about them.

But in a corner of her heart, equally dusty and hidden away, she had also stored her dream of returning to the Cornwall of her childhood, not as a visitor, trammelled by the ever-decreasing weeks, then days, then moments, of fleeting holiday time, but as a true, wild denizen of the county.

This dream had got her through some hard times. Through heartbreaks and disappointments, redundancy and then – shockingly – the loss of not just one but both of her parents. A car accident in France: impossible to process. Gina suddenly found herself simultaneously orphaned and burdened with responsibility for the family home, a barn conversion outside Amersham, as well as with her parents' half-feral black cat, Roxy. Unfortunately, Roxy took an instant dislike to Dan. The feeling was mutual.

The cat gave him an unfriendly stare, and when he sat down at the far side of the room, jumped up onto his lap, turned her rear towards him and fluffed out her tail, casting out dander, causing him to sneeze and sneeze.

He rounded on Gina. 'You didn't tell me there was a bloody cat! You know I'm allergic.'

'I did tell you: you just didn't listen.'

Dan stormed off, put on his trainers and Lycra and literally did a runner, disappearing into the lanes around the village on an excursion from which he didn't return till nightfall. Gina, gnawed to the bone by anxiety, imagined him crushed by a tractor or hurled into a ditch by the bonnet of a speeding car. When he finally returned unscathed, Gina lost it with him. 'You're a monster!' she yelled.

Dan stared at her. She'd never dared to shout at him before. Appalled, he went to sleep on the sofa downstairs.

As she dozed, Gina felt movement, and someone, or something, settled up against her. She woke for a moment, then plunged into a deeper sleep than ever, a sleep in which she dreamed she was flowing across an unfamiliar heath; or maybe she was in the landscape and *it* was flowing past *her*. It was surreal: she was large, she was small, she was terrified, then ravenous. There was blood, and the smell of death, and she wasn't alone.

As she came slowly to the surface of consciousness, she realised she really wasn't alone, but it wasn't Dan there beside her, but her parents' cat, Roxy. She was sitting very upright, staring at Gina with golden eyes as if trying to communicate something grave and life-changing, like a message from beyond.

Gina's father had adored Roxy. He had acquired the cat from a rescue centre where she was on death row, due to be euthanised unless she was adopted.

'She's always running away: we never know where she's gone,' was the complaint of the woman who'd deposited the cat there. 'I was about to choose this little tabby,' Gina's father said, 'but then I turned around and this rough-looking black cat was watching me intently, as if her life depended on it. Which it did: so I brought her home.'

Gina's father was a kind, steady man who adored animals; her mother put her energy into people – foodbanks and fundraisers, jumble sales and fun runs. It seemed unfair that such decent people should have been snatched away, leaving both Gina and Roxy bereft. And now she and Roxy were all that were left, and the world felt a lot darker.

Gina found a decision hardening in her heart, one she'd been avoiding for months. Roxy needed a home; Dan hated cats. The two of them were incompatible and one would have to go.

She caressed the cat's bony head.

'Would you like to come and live with me in Cornwall?' she whispered, and Roxy purred and purred.

*

The months that succeeded this question passed in a welter of unpleasantness and bureaucracy, and battles with Daniel over their shared possessions. Every time she faltered, though, the imperative of the dream of Cornwall took a firm hold of her and guided her back on track. Taking the plunge to go fully freelance, Gina moved into the family house till the sale went through and she had dispersed the paraphernalia of her parents' lives. Memento mori filled her days and disturbed her nights. And one morning she entered the kitchen to find the torn and bloody remains of a rabbit under the table. Just the hind legs and scut: everything else consumed, presumably from the head down. After that, a vole, a shrew, a harvest mouse; then nothing except disapproving flat-lidded looks from Roxy at Gina's lack of appreciation for the offerings.

As the sale went through, Gina searched online property sites. The shocking thing, though, was the price of Cornish houses anywhere near the coast. And somehow, the coastal scenes seemed too saccharine, too tamed for the benefit of tourists: her childhood dream had palled. She wanted, she realised now, to live in 'real' Cornwall. Wild and ancient Cornwall. Which was why, as the chill of autumn nipped the evening air, she found herself standing outside a granite cottage on the edge of Bodmin Moor with a bunch of keys in her hand. Behind her on the road sat a hire van crammed with the trappings of her previous life and a complaining Roxy in a cat carrier on the passenger seat.

Roxy had not enjoyed the journey. Within moments of leaving, she had set up a tooth-grating yowl punctuated by the heavy breathing of an animal threatening to expire of hyperventilation unless the vehicle was stopped *right now*. And then, contradictory, in the way of all cats: *Hurry up, hurry up, hurry up.*

Now, with the van's doors firmly shut and the late-afternoon light failing, it was quite, quite silent. Not even a bird sang.

Through the trees Gina could see the distant glimmer of lights from the village she had walked around in the summer, when a benevolent sun had beamed down on the cluster of little houses and the great Celtic cross in the graveyard of the ancient church, and she had thought how pretty it was. Now she thought: those lights seem a long way off. On that first viewing of the cottage, so quaint and alluring, with roses and delphiniums out front and a back garden that seemed simply to melt into the vast wildness of the moor, Gina had lost her heart.

Now, however, she could feel the presence of the moor lurking behind the house, like a big sleeping animal, and she couldn't help but wonder if she had lost her mind.

She unlocked the front door and stepped inside. An even deeper silence met her here, a feeling of being watched. The darkness crowded in on her. Gina felt around for the light switch and flicked it on. Nothing.

At once, panic engulfed her. She was, she told herself, ready for this new chapter in her life, one as a single, independent woman with a cat, a freelance career, and some money in the bank; but what she was not ready for was a remote cottage on the edge of the moors with no electricity and – as she checked her mobile phone – of course, no signal.

A scream of frustration bubbled up inside her and she stifled it – not so much out of consideration for the neighbours (for there were no signs of life at either of the other two houses in the terrace, which she realised belatedly were probably holiday lets or second homes) as from a deep-seated reluctance to draw attention to herself from other moorland life. Summoning her courage and practicality — both of which she'd had to acquire by rather faster degrees than she'd have preferred over the past few months — she enabled the torch function on her phone and located the fuse box, discovering that the estate agent must have turned the electricity off at the mains. She levered the master switch down and at once the place flooded with light.

Gina went through the cottage, lighting every room against the encroaching darkness, selected the one where she would keep Roxy till the cat was used to her new domain (the last thing she wanted was for the animal to make a heroic trek hundreds of miles back to its previous home as displaced pets sometimes did) and went to fetch her from the van.

The cat carrier was empty.

Gina stared at the void within, at and under the passenger seat, at the crammed immensity of the rental van. Then she got back in, shut the door behind her and listened — for a yowl, a purr, even the sound of breathing — but the van felt as devoid of life as the cottage felt full. She got out again, shone her phone torch around, called and called, her voice shrill with frustration and fear.

Had she hallucinated the presence of the cat in the car and somehow, in an episode of stress-induced memory loss, left Roxy behind? But the muscle memory of hefting the carrier was strong as was her recollection of the howls of protest all the way down the A303. The only time she could recall the cat falling quiet had been as they approached, then passed, the ancient sacred sites of the Salisbury Plain. But she had driven the whole five hours of the journey without a stop, impelled by Roxy's will to reach their destination, so there was no way the cat could have escaped.

Full dark had fallen now, and a thin moon had risen in the velvety black sky. Gina realised she could make out every constellation of stars her father had ever taught her: the Plough and the Great Bear, Orion the Hunter, Lepus the Hare, and the flickering seven sisters of the Pleiades, winking in and out of sight as if they existed in two cosmic worlds at once. How she missed her dad. Feeling utterly bereft, and utterly guilty, Gina let the tears fall. She had never felt so alone. Here she was, in a new home which didn't feel like home at all; in another country, some said, a world away from anywhere she knew, and without a single friend or neighbour. What had she been thinking?

It was hard to give up on Roxy and go to bed. Gina went out time after time, calling for her lost cat, but there was no sign or sound of her. She closed the front door, then opened it again. How awful would it be for Roxy to return from wherever she had gone to find the door locked against her. But she was a woman on her own in a remote place: anyone could chance by and murder her and no one would even know ... Indecision gripped her, tearing her apart. At last she left the front door jammed slightly ajar, placed a bowl of wet cat food within sniffing distance, then wrapped herself in a duvet in the largest bedroom and tried to sleep, her senses hyper-alert, picking up inexplicable movements and noises just on the edge of her awareness – creaks and scuffles, heavy breathing, disembodied cries far off, and sometimes nearby, sounds of running feet, of fear and triumph.

And the next morning when she went downstairs, the cat food was untouched.

*

Between the myriad tasks of settling in, she walked for miles to the nearest villages and hamlets, knocking on doors and showing people photos on her phone of the lost cat. It was, at least, a good way to get to know her new community. Most people were kind and promised to call if they saw Roxy – also informing Gina of the places you could get a signal if you held your phone up, or climbed a hedge – and the local vicar told her to come and use his Wi-Fi connection whenever she liked. But one or two people looked at her askance and seemed nervous.

'Black cats are unlucky,' said an elderly woman whose face was as seamed as a dried apple. 'I don't hold with 'em. Get yourself a dog, I say, a good guard dog's what you need where you are. Strange goings on up that way.'

A farmer warned her, 'Best not go out on the moor at night. We been losing sheep. Don't give your little cat much chance of survival. There's something unnatural out there.'

When she asked what he meant by 'something unnatural', his expression became shuttered and he said, 'Don't speak of the Devil if you don't want 'e to appear.' The hairs on her forearms rose.

The vicar, when she took him up on his offer a few days later, laughed off the remarks. 'They're a superstitious lot around here, and they do love to spin a story.' He wasn't a Cornishman himself, he explained, rather apologetically. 'I came down from Bath.' He laughed. 'But if you like a strange tale, go into one of the moorland pubs – the Pipers or the Sword of the King – and buy one of the locals a pint of Doom Bar.'

That's exactly what Gina did. The Sword of the King didn't disappoint, but it wasn't an elderly local who regaled her with stories, but a group of ramblers, breaking their day's walk with hot chocolate and a pasty.

'I was walking out past the Hurlers one evening just after sunset,' said one, explaining that the Hurlers were concentric circles of granite stones erected by ancient peoples: no one knew what for. 'And I had this sensation something was watching me. Not human; something ... otherworldly.' The man's anorak was well worn; his face weather-beaten: he looked to be a seasoned walker, not someone given to telling fanciful stories. 'I didn't hang around.'

Emboldened by his confession, another man, younger, with a shock of ginger hair, introduced himself as Max. 'You've got to take care on the moor. It's beautiful during the day, but people have all sorts of odd experiences there. I mean, it's a truly ancient, atmospheric place. Stone circles, burial chambers, traces of settlement for over six thousand years.'

'Those stones channel energies,' an earnest young woman with multiple ear piercings added. 'You can feel them for yourself if you tune into them. It's the combination of the passage of so many lives across millennia with the primal wildness of the moor.'

The landlord leaned over the bar. 'Thank you, Karenza.' He rolled his eyes as if to communicate to Gina that he was not endorsing such a woo-woo theory. 'Dozmary Pool's not far from here – where King Arthur told Sir Bedivere to throw his sword Excalibur when he was mortally wounded in battle – that's what gives this pub its name. Legend.'

But the other walkers had warmed to the supernatural theme.

'There are ghosts, too,' said a woman wearing a striped beanie. 'Poor Charlotte Dymond was murdered by a jealous lover on the slopes of Roughtor, and he was hanged at Bodmin Gaol. It's said their spirits both roam the moor.'

'Then there's the Beast of Bodmin ...'

A collective groan swept through the group. 'Such nonsense,' a woman said.

'No, really, there have been loads of sightings,' Max said. 'For years – decades, in fact – there've been rumours about a giant cat roaming the moors, taking sheep, even cattle, frightening walkers. A motorist whose car broke down took a shortcut across the moor to seek help, got lost and stumbled about in the dark, fell in a bog, then swore he was chased by a big cat. Said it was a jaguar or a panther or something, but bigger, with eyes that glowed like headlights—'

'Sounds more like the Hound of the Baskervilles,' one of the walkers offered, and everyone laughed.

'The sightings come in spates – several one year, then nothing the next. Dozens of them. And I—' He swallowed, looking at Gina, who nodded encouragingly.

'Go on, please.'

'A couple of years back I camped out on the moor for a week, up your way, in fact, because that was where the last sighting had been reported. On the third night I heard this sound, like nothing I'd ever heard before, and I stuck my head out of the tent and there was *something* there. I managed to capture a few fuzzy shots – it was moving fast, but I swear you can make out a larger than usual catlike animal ...'

A woman in a smart rain jacket guffawed. 'Reckon you were smoking wacky baccy.'

'There could be a completely rational explanation. People may have released big cats onto the moor,' an older man said. 'You know – from zoos that have gone bust, or pets bought illegally that have got too big to keep.'

'Or it might all just be a load of bollocks,' said the woman, draining off her glass of wine. 'Probably generated by local publicans to rev up trade, eh, Rob?'

The man behind the bar gave her a narrow look, then said to Gina, 'There was sufficient evidence for a squad of RAF Reserves from St Mawgan to spend a day on the moors with night-sight equipment not so long ago—'

'Not so long ago? It were twenty year back, Rob, you're going senile!' one of the regulars chuckled. 'The Beast's out there for sure – maybe more than one of them – but they couldn't find it because the mist come down. Canny creatures, felines. If they don't want to be seen, they won't be seen.'

The idea of Max having seen the Beast close to her cottage gave Gina a sudden upwelling of fear for Roxy. Tears sprang to her eyes. Embarrassed, she searched in her bag for a tissue, and by the time she found one, the walkers were preparing to carry on their way.

Max hung back. 'I walk the moors a lot, so if you'd like some help looking for your lost cat?'

Gina smiled. 'That's really kind …' The 'but' hovered in the air between them.

He nodded. 'Okay, didn't mean to push myself upon you, but take my number …'

He had a nice smile, Gina thought, and it might be good to have someone she could call upon, so they swapped numbers and she watched as he ducked through the low door to join the other walkers outside.

'He's a good lad, our Max,' the publican said. 'Can turn his hand to most things.' Other locals vouched for him as well.

Gina thanked them, then finished her drink and headed outside to grab her bike. She pedalled off in the opposite direction from the walkers.

Low afternoon light burnished the upland banks of heather and gorse, elevating their dusty purples and golds to glowing, Byzantine hues. She concealed the bicycle in the furze and took a well-worn footpath that brought her up onto an open sward dotted with standing stones. She trod the close-cropped grass, following the stones as they wove their dance across the moor. Some reached only to waist-height; others dwarfed her. Standing in their lee, she felt the chill of the shade they cast, but also another sort of cold, one that spoke of a place inimical to, or at least unmoved by, the brief passage of human life. She reached her hand towards one of the rough pillars and was surprised to receive a sort of mild electric shock.

'Sorry,' she whispered, as if contact with her had somehow injured inanimate stone, and snatched her fingers away.

For a second, just the briefest whisper of time, she was sure she caught a response. Subvocal, mind to mind. *We see you*, it said. *We feel you. We know you.*

Gina looked around, but there was no one in view. The quality of the light had changed. She redoubled her pace, passing between the two highest menhirs set like sentinels to guard the site almost at a run, with a growing suspicion of a presence becoming immanent in the darkening air.

Nearing the road, and the stand of gorse in which she had hidden her bike, Gina caught her foot on something – a tussock she hadn't seen in the gloom – and almost went flying. She looked down and rather wished she hadn't, for it was not a grassy tussock that had tripped her, but the unmistakable back end of a small sheep – a woolly rump, a pair of delicate hind legs, a daggy tail – and then her eye snagged on a tangle of entrails spilling pink and brown from the red innards. The whiff rising from the disturbed remains was not of decay, but rather a meaty tang that coated the back of her tongue and throat, making her retch. The partial animal was flung almost performatively across the footpath, and she was quite sure it had not been there when she had come onto the moor. A frisson of primal fear ran through her and she sprinted for the spot where she had stashed her bicycle, giving gasps of thanks to an unseen god that it was still there, and pedalled the five miles home as if pursued by the very Devil.

*

The weather turned wet and windy, and Gina despaired for her lost cat. How could Roxy possibly survive in these conditions? Even though the cat was a good hunter, she'd be soaked through, cold and miserable. Driven by this thought, at the end of every workday, Gina put on a waterproof that was growing increasingly baggy as all the exercise and lack of appetite diminished her, and searched in ever-increasing circles, calling, listening.

'I'm sure poor Roxy's out on the moors, dead of hunger or killed by a fox.'

'It's actually quite rare for foxes to attack cats,' Max said. It was the third time he'd accompanied her. 'And even spoiled pet cats are wild little hunters at heart.'

'But maybe she's been hit by a car. I mean, she's black: as hard to see as a shadow.'

'Cats are wily animals. Don't give up hope.' He had given her a sturdy torch with a rubber handle to use on her nocturnal searches. 'It also doubles as a club,' he joked. 'In case you stumble across the Beast.'

The torch had a powerful beam: it illuminated a dead mouse on her path, its arc of light bright enough to show the bloody puncture wounds in its throat, and hope leaped up in her. But no Roxy appeared. Other murders followed, strewed close to the cottage: a vole, two rats, a crow; finally, a brightly plumed pheasant, breast ripped open and head gone, a lurid message from the Cornish hinterland.

On an evening when Gina was out on her own, since Max was putting up shelves for an elderly neighbour, the torch reflected shockingly off a pair of eyes amidst the furze, lambent as headlights. She gasped, and then they were gone. Too tall to be a fox or badger. Maybe a stray dog?

*

And then it snowed.

Gina wasn't used to country snow. The falls she'd experienced in London came and went in a blink, giving way to grey slush and lethal pavements, but when she opened the curtains in her moorland cottage one morning, it was to see a changed world, as if her home had been picked up by a giant hand and deposited in the tundra. Her first thought was of Roxy, a cat that loved to curl up by the fire. She might freeze to death. Gina pulled on her wellies and headed out of the back door, over the low wall and onto the moor, where gorse bushes and outcrops of granite were all that interrupted the swathe of white. She struck out for the top of the tor, marked by a single standing stone like a finger pointed to heaven, where she could get the best view: surely a black cat would stand out starkly against this frozen panorama?

She stared in every direction, straining to pick out a small animal in the vast whiteness, but the whole scene was empty of life. Disappointed, she turned and started to make her way back down to the cottage, literally retracing her steps, the only marks to spoil the pristine snow. Except that they were not the only marks now. Another set of prints had sprung up alongside her own, and they were not human.

Her heart clenched.

These were the tracks of a huge creature.

Gina whipped around, suddenly terrified, half-expecting to see the legendary Beast preparing to leap upon her, ready to rip out her throat and devour her from the head down. The air shimmered like a miasma, and for a moment she was sure she saw something shadowy and menacing; then it was as if the world tilted, and the figure dwindled and was gone, winking out of existence as tantalisingly as the Pleiades.

The snow kept falling, and Gina's pulse hammered in her ears. She felt odd, dizzy, displaced; maybe even a bit mad.

*

'I'll come right over.' Max's voice on the phone was eager. He didn't once ask her if she might be imagining things. Instead he simply stated, 'I'll bring my Nikon. It's good at low-aperture settings.'

Together they reclimbed the hill, but Gina was disappointed to see that the spoor was no longer distinct: new snow had blurred the imprints. Even so, Max hunched over them, taking photo after photo, while Gina illuminated them with the flashlight.

'You can see whatever made these is big,' he said, looking up at her, eyes shining.

The tip of his nose was red from the cold and the low-spectrum light caught the ends of his auburn hair, turning them to flame. He looked resplendent, Gina thought. She loved that he hadn't treated her as if she was crazy when she told him what she'd seen: even she was beginning to doubt the evidence of her own eyes. She leaned in and kissed him, and for long moments they stood awkwardly locked together, hampered by equipment and winter coats.

Then the air was full of noise, a great roaring whoosh of sound. A rumble that started beyond, and became trapped in the breastbone, where it reverberated till their blood shook. There was something with them; something behind them; something all around.

They broke apart and Gina found herself running – not as any sensible person would, downhill, towards the safety of her cottage, but for no reason she could think of, since instinct had taken over from thought, for the top of the tor and the marker stone there: a rugged pillar of rough granite patched with golden rosettes of lichen. Panting, she pressed her back to the stone, and as she did so, a vast creature materialised before her. Like the granite, it was patched and patterned. The word that came into her mind was 'jaguar', and that didn't seem in the least ridiculous, especially when it stepped towards her, so close that she could smell the rancid stench of its last meal.

Her knees turned to water. This was it: the way she would die. She could not outrun a big cat, could not overpower it, had no defences against its merciless teeth and claws. It would kill her now, devour her from the head down, and her mauled corpse would be left for some farmer or rambler to stumble upon: tangible, undeniable evidence of the existence of the Beast of Bodmin at last. It might even be Max who found her. Unless the Beast took him too ...

She closed her eyes and awaited the inevitable.

Hot breath on her face. The rank smell engulfed her.

Then:

Come, the Beast said, without words, into her mind. *Run with us.*

Gina's eyes fluttered open in shock. She took a step, and the world became a maelstrom of sound and movement, and suddenly she was running, growing, changing, filled with power and grace, and the jaguar was loping beside her, and beyond the jaguar was a huge tawny lioness – a barred feline with a long body and a wedge-shaped head for which she had no name – and a great, grey cat with vast, soft paws that seemed to dance across the snow, tufted ears and eyes outlined as if by kohl.

She did not know whether they ran for seconds, for minutes or hours: the movement was more flow than effort, joyous, natural, transcendent. Gina felt as if she inhabited her truest self, bigger, wilder, at one with all others in this shared, wild life. And as they ran, she heard them revelling in their domain.

We run! was what she heard in her mind, though the sound lay somewhere between a roar and a howl. *You are one with us now, one of the wild. We are the Beast; you are the Beast!*

And then, as abruptly as it had started, it was over, and Gina found herself standing on the other side of the tor, the one overlooking distant woods and the village, trembling all over, once more her own, usual human self.

Something bumped against her leg, and she looked down, and there was a small black cat regarding her intently.

'Roxy?' Gina dropped to her knees, all the air going out of her lungs. But how could this be? It was impossible! The creatures she had run with were giant and wild, and this was ...

Watch.

Roxy took a few fastidious steps, lifting her paws clear of the snow and giving each one a little shake, and then she leaped into the darkening air, and disappeared.

It was as if Gina had barely even blinked when a huge tawny head re-emerged and dropped a fat rabbit at Gina's feet. Another blink, and the lioness dwindled and became Roxy again. The rabbit's muscles shuddered with tremors of intent, and then it leaped up and bounded off down the hill.

Roxy stared at her with flat-lidded disapproval, and it was that look that convinced Gina. She reached her hand into the space from which her lost cat had emerged, retracted it once more, and watched with fascination as her arm shrank back to human size. What the hell had she become inside the wild highway? She had not felt monstrous, though: she had felt wonderful, powerful. A sense of loss crept over her. A gift had been given, then taken away. A promise of something greater, more essential. Now she was just Gina again. And Roxy – for now – was just Roxy. Or was she?

She bent and picked up the black cat, buried her nose in the snow-flecked fur and felt its purr run through her. This little cat looked like Roxy, smelled like Roxy, but Gina couldn't shake off the otherworldliness of her experience. She shivered. 'Is this what the legend is about?' she wondered aloud. 'Are you all the Beast of Bodmin – ordinary cats transformed?' For that was how she had felt when she had joined them – like some sort of ur-woman, fleet and strong and filled with a river of shared energy. It made a sort of delirious sense, was both terrifying and seductive. Roxy made no answer, just fixed her with a golden gaze that spoke of triumph and satisfaction.

In that moment, Gina questioned whether the decision to move onto Bodmin Moor had been fully her own. This should have felt chilling, but somehow all she felt was gratitude. Her transformation had been exhilarating, ecstatic. The fulfilment of a long-buried dream. She wondered what her primal self had become, how she had looked, whether she had been magnificent or monstrous. Maybe both?

And then it occurred to her that Roxy had brought her and Max – the man who believed in the Beast – together. Had there been a degree of contrivance to their meeting or was it sheer serendipity? What would Max become when she brought him here, as she knew she would? Anticipation of running with him along the highways set her veins afire, warmed her from the soles of her feet to the roots of her hair, and everywhere in between.

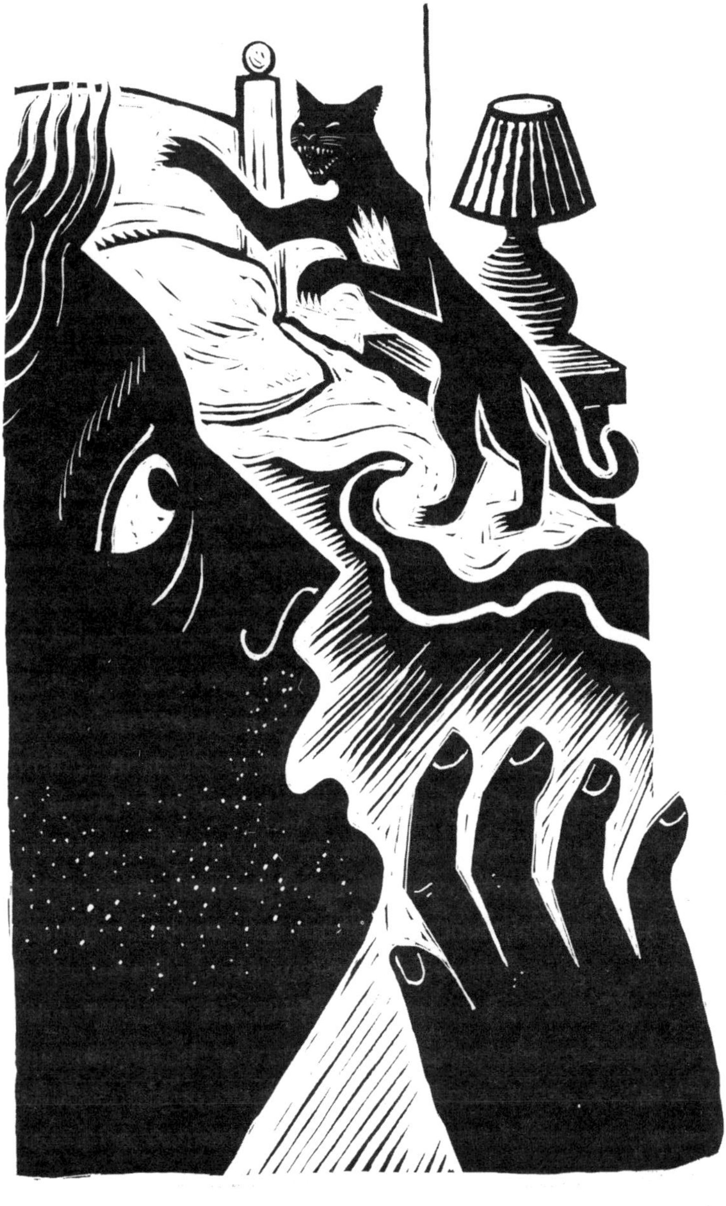

These Things Happen

DAN JONES

'Sorry to wake you, sir.'

Nick opened his eyes groggily as the stewardess touched his arm and pointed to his seatbelt. The plane was starting its descent.

'Fifteen minutes until we land,' she said brightly.

The girl reached for his glass. Nick got there first. He drained the dribble of whisky that was left before he handed it over. She eyed the shooting script on his lap, still open on the title page.

Secrets of Auk Island
Season 19, ep04
CURSE OF THE TEMPLARS [working title]

'*Auk Island*? My boyfriend watches that.' She smiled. 'On the Ancient Eras channel. You work on it?'

She bustled off. Nick looked half-heartedly at her arse, then glanced away. He had enough trouble with that sort of thing as it was. The plane lurched, buffeted by the

North Sea winds. Nick broke a sweat and tried to concentrate on the script – what little he had written. It was, as usual, tendentious bollocks.

This episode was about the Knights Templar: medieval warrior monks who were burned at the stake by some uptight French king for rogering each other, hoarding gold and worshipping Satan when they were meant to be fighting the Crusades.

They were a *Secrets of Auk Island* favourite. But even by *Auk Island* standards, this story was pretty dumb.

The Templars allegedly worshipped animals. The French king who abolished the Order said they summoned demons from hell into beastly form. Did these hellish beasts escape from France with renegade Templars and populate the Scottish isles ... ?

Christ, thought Nick, rubbing his eyes. It was hard to believe people watched this shit.

It was even harder to believe he made it. This wasn't exactly what he'd got into the telly game for. But he was the wrong side of forty-five and these days it kept him in work. He knew the production company found it hard to get other directors to come up here, to this weird island miles off the Scottish mainland. Or at least, to come back more than once.

A lot of them said they got a creepy vibe from the place. Not that the wankers ever managed to catch anything on camera. More likely, they were making excuses because they were too proud to do the job.

Nick had stopped being proud a long time ago. And he'd never heard anything go bump in the night in his life. Then again, he thought, as he belched into his mouth and tasted cheap airline Scotch, he didn't exactly have trouble getting off to sleep at night.

Bored of the script, he pulled out his phone. He thought about texting the girl from his local, see if she was up for something when he got back. He looked at her last message to him:

your disgustin. fuck off

He tried his wife instead.

Landing now.
Thanks for holding the fort while I'm away ... again.
Hope the kids are behaving!
See you soon

He typed a kiss, then two, then deleted them both. Just as he pressed send, the 4G signal disappeared from his phone.

The plane bumped down and trundled to the end of the runway. In the little shop by baggage claim, Nick bought a bottle of the cheapest local whisky and sixty fags. Then he got in the only taxi outside the airport, throwing his rucksack and camera cases on the back seat next to him.

'Where to, pal?' The driver didn't look round.

Nick slumped and looked at the call sheet Ingrid had sent him. Skarramoray Guesthouse, he told the man. He didn't remember staying there before.

'Twenty minutes,' said the driver. He put the car into gear and pulled away from the airport. Neither of them said a word until they got there.

*

The guesthouse lay on the far north coast of the island, surrounded by nothing but wind-blasted rocks and outcrops of tough salty grass. It was as far as it was possible to get from the only town, where they normally stayed, and where there was at least a crappy newsagent and a couple of shit pubs.

From the outside the place seemed clean and in good repair, but still. Nick shook his head. Ingrid was supposed to be an experienced production assistant. Why the hell had she stuck them out here? He guessed it was cheap.

His mood barely lifted when he walked through the front door. The place was done up like a fucking shortbread tin. Tartan wallpaper clashed with tartan carpet. There were bits of taxidermy on the windowsills and yellowing, foxed watercolour prints of Scottish island scenery everywhere. It smelled of wet coats.

Nick checked in, noting that his name was one of only three in the reservations book – the other two being Ingrid's and someone called Jeremy Sutton. He discovered the time of breakfast, the location of the bar and the fact that there was no Wi-Fi. Then he hauled his luggage up three flights of narrow stairs, separated by creaking corridors carpeted in more of the same musty red tartan. As he climbed, it grew stuffy and hot.

His room bore the name 'Rosslyn' on the door. It took him five minutes to get the key to turn in the stiff lock. He was on the verge of giving up and returning downstairs when finally it bit and the door opened.

The room was dingy, with a steep sloping ceiling formed by the eaves. A skylight and two dusty lamps provided the only light. And it was even warmer than the corridor, as though positioned above the boiler for the whole guesthouse.

Nick threw down his cases by the bed. His forehead was beaded with stale whisky sweat and his hair was plastered to the back of his neck. 'Jesus,' he said out loud. Everything about the room made him depressed: the low ceilings, the stuffiness, the thin mattress, the cracked mirror above the sink.

He looked at his watch. Apparently the bar was open from 5 p.m. It was now twenty past. Nick grabbed his wallet, one of the packs of cigarettes and a lighter, and debated whether or not to lock the door.

The camera gear was in there. Insurance said he was supposed to leave it somewhere secure if it was out of his sight. But the place was almost empty. Could he really be bothered wrestling with the key again later?

Nick pulled the door shut but didn't lock it. He almost ran down the three flights of stairs to the bar.

*

Ingrid was there, sitting at a table in the corner talking to a man Nick immediately made as their expert for the shoot. He was like a cartoon professor: mid-sixties, maybe, bald on top of his head but with the grey hair on the sides grown to his shoulders. He had bushy mutton-chop whiskers and big unfashionable glasses. He wore a cravat and waistcoat. A long tweed coat hung on his chair, and a heavy, brass-tipped walking cane lay on the floor nearby. Nick disliked him on sight.

The other two looked up as he came into the bar and Nick waved as he walked over, taking stock of the room. It was a decent enough place, hung with old prints and more taxidermy: a couple of stuffed puffins, an otter, and on the windowsill one of the biggest cats Nick had ever seen: almost the size of a dog. The cat had large yellow marbles for eyes and on its chest a white patch that stood out starkly against its black fur. Its coat seemed oddly thick and glossy, given that its guts were made of sawdust.

It seemed to be eyeballing him.

Nick eyeballed the bar.

'Hi, Nick,' Ingrid said breezily, though he could tell she was inspecting him. 'Good flight? Are you hungry?' She and the old geezer had just finished a meal.

'Not bad,' Nick said. 'Bumpy.' He looked at the plates on the table, streaked with grease and ketchup. 'I've eaten,' he lied.

The professor stood up formally to greet him. 'Jeremy Sutton. How do you do?' He bowed slightly.

'Nick. I'm the director. Thanks for making it up here.' Without waiting for a response, he went to the bar and ordered a pint. While he waited for it, he studied Sutton out of the corner of his eye, wondering again what had got into Ingrid. Historians on telly these days generally had piercings and tattoos and looked about fifteen. This dozy bird had gone and booked Hammer Horror Van Helsing from Cambridge high table.

He slurped the pint as he came back to join them. Ingrid and Sutton were now gazing around at the pictures on the walls, and Sutton was pointing something out. He had a large gold ring on his hand, engraved with a weird-looking cross.

'So,' Nick said. 'Interesting choice of hotel, Ingrid. Nice ... animals.' He nodded at the stuffed cat. 'What are we talking about?'

'Well, Jeremy was just explaining that there's some interesting new research on the accusations about the Templars and their dabblings in the occult,' said Ingrid. 'He suggested we stay at this place, actually. He's been here once or twice before.'

Nick half-listened as he let the beer take hold. Fair play to her, Ingrid was looking decent. She was in standard film-crew gear: cargos, fleece, walking boots. Hair pulled back in a ponytail. Hardly any make-up. Not exactly sexy, but there was something there.

He gulped more of his pint. 'Go on,' he said. 'Or save it for the camera tomorrow, if it's good.'

'Jeremy was just saying—'

The professor took over. He spoke in elaborate, grammatically perfect sentences.

'Most modern scholars of the history of the Knights Templar have doubted the truth of the claims made against the Order by the kings of the Middle Ages, not least the accusations of the brothers' taste for blasphemous acts, including worship of satanic deities, often in bestial form.'

'Right,' said Nick. 'Yeah.'

'No doubt in France, where the Templars were rigorously sought out and destroyed, these accusations were meant to frame them as idolators and were largely false. But here in the Outer Isles, where sources suggest a few renegade brothers fled during the destruction of the Order, it may be that there was more ... substance to this rumour.'

Nick laughed. He had been expecting whatever expert they brought along to dismiss all this talk of animal—demon worship as bollocks. But this old codger actually seemed to be standing it up.

'Hold on a sec,' he said. He went to the bar and ordered another pint, then added a double Scotch chaser. Sutton waited for him. Nick sat back down and for the first time since he had taken off that morning, he relaxed.

'The original accusations against the Templars mentioned worship of satanic idols, but also of a demon in cat form,'

Sutton continued. '*Those* accusations were never followed up in the trials of the Order's members.

'Yet in the Scottish Isles, within years of the Templars' alleged flight here, we begin to hear stories of the *cat-sìth*: a hellcat, if you will pardon the colloquialism, which bears in my judgement a remarkable likeness to the alleged feline demons worshipped in France. It roams at night. It attacks humans. It associates with other creatures of the dark world and must be placated so that it does not summon them to help it do harm. So the *myth* may not be entirely that.'

Sutton sipped from his own half-pint of bitter and raised his eyebrows, as if to say: *QED*. Ingrid looked encouragingly at Nick.

He laughed. '*Da Vinci Code*, eat your heart out.' He got up and picked up the stuffed cat from the windowsill. He held it at arm's length. 'Miaow,' he said, grinning. 'I'm coming to scratch your bollocks off.' He attempted to make the cat wave its stiff, dead paw.

Sutton looked aghast. Ingrid was staring at the table.

'Never mind.' Nick put the cat down and thought for a moment. If the professor was into this woo-woo cat theory, it could actually be TV gold. They could get it all on camera in one go the next morning and be wrapped by the middle of the afternoon. He might even be able to get down to the town in the south of the island for a few pints.

He turned his cigarette packet over on the table. It was worth a try. 'Ingrid, why don't we start tomorrow at the usual spots – the Neolithic burial site, the cliffs. Generic places. Wheels up at eight a.m. Maybe get the drone up if the wind isn't too strong. If it is, we knock off GVs. Eighteen mill for the big wide, two hundred mill to pick out moody wildlife and shit. You get a time-lapse going down on the beach.'

Sutton awkwardly rearranged the cutlery on the greasy plate in front of him. 'You don't want to film ...' he began.

Nick jiggled his leg impatiently. 'Yeah?'

Sutton bit his lip. He seemed ruffled. 'Well, there is also a medieval site—' he began before Nick cut him off. He had told them the plan and now he wanted a fag.

'Wheels at eight, yeah?' He stood up, staggered slightly, but caught hold of a chair.

'Can I get you anything else, Jeremy?' asked Ingrid, her voice tight. She wouldn't look at Nick.

The professor brightened. 'Most kind,' he said. 'But I must retire for the night.' He stood, put on his coat, retrieved his cane from the floor beside his chair and bowed.

As soon as he left, Ingrid went up, too. She didn't bother saying goodnight.

Nick shrugged and looked around the bar. Even the barman had momentarily vanished. 'Just you and me, mate,' he said, looking at the glossy-coated stuffed cat, with its gleaming yellow eyes and long, exposed claws. Its eyes seemed to glitter back at him.

When the barman returned, looking sullen, Nick ignored his obvious wish to close up and drank several more pints with double whiskies. He went outside and chain-smoked three cigarettes, came back in for a nightcap then stumbled up to his attic room.

He thanked his earlier self for not locking the door before falling asleep face down on his bed with his clothes on.

*

He woke up feeling awful. The lights were on and he had sweated through his clothes. It was 7.46 a.m. He would have no time for breakfast – not that he could stomach any.

Nick stood up, changed his sweaty T-shirt, pulled on a fleece and splashed his face at the bedroom sink. The water was cool, and though he guessed he had pissed in the sink before passing out the night before, he bent down to gulp from the tap.

Once he had got a few mouthfuls down, he stood up and looked at himself in the mirror. He looked fucking terrible. His eyes stung like they had sand in them. He leaned in to the mirror, pulling at his lower lids.

Then he saw something on the bed behind him.

'Jesus Christ!'

Nick recoiled from the mirror, half-tripped over his own feet and sat down heavily on the bed. Then he jumped up again, shrinking in horror from the thing beside him.

The cat from the bar glared up at him with its yellow marble eyes.

It was somehow balanced on its hind paws, as though it were rearing up, alive.

'Fuck!' said Nick. 'What the *fuck*?'

He stared back at the cat for a moment in disbelief. By daylight the thing was really creepy. A piece of rough red leather, which passed for a tongue, lolled from its mouth. Its teeth, which seemed to be real, looked razor-sharp. Its tail, which he could have sworn had been sticking upright the night before, curled behind it in a lifelike posture that made him feel ill.

He must have brought the bastard thing up with him last night when he was wrecked. Wrenched it into that idiotic pose. What had he been thinking?

Nick shook his head and laughed uneasily.

He'd done stupider things in his time.

But still.

Bloody hell.

He would have to take it back downstairs, or else the cleaner would find it while he was out.

Nick looked at his watch again: 7.56 a.m. He had said wheels up at eight.

Leaving his door unlocked again, Nick hurried downstairs with the camera cases in his hands and the cat tucked under his arm, preparing a joke to make if he saw anyone on the way. Its fur was greasy and slipped under his grip, feeling, somehow, repulsively alive.

Fortunately, he saw no one on his way down. Breakfast had been served in another room. The bar was empty, with the curtains still drawn. Nick snuck in and put the cat back more or less where it had come from. He wiped his hands on the back of his trousers and shuddered. Then he hurried out to the rental car without looking back.

Ingrid and Sutton were waiting for him, with the engine running.

*

It was a blustery day on the island. Squalls of light rain spattered the car's windscreen as Ingrid drove them up to the spot he called the Neolithic burial site – not that he was sure it really was. It was just the spot where they usually filmed pieces that had no obvious connection to anything on the island, which was almost everything they did.

Over the years Nick had used it as the backdrop for wonks like Sutton to talk about everything from how Auk Island 'might have been': the birthplace of Viking gods; the real location of Atlantis; where the Nazis came to hide a nuclear bomb; and the secret hiding place of Marie Antoinette. They had even actually talked about Neolithic burials there once.

The point was, it was easy to get to and looked moody on camera. He was past giving a fuck about anything else.

From the silence in the car, he could feel Ingrid was still annoyed with him, probably about having pooh-poohed the professor's suggestion of filming somewhere else. He decided against telling her anything about the stupid cat.

He doubted she'd see the funny side.

They drove on, Ingrid concentrating on the road and Sutton staring out of the window at the rugged countryside. The professor switched back and forth between looking through his glasses and using a small pair of binoculars — antique-looking things — with a case of leather trimmed with brass.

Nick checked his phone.

They must have driven through a patch of signal, because he had more than twenty emails: all junk or crap that could wait. There was a text from Ingrid saying she'd arrived at the guesthouse, and a message from his wife. He opened it.

Okay

There was also one from the girl in his local.

I said fuckin leave me aloun. Fuckin creep

He scrolled back, confused. It looked like he had sent a couple of messages to her late last night. They were pure nonsense.

Not for me

—venged on my

O Lord!

He must have been in a worse state than he thought. He winced and put the phone away. Maybe he should take it easy tonight.

When they parked at the burial site, Ingrid went down to the beach to set up a time-lapse. Nick stayed up at the main site — a grassy mound with boulders strewn over it, which rose from the headland at the top of the cliffs. He put a clip-on mic on Sutton then let him hobble off with his walking cane and binoculars. The professor seemed fascinated by something further around the coast, where a few old stone walls were visible, overgrown with bracken and weeds.

Nick lit a cigarette and started working out a shot list in his head. After a while, he called the professor back.

'I thought we'd do the first half of the interview here,' Nick said, pointing to an outcrop of rock where Sutton could lay down his cane and sit while they filmed. 'Talk through some of that stuff you were mentioning last night.'

'Very good,' said Sutton politely. 'But if I may ask …'

'Yeah?'

'I wondered why we are filming here?'

This again. 'Well, it looks dramatic in the back of shot. As far as I know, there's not much evidence the Templars were ever here, so …'

The professor looked faintly puzzled.

'Something wrong?'

'No, indeed,' said Sutton. 'It's just there is in fact a medieval site on the island. Or what I believe appears to be such. And if our subject matter is the Knights Templar and their … cats, look over here.' He gave a faint, peculiar smile, handed Nick his binoculars and pointed to the spot he had been studying.

Nick sighed and snuck a look at his watch, thinking of the pubs in the island's town. But then he looked through the binoculars, adjusted the focus and panned across the clifftop.

Though small, the binoculars were powerful, and at first it was hard to locate the spot. But then his gaze rested on it, and as it did so, he gasped.

Viewed through the lenses, the stone walls that had seemed broken and overgrown were in fact fully intact, built to about twelve feet high, with an arched wooden door, little windows and a slate-tiled roof. The windows were glazed with diamonds of leaded glass, but a flickering light seemed to glow through them and Nick thought he saw the silhouettes of people moving within.

His heart was pounding, but he could not look away.

He watched as the door opened.

Something – half-human, half-animal – was standing in the doorway. It had crooked legs, a long naked torso and a skull-like head from which long horns stuck out.

Around its hideous legs stalked a huge black cat.

Nick let out a yell. He let go of the binoculars, which clattered onto a stone by his feet. His hands were shaking. He was once again covered in sweat. 'What the fuck—'

'Oh, dear ...'

He looked around him in a daze. He could feel the veins in his neck straining as though they were about to explode.

It took him a moment to catch his breath, and when he did, he saw that Sutton was holding his binoculars and looking at them with dismay. The glass in one of the lenses was shattered.

At that moment Ingrid arrived from the beach. 'Everything okay?' she said, looking concerned. She saw the broken binoculars. 'Oh, Jeremy! What happened?'

Sutton was clearly annoyed but did his best to be gracious. 'It is, ah ... well. No matter. These things happen.'

Ingrid turned them over in her hands. 'I'm so sorry,' she said. She glared at Nick, then put her hand gently on

Sutton's arm. 'I'm sure we can get them fixed. And if not, we'll see if the production company can pay for a new pair.'

'Most kind,' said the professor, his voice tight. 'But I'm afraid they are one of a kind.'

Ingrid looked at Nick, questioningly this time. But he avoided her gaze. He was instead looking back along the coast, to the spot where he had just seen … whatever the fuck it was.

All that stood there now were stone ruins, overgrown with weeds.

'Nick?' said Ingrid, her voice a mixture of impatience and concern.

He went to the camera and made a show of adjusting the settings.

Eventually he felt calm enough to look up at them. 'Sorry about that,' he mumbled. 'Hand slipped.'

For a moment no one said anything.

'Let's turn over in five,' he said, trying to sound authoritative. But he could hardly stop his hands from shaking as he lit another fag.

*

Nick started the interview by throwing Sutton a few easy questions about the Templars, the medieval Church, their downfall, and popular belief in the brothers' worship of the occult.

He had to admit, the professor was good. His cravat and glasses worked on camera. Though Nick could tell he was still vexed about his binoculars, he gave elegant, succinct answers and did not mind going through each stage of the interview twice so Nick could film in different shot sizes, to make the footage easier to edit.

Nick, however, was feeling worse and worse. His mouth was dry and his head was pounding. His stomach was full of acid, which kept creeping up to the back of his throat.

He realised he had not eaten for nearly twenty-four hours. More than once he lost the thread of what the professor was saying, asking him the same question twice or else forgetting his next question. On the close-up shots, he kept screwing up the focus.

He could feel Ingrid growing uncomfortable.

But he could sense something else, too. He felt quite sure there was someone watching them. As though eyes were boring into him from somewhere nearby, moving around, always behind him.

'... accounts say that demons raised by the Templars could transform into a cat-*sìth*, and in turn the cat-*sìth* was capable of commanding ... Ah, I think your camera may be experiencing some technical issue.'

'Huh?' Nick realised Sutton had broken off his eloquent monologue and was looking at the body of the camera, where a red light was blinking rapidly.

'Shit,' he said. 'Battery.'

Ingrid went to the car to get a fresh one. Nick blinked hard. 'You know what?' he said. 'I think we've got it here. Thank you, Professor, that was ... yeah. That was great.'

He shouted to Ingrid, near the car. 'Bring the long lens and the sticks. We're done with sync. Drone can wait 'til tomorrow.'

Ingrid gave him a thumbs-up.

The professor looked blank. Nick took his microphone. 'I'm going to shoot some GVs ... ah, general-view shots. Stuff we can put voiceover on top of. You can sit in the car for twenty minutes, stay warm.'

'Very good.' The professor picked up his cane and walked slowly back to the vehicle. At one point he glanced back and gave Nick the same flicker of a smile he had earlier.

Nick pretended not to notice, glad to be rid of him.

*

With the others gone for a moment, Nick stuck an unlit fag in the corner of his mouth and got to work on the GVs. A storm was rolling in and the sky looked nice and dramatic.

He started with wide shots, then changed lenses to pick out detail. He filmed gulls circling. Moody clouds. Foam on the waves.

He deliberately avoided pointing the camera in the direction of the medieval ruins on the far clifftop. But somehow he felt their presence. As though it was from there that he was being watched. He glanced towards the car. Ingrid and Sutton were both inside, the professor drawing something like a diagram with his finger on the steamed-up passenger window. It looked a little like the cross on his signet ring.

Taking a deep breath, Nick turned the camera back towards the medieval site on the cliff and squinted through the viewfinder.

His stomach plummeted. Through the camera's high-quality lens, he could see it all in terrible detail.

The church, complete and in good repair, a sickly light burning in the windows. Flickering shadows which could only be cast by moving figures – some sort of ceremony? And in the doorway, the thing. It was facing into the building this time, and he could see now that it had leathery wings folded on its back and furry animal legs, with thick black bristling fur covering them, tapering to hooves. Its head was a triple-faced skull, topped with curling horns.

And there was the cat, the fucking cat, stalking around its feet, leaning into its lower legs and whipping its tail back and forth.

Nick's whole body was shaking but he kept the camera trained on the church, unable to look away.

A red warning light started blinking in the top right-hand corner of the viewfinder display, indicating this battery, too, was running low. After a few seconds, it ran out. The camera shut down and the display disappeared completely. It was as though the hideous image the lens had picked up had drained it to nothing.

He stared into the blackness of the dead viewfinder for what felt like a long time. Then he sank to his haunches and lit his now-damp cigarette.

A hand pressed his shoulder.

'Nick. What's going on?' Ingrid sounded concerned and embarrassed in equal measure.

Nick shut his eyes and pointed to the camera. 'There's something ... I saw something. Put a new battery in and roll the footage back. Ingrid ... I ...'

Sutton had now come to find out what was happening, and he and Ingrid stood by the camera and looked at the little LCD screen as she scrolled back through the thumbnails of the shots Nick had just taken.

'I don't ... Nick, I don't see anything,' said Ingrid, peering at the little screen. 'Just sea, the cliffs. Birds.'

Nick was still in a squat. He shook his head. 'I saw it. I fucking saw ... *it*.'

With some effort, Sutton laboured to his knees beside him. 'Might you describe this ... apparition?' he said, gently.

'There was a church there. A fully built church. And there was this thing with ... legs ... and horns.' Nick's voice sounded thick, like someone else's. 'But the worst thing was ... there was a cat. Christ! A fucking massive black cat.'

Sutton nodded. 'Fascinating,' he said. He sounded satisfied, even excited by Nick's description.

Nick looked around at him, suddenly irate. 'What the hell do you mean, fascinating?' he said. 'What's going on here? It was in your binoculars. Now it's in the camera only it's ... I can't find it. Have you seen this thing before?'

A few fat raindrops began to fall. The wind was picking up.

Sutton said nothing. He seemed to be lost in his thoughts and not to have heard Nick at all.

'For fuck's sake,' said Nick. 'For ...' He tailed off. He didn't know what else to say.

'Nick,' said Ingrid, 'I think you need to eat. Come on, let's get this gear into the car before the rain comes in.'

Nick suddenly felt exhausted and dazed. Somehow defeated. Ingrid was right. They couldn't let the gear be rained on. Maybe he'd imagined the whole thing. He was pretty hungry and hungover. He had Templars on the brain. He needed a break.

'Okay,' he said, standing up and nodding. He picked up the camera and stumbled numbly towards the car. 'Yeah. Yes. Okay,' he heard his voice say. 'That's a wrap on today.'

He looked back at the opposite clifftop. There was nothing there. Just tumbled rocks. He shook his head. He felt like he was losing the plot.

'Let's go and get a drink,' he said.

*

When they got back to the guesthouse, Ingrid and Sutton went to their rooms. Ingrid took the camera and said she would back up the day's footage onto a hard drive.

Nick had thought about going to his room to sleep for an hour, but instead he went straight to the bar. Whatever he had seen, or imagined he had seen, up there on the cliffs, it felt like it had left a mark on his brain. He needed to forget about it.

By the time the others appeared, he had drunk three pints and eaten two packets of peanuts. He was beginning to feel normal again.

The bar was warm and a fire was crackling in the grate. He looked around. Something was different.

That stuffed cat was missing. He must have put it back in the wrong place. Or maybe someone had seen sense and hurled the ugly thing in the bin, where it belonged. He felt incredibly relieved that it was gone and he was freed from its ugly yellow glare.

He ordered another pint.

Then, for the first time since the morning, his phone buzzed in his pocket. He pulled it out. It was a message from his wife.

What?

How much are you drinking?

He belched guiltily. Then his flesh began to crawl as he saw the string of messages before hers, apparently sent by him.

Not for us
Not for us O Lord
Nekam Adonai
Vengeance we will have vengeance we
Lord
to the generation to the thirteenth
Is e an cat an tighearna

Within the year
To spit on the Cross
God will avenge our death

He stared at the screen, perplexed, then typed a message.

Sorry. Phone went mad. Predictive text I think?? How are the kids? And you?

The message went through and the phone blinked three dots to indicate that she was replying.

...

...

But then the dots disappeared, and his 4G symbol vanished too. She was gone.

As Sutton settled himself at a table, laying down his walking cane and hanging his coat, Ingrid came and stood at the bar beside Nick.

'Drink?'

She ignored him. 'Nick, what happened today? Is anything wrong? At home maybe?'

He turned and faced the beer pumps, leaning on his elbows. 'I'm telling you, I saw something.'

'Saw something? Saw what?'

'I know it sounds crazy. But there was this ... Like I said. There was a church. And a ... I dunno. A sort of ... thing. Not an animal. Like, a ...' He felt embarrassed even to say the word. For all that he had tossed around tales of demons, monsters and strange goings-on during his *Auk Island* career, now it came to it, he felt ashamed to admit what he thought he had seen. 'Like, something. I don't know.'

Ingrid looked dubiously at the pint in his hand. 'How much are you drinking, Nick?'

'It's not that. I'm telling you.' He realised he was pleading.

She paused and bit her lip. 'I went through the footage just now. I couldn't see anything out of the ordinary. Nothing. Just random GVs. I know it's not my place to say it but some of them were pretty out of focus.' She cleared her throat, uncomfortable at criticising his camera work. 'Just in case we want to reshoot tomorrow.'

Nick hung his head for a moment. He felt it was futile to argue with her. 'Okay. Yeah. Yeah. Maybe it was something else. A goat or ... something.' He drained his glass and ordered another.

'Yes, maybe.' She paused. 'Christ, Nick, go easy. Come and have some dinner.'

He followed her unsteadily over to the table. The professor greeted him politely, but Nick thought he was looking at him in a curious way. They ordered food at the bar and made small talk while they waited for it to come.

Nick had chosen a homemade game pie and it arrived at the table steaming, slicked in glossy brown gravy, with a pile of vegetables on the side of the plate.

The sight of it made him feel nauseous. He moved the food around his plate, managed to fork only a few mouthfuls into his mouth before pushing it away.

He could feel Ingrid and Sutton watching him. They had finished their meal. He had barely touched his. The barman took the plates away with a look of disappointment when he picked up Nick's.

'Well,' said Ingrid, 'I think I'll turn in. Nick? Maybe you should get some sleep.'

He mumbled something indistinct and made no move as she and Sutton gathered their things and got ready to leave. He avoided their eyes, staring into his pint.

But before they left, the professor put his hand on Nick's back.

'You really saw something today.' It was not quite a question.

Nick nodded without looking up.

'I don't know. Christ, I'm so tired. It could have been. I—' He was going to show them his phone. The messages. But he fumbled it as he tried to take it out of his pocket and it clattered to the floor.

Ingrid had her arms folded and was looking at him coldly. But the professor had a strange expression on his face.

'May I give you some professional advice? It may amount to nothing, but perhaps it will.'

Nick looked at Sutton, feeling suddenly very desperate. He felt he might cry.

The professor narrowed his eyes behind his large glasses, as though he were studying a rare document. He turned the gold signet ring on his finger and straightened the flared lozenge with its engraved cross.

'You have upset someone,' he said. 'And you have only yourself to blame.'

Nick looked up at him, now genuinely afraid.

The professor seemed earnest, but not angry. He placed a delicate hand on Nick's shoulder and squeezed it lightly.

'Lock your door tonight,' said Sutton. 'And do not open it until the morning.'

*

It was pitch black in his room when he awoke and no longer warm and stuffy. In fact, it was so cold he was shaking.

He did not remember going to bed.

Nick shuddered and clung to the sheets, wrapping them around him. They were wet and he realised he was naked beneath them. The springs of his thin mattress creaked as he shook with the cold.

He tried to recall the last thing he could. Smoking outside? He could taste whisky. Fuck. What the fuck was wrong with him? What time was it? He put an arm out of his bed and felt around for his phone. He could not find it.

Then he froze as he heard a sound. There was scratching, like a rat's. In the dark he could not tell where it was coming from.

Slowly, his eyes adjusted to the bleak dark. The skylight in his room was wide open, and rain was blowing through it.

The scratching came again, and as it did, the professor's words came back to him.

Lock your door tonight.
Do not open it until the morning.

Had he done so? He had no idea.

But now there was no doubt: the scratching was coming from the direction of the door. It was getting louder. No rat would make a noise that loud.

Nick's teeth began to chatter. He curled up in a ball, dragging the wet sheets around him. The scratching grew even louder. So loud now that he felt it was piercing his brain.

'Go away,' he whimpered. 'Leave me alone. Please—'

The handle on the door began to rattle, turning back and forth. At first the movement was gentle, as though someone were trying to enter stealthily. Then it grew violent.

'Please—' Nick was crying now, sobbing as his teeth chattered in the cold.

The key was rattling and now the locked door was being pulled back and forth, as someone – or something – tried to break it open.

With a shriek, Nick uncurled himself and leaped out of bed, stumbling to where he thought the door was. But in the blackness he tripped and fell hard, banging his head on the radiator with a loud clang.

He rolled, dazed. The darkness in the room was shot with green light and stars danced around before his gaze.

He groaned.

And then it was on him. A scratching ball of claws and fur, howling as it ripped at his face and throat.

Nick shrieked and grabbed at the thing that clung to him, which was tearing at his skin, sinking its teeth into his cheeks and trying to scratch his eyes out.

He could smell something terrible, a rotting stench worse than death, fouler than anything he had ever known. Somewhere he could hear men chanting – a sound that seemed to swirl and gather, an awful cacophony that tore at his brain.

He tried to scream again but now his voice only came out as a whisper. His hands were numb with cold and he could not get a grip on the beast that was attacking him.

The rattling of the key in the lock now reached a crescendo, drowning out the chanting, and as Nick rolled and fought on the floor, the door flew open.

Light from the hall flooded the room, silhouetting a figure with what seemed to be wings spread at its back.

The figure sprang towards Nick and, with a roar, it swung something hard and heavy at his head.

Straight away the scratching at his face stopped. But in its place a powerful draught whipped through the room.

Nick howled again in terror and wrapped his arms tightly around his head, curling up on the floor, naked and stricken with fear, awaiting the monster's next blow.

Yet nothing came. All he could hear was the whistling of the wind and the panting of his own breath, juddering in rhythm with his pounding heart.

Professor Jeremy Sutton stood over him, with his brass-tipped walking cane in one hand. Over a pair of paisley pyjamas the professor wore his overcoat, which was billowing like wings in the wind gusting through the skylight and out by the open door.

'Extraordinary,' said Sutton.

Across the room, lying on the floor with stuffing spilling from a hole he had knocked in its side, was the stuffed cat from the bar. Its yellow marble eyes gazed up at the slope of the roof, blind and cold. But its teeth and claws were still bared.

Nick blinked and touched his face, which was scratched and bleeding. Beneath his nails were strips of his own pale skin.

He covered his eyes with the crook of his elbow and wept.

'Fascinating,' said Sutton, sounding amused. He continued to inspect the room: the soaked sheets and clothes strewn around the floor, the glasses filled with ash and cigarette butts, the empty whisky bottle and the sink blocked with vomit and full to the brim with dark, pungent urine.

On the floor, Nick was now on all fours. He was still naked and shaking with cold, but he was crawling as best he could towards a light blinking in the far corner of his room.

It was his mobile phone. Though the glass screen was spider-webbed from being dropped many times, it seemed that a series of messages was coming through.

When Nick picked up the phone, he found they were all from his wife.

I've had enough of this, Nick.

We all have.

When you come home we need to have a serious conversation.

This isn't working anymore.

Sutton watched him reading for a moment with a look of sympathetic pity on his face. Then he glanced up from the sink to the cracked mirror, just in time to see a horned skull duck from view.

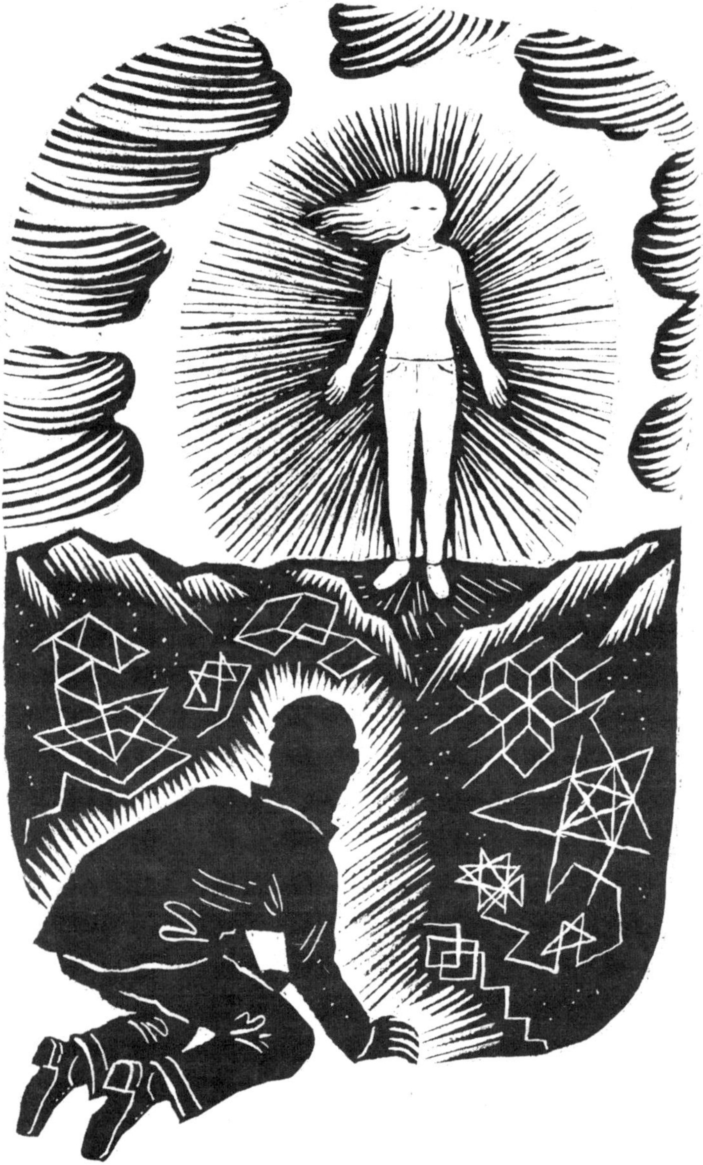

The Doctor's Wife

ABIR MUKHERJEE

Sunday

The cold wasn't a problem, nor the gale slicing like a knife straight from the Arctic. Worth it just for the view: for the greens and the golds and the light of a pale sun reflecting off the waters in the glen below.

Above, thin clouds peppered an ice-blue sky. A bird circled. An eagle, maybe, or a hawk. He hoped it was an eagle. Birdwatching wasn't something you did back home, but he might take it up here.

The passenger door opened, Mel struggling against the force of the wind.

'Get back in, Steven.'

'A minute,' he told her, and breathed in fresh air that smelled faintly of shit.

What a view. And only three hours from Glasgow. Hard to believe it was the same country.

He got back in, smoothed down his hair and started the engine. Not much further to go, at least per the satnav.

Forty minutes, give or take, unless they got stuck behind another bloody tractor. The car was too warm: Mel's choice, but he wasn't about to argue. He should have listened to her and taken his coat off when he got back in, but he hadn't because he knew best, even when he was wrong. Better just to keep going. He looked over at Mel, sitting there sullenly with her arms folded, looking out the side window at the trees as fixedly as if they held the secret to life. Best to leave her to it, stewing in her low-intensity pissed-offedness and the heat of the car.

He couldn't blame her, to be fair.

Six months, that's what he'd told her. Six months, a locum job, good money, and good Highland air. She could get a job at the local school, or at least one in the nearest big town – Inverness or Granton. He'd expected more time to bring her round to the idea, but that email last week had laid waste to his careful preparations. 'Change of plans. You're needed urgently.' And then, instead of having a month for Mel to make peace with the whole thing, say her goodbyes to kith and kin, he'd come home and told her it was all happening now, three weeks before Christmas.

Still, he'd make it up to her, somehow.

The sun was getting low. The bird was still in the sky, following them or leading them, he couldn't tell, its black wings outstretched like Christ upon the Cross. The road meandered down from the hills.

'That must be it,' he said, pointing out through the windscreen. A shortbread-tin village with a stream running through it, cottages to either side with lights twinkling in windows and wisps of smoke snaking from chimneys.

'Pretty, eh?'

She gave a nod, which felt to him like a victory.

The satnav, god bless it, led them to a pebble-dashed cottage at the end of a gravel driveway, small windows to either side of a pair of dark blue storm doors that looked to be bolted tight.

He killed the engine and for a moment they sat there, listening to the wind and silence and the ticking of the clock on the dashboard.

'Nice, eh?'

If Mel agreed, she kept it to herself. He reached for his phone, looked up a number and pressed call.

'Hello, is that Maggie? … Yes, that's right, Dr Gibson … We're at the cottage … right … great … See you soon.'

He ended the call and turned to Mel.

'She's coming over with the keys.'

*

Sure enough, five minutes later, a short middle-aged woman in a blue parka, shopping bags in hand and head down against the wind, struggled up the driveway. He got out of the car.

'Maggie?'

She beamed at him.

'Aye, the practice manager. And you must be Dr Gibson. Welcome to Glentorrance.'

'Steven,' he said, then pointed to the outline behind the windscreen. 'And that's Mel.'

The woman aimed a wave and a smile in his wife's direction, which proved enough to persuade Mel to open her own door and get out the car.

'Lovely to meet you.' Maggie fished in her pockets. 'Here we go.' She walked up to the door, stuck a key in the lock and turned it twice.

'Come on in out of the wind.'

*

The cottage was nice enough: bland and beige and probably unchanged since the nineties. A few paintings on the wall and the radiators on. Warm and toasty and damp-free, so already better than his flat in Finnieston.

Maggie gave them the tour and explained the self-explanatory: sitting room, dining room, kitchen. 'Upstairs there's two bedrooms and the bathroom. Cup of tea?'

It didn't feel like a question.

As she conjured milk and sugar from shopping bags and Mel examined mugs for hygiene, he wandered back through to the lounge, to the worn and faded Chesterfield and the boxy television and the cardboard boxes packed and stacked in a corner. The room was drab, the only colour coming from the paintings on the walls.

Watercolour landscapes. Highland scenes. Mountains and glens, all quite similar and bought together as a job lot, probably. But it was the other paintings that caught his attention. Two of them, not landscapes but portraits. The same woman. Something about the figure looked familiar, even though the face was vague and indistinct.

Outside the day was dying, the last of the colour being wrung from the sky, the drystone boundary wall just a black line amidst the charcoal. Beyond it a streetlamp, flickering to life, its light a milky pink.

'Tea's ready, doctor.'

He turned.

Maggie was standing at the door with a mug in each hand. No sign of Mel. She was probably busy organising the kitchen.

'These boxes?' he said.

'Aye, sorry about those. They're Dr Chakraborty's. They're going to be shipped out to India in a few weeks, but what with him leaving early, it's all got left here for now. I hope it's not too much of a bother.'

It wasn't a problem, not in the grand scheme of things, and anyway he'd be at work most of the time. But Mel would be around, fixing up the cottage, at least until the new school term. Shit. It would probably piss her off.

'Is there anywhere they can be stored in the meantime?'

His new colleague gave a shrug.

'There's the garage round the back, if you don't mind moving them?'

He supposed he'd little choice. He'd do it tomorrow, or at the weekend more likely. Tomorrow was work. First day, new surgery. First time working outside of Glasgow.

He followed Maggie back to the kitchen where Mel was stowing the contents of the shopping bags into cupboards. Maggie drained half her tea into the sink and rinsed her cup.

'I'll leave you in peace,' she said, and he walked her to the front door.

From her coat pocket she fished an envelope. 'Keys to the surgery and the code for the alarm.' She held it out for him. 'See you tomorrow then, doctor.'

'Aye,' he said. 'Looking forward to it.' And he was. A brave new world – that's what Glentorrance was to him.

*

He watched as Maggie made her way down the drive and disappeared into the night. Frost glistened in the lamplight. Breath turning to mist, he headed outside, shuttling between car boot and hallway with bags and cases and essentials hurriedly packed. It didn't take too long. A few minutes and they were cluttering up the hallway like it was an airport check-in queue. He opened the front door one last time.

'Ye gonnae leave that all sitting here?'

Mel's voice behind him.

'Just going for a smoke,' he told her. 'I'll take 'em up when I'm done.'

He stepped outside, closed the door behind him and sparked up. His hands started to tingle. It was going to be a cold one, what his dad would call *brass monkeys*.

Above him the sky was a celestial tapestry, the stars shining brighter and whiter than they had any right to. Nights like this, in places like this, they made you look at the universe differently. He took a pull on the cigarette and exhaled heavenward.

In the distance, in the shadows beyond the streetlamp, something stirred. A fleeting wisp of something, red against grey. He tried to make it out but there was nothing to see. Whatever it was, assuming that it had even been anything in the first place, was gone.

Dr Gibson finished his cigarette, cleared his lungs then breathed in, and this time there was no smell of shit.

Monday

The alarm went off at six. He fumbled for it in the dark. He hadn't slept well. First night in a new bed was always difficult for him. But it was the dream that really troubled him. It had been so vivid: a woman on a mountainside, leading him to a ravine … a body at the bottom of it, and as he looked down at it, the woman turned to him and he saw she had no face.

Mel stirred beside him. She reached over and put her arm round his chest.

'Ten minutes more.'

It was tempting. The world beyond the bed was dark and cold.

'Can't,' he whispered. 'You sleep, though.'

The surgery was close, but then everything in the village was close. A fifteen-minute walk, he reckoned, from one end to the other. The sky was gunmetal grey, the air a mix of sleet and drizzle. He pulled his coat tight around him and, with the last vestiges of the dream still haunting the back of his mind, set off down the drive and on towards the surgery.

The door was unlocked, which came as a shock, Maggie there already, behind the reception desk, a mug of something steaming away next to her. She brightened at the sight of him.

'You're early, doctor. You could've come in a bit later.'

'Couldn't sleep,' he told her, 'so I thought I might as well make a start on things. It's all happened a wee bit fast.'

He watched as her lips thinned and she looked to the floor.

'Aye. I'm really sorry about that. It all came as a bit of a shock to me too. Adi ... that's Dr Chakraborty ... he'd been here such a long time. I always thought he'd retire and live in the village. When he said he was going to leave, it surprised a lot of folks, and then, to go in such a hurry, without so much as a ...' She looked up again and put on a weak smile. 'Anyway, as you say, there's a lot to do. I'll show you through to the consulting room.'

*

The rush started at nine and didn't let up. Some patients had welcomed him. Others had been more guarded. That was par for the course though, wasn't it, in places like this? Places where everyone knew everyone else and outsiders were accepted slowly. Still, if the morning's patients were anything to go by, the last doctor, Chakraborty, seemed to have been accepted. They'd all asked about him; all interested in where he'd gone and why so suddenly. He'd told them what little he knew: that the good doctor had apparently decided to go back to India; and no, he'd no idea why the man had left so suddenly.

The glut of patients continued. It had surprised him somewhat. You pretty much expected it to be non-stop in big cities like Glasgow, but out here in the countryside, weren't things supposed to be a bit more sedate?

'We're backed up for the next week or so,' Maggie said between patients. 'On account of having to reschedule Dr Chakraborty's appointments from last week. It'll take a while to get back to normal.'

He told her it wasn't a problem, and really, it wasn't. Folks were different here, more polite, more personable. Still, by five p.m., he was feeling it. The world outside was black. He caught his reflection in the dark glass of the window. Maybe it was the lack of sleep, or the strain and upheaval of the last few days, but he looked older and pallid, drained of colour like a ghost. For a moment it felt like he was looking at a totally different man. A shiver passed through him as though, as his mother would say, someone had just walked over his grave. He shook the thought from his head. He needed to pull himself together. Do some exercise, cut down on the fags.

At least the appointments were done. An hour and a half of the afternoon walk-ins to go and then he could call it a night. He should phone Mel. See how she was getting on. An attempt during his lunch break had gone to voice-mail. Lack of reception probably. It was patchy up here among the hills. Before he could consider it further, the door opened. A young woman entered. The sight of her took his breath away. Late twenties or early thirties, he thought, long, flowing auburn hair and the kind of green eyes you might get lost in. She was dressed in blue jeans and red T-shirt. It hardly seemed like the weather for it, but then these Highland lasses were supposed to be tough.

The sight of him, sitting there, seemed to confuse her.

'Where's the doctor?'

'I ... I am the doctor,' he told her.

Her features darkened.

'No. You're not.'

The thought that he might have disappointed her stung, and the recognition of that irritated him further. He was too old for this, wasn't he? The urge to impress a beautiful woman. Or maybe one never grew out of it. Maybe it was hard-wired into the straight-male psyche. And suddenly he wanted her to be happy. Why, he didn't know, but he'd give anything to see her smile.

'I'm the new doctor,' he said. 'Dr Chakraborty retired. He's gone back to India.'

For a moment she simply stood there, staring at him as though he was speaking a different language.

'That's not possible. He wouldn't leave.'

He felt his stomach knot. Her disappointment seemed like a rebuke aimed directly at him. But why?

People sometimes got too attached to their doctors. They taught you about it at medical school. Girls and boys, often from broken homes. The doctor sometimes became a proxy father figure. Was that what this was?

'Maybe I can help?' he said. 'Why don't you take a seat and tell me your name?'

She shook her head.

'No. I'll come back.'

She was halfway out the door before he even thought to persuade her otherwise, and honestly, he was too tired even to try.

*

At six-thirty, Maggie knocked and stuck her head round the door.

'That's it for the day, doctor. I promise they'll not all be as hectic as this one.'

'It's not been that bad,' he told her, more reflexively than out of any real conviction. 'I'll say one thing: the old doctor seems to have been popular. So many people asking after him.'

'Aye,' she said. 'That he was. Shame *he* didn't see it.' She gave a shrug. 'Shame he didn't even say goodbye to them.'

There was an edge to her voice. Hurt or dislike, maybe? He didn't care enough to pry further.

'Anyway,' she said, 'I'll say goodnight. Are you okay locking up like I showed you?'

'Aye, fine.'

'And the code for the alarm?'

'Still got it.' He read it off a yellow Post-it stuck to the foot of his monitor, and if she had any qualms about the blatant lapse in security, she kept them to herself.

Thirty minutes more, he told himself, to finish up on paperwork. An hour, max, and then he'd head back. Still, it was worth texting Mel. He picked up his phone.

Home within the hour. All OK? xx

The response came a few minutes later.

Not really. Please come home

He tried calling her, but the reception on his mobile was shitty. He tried from the landline and only got her voicemail.

He texted her.

On my way xx

*

The air outside hit him like an insult. There was snow coming. The forecast said as much. The path to the road was already treacherous, frost glistening in the lamplight. Someone would have to grit it before the morning.

As he looked up again, he caught sight of someone. A woman, standing in the glow of a streetlamp maybe two hundred metres away, staring straight at him, or at least that was how it felt. He looked closer. Blue jeans. Red

T-shirt. A frisson of something passed through him. A frost-induced shiver, that's what it was. Nothing more. She, though, seemed impervious to the cold, her arms bare to the elements. The breath seemed to leave him. He slipped on the path and lost his balance. By the time he'd recovered and looked over again, she was gone, disappeared into the blackness of the night.

Did she think he'd been lying to her? Did she think Dr Chakraborty was still there? Was that why she'd been waiting? Poor thing. He'd need to ask Maggie about her. If she came in again, he'd make sure to have a chat with her. Now, though, he needed to get back. Mel was waiting for him.

*

At the cottage all the lights were on.

'I'm home,' he said, closing the front door behind him. The hallway was full of boxes. Mel came rushing down the stairs. She flung her arms round him and buried her head in his chest.

'You okay?'

For a moment she said nothing.

'Mel?'

'I'm okay,' she said eventually.

'What's happened?'

She released him.

'It's just … I don't know. It's been a long day. I've been trying to get this place sorted, trying to clear out the old guy's stuff.'

'And?'

'It ... It's hard to explain. Those paintings are freaking me out. That woman without a face ... it's fucking creepy. Who puts stuff like that on their walls? And there's more of them. Look.'

She gestured to a box. 'There's about ten of them in there. Sketches and things – all the same. I reckon the old guy drew them. It's weird. I even had a dream about it.'

'What?'

She shook her head.

'It doesn't matter, but Steven, I don't like it here.'

She was being too hasty, of course. She hadn't given it a proper chance. Besides, the rent was next to nothing and at the very least, six months here would go a long way towards a deposit on a decent house back in Glasgow. They'd be able to leave the shitty little flat in Finnieston. Wasn't that what she wanted? But he wasn't about to say any of that, not just now.

'Let's talk about it later,' he told her. 'I'll take the pictures down.'

She gave him a nod.

'All of them, the mountains too. Or the mountain singular, rather.'

'What?'

'It's the bloody same one – in every picture.'

'Really?'

Her eyes widened.

'You must have seen it? Different angles, different seasons, different weather, different times of day, but they're all of the same mountain.'

'Maybe the old doctor just liked that place?'

'Then why didn't he pack them all away with the rest of his shit? Why leave them on the walls?'

It was a good question. One he didn't have an answer to. Maybe the man had been going senile. It happened. Early-onset dementia. And as he thought of Chakraborty, the image of the woman in the red T-shirt came into his head. Her, her green eyes, and suddenly his questions evaporated.

'Look,' he said, 'don't worry about it now. I'll take 'em all down in the morning.'

Mel wandered through to the kitchen. He took off his shoes and stowed them in the alcove under the stairs, beside more boxes of Chakraborty's things. He reached for the one Mel had pointed to and opened the flaps. Inside was a jumble of thick paper, some sheets rolled up, others stacked in a pile. He pulled out several of the sketches. Mel was right. All portraits of the same woman. At the foot of each, one solitary word.

Daini.

Was that the artist's name? Maybe Chakraborty's middle name? He stowed them away and made his way to the lounge. He checked the paintings on the wall. Sure enough, both portraits bore the same word at their base. He moved on to the landscapes, the scenes of the mountains, or mountain singular, if Mel was right. But the word was missing. In fact, there was no signature at all.

*

Dinner was microwaved meals that Mel had picked up from the corner shop and a bottle of red in front of the TV. The wine helped soothe things, Mel stretching out, putting her feet up on him.

Sleep too, maybe on account of the wine, came quickly, and with it once more, the dreams. He was in the hills somewhere, a village in the glen below him with a stream running through it. The sky was blue, the sun high in the sky. He was on a blanket – a tartan rug – lying back, looking up at the sky. Mel was beside him – he could feel her, the warmth of her body, the touch of her hand in his – though he couldn't see her. And then the skies started to darken. The sun turned black, swallowed whole by the night, replaced by a yellow moon. The wind rose. He reached for Mel, but she was no longer there. He got to his feet, spun round. She was moving away from him, almost at the tree line. He called her name, shouted for her to stop, and she turned, but now she had no face.

Before he could react, she'd moved off again, further from him, and then he heard his own name, carried on the wind and coming from beyond the trees. He ran towards it, reaching the tree line. Once more he heard it. His name. He kept going. Further into the forest, until there, in front of him, a figure, retreating between the trees. Not Mel. He knew it instinctively, but that seemed suddenly immaterial. He had to follow. He did not know how far or for how long. Time seemed suddenly superfluous. The figure reached the edge of a precipice, stopped once more, turned and gestured him closer. He didn't know how, he had not moved, but suddenly he was there, at the edge, looking down into a ravine, at the bottom of which lay the broken figure of a man.

Tuesday

The alarm went off at its usual time and he felt like he hadn't slept at all. He held Mel tight for a moment – why, he wasn't sure – then forced himself out of bed.

He followed Maggie's advice and took his time this morning. Besides, he was knackered and that dream kept playing in his mind. The faceless woman, the man lying there at the bottom of the ravine. He didn't normally have nightmares that vivid.

The snow was falling as he left for work, its flakes hued amber in the glow of the streetlamp and settling thick and silent on the street. Black coffee and Highland air seemed to do their thing, though, and he was almost himself by the time he got to the surgery. Maggie welcomed him with a smile.

'Settling in okay, Dr Gibson?'

'You need to start calling me Steven,' he told her, and avoided answering the rest of the question.

The day was hectic once more. Too many patients, not enough time. Now and again, though, his thoughts drifted back to the dream. The woman whose face he could not see and the face of the man, which was all too vivid, lying there at the foot of the precipice.

It was gone six by the time he'd finished with the last walk-ins, and he was typing up his notes on the system when the door opened. He turned to see the young woman from the previous evening. Same jeans, same T-shirt.

Once more, the sight of her sucked the air from his lungs. Her eyes seemed to pierce his skull.

'Can I help—'

'Where is he? Where's the doctor?'

'I told you, Miss ... he's not here anymore. He's left.'

'No!' She spat the word vehemently. 'He can't have left. He wouldn't. He's here.'

He felt a pang of indignation, of jealousy even, but that was ridiculous. He didn't know anything about this woman, still less about her relationship with the old doctor. But why was she so concerned about the old man? Someone who hadn't even bothered to say goodbye to her.

'I'm the new doctor,' he said, more firmly. 'Now if you'll tell me your name, maybe I'll be able to help you.'

She paused for a moment, then shook her head.

'No. Not while he's still here.'

With that she turned and stormed out.

He shouted after her but knew instinctively that she wouldn't listen. He lifted the receiver of his office phone and pressed the button for reception. If the woman wouldn't tell him her name, he'd ask Maggie. Except she didn't answer. The phone continued to ring. He got up, left his room and made for reception.

'Maggie.'

She appeared from the kitchenette, mug in hand.

'Sorry, doctor. I was washing the cups.'

'Did you see the woman who just left?'

Maggie shrugged. 'Woman? The last person was Mr Hazelton, from Rosebank.'

He shook his head.

'After that. Just now. The woman in the red T-shirt ... I need to see her records.'

Maggie furrowed her brow.

'I didn't see anyone after Mr Hazelton. I was in the kitchen.' She tutted. 'Folks know better than to wander through when I'm not at the desk. The nerve of some people.'

'She came in yesterday, too. Wearing the same thing.'

'Really?' Maggie puffed out her cheeks. 'Can't say I remember.'

'She seemed convinced Dr Chakraborty was still here.'

'Well, that's just nonsense. What does she think he's doing, hiding somewhere?'

She disappeared into the kitchenette and re-emerged with her coat.

'Anyway, it's home time, doctor.'

'Maggie,' he said. 'Before you go, I was wondering if you could tell me a bit about Dr Chakraborty.'

The question seemed to surprise her.

'What do you want to know?'

He gave a shrug.

'What sort of a man he is. How he came to be here. Anything, really. I want to connect with the patients, and I was wondering how he managed it.'

She came over to where he stood, placed her coat over the back of her chair and gave an embarrassed laugh.

'It wasn't easy, I can tell you that. I remember when he first came to Glentorrance. Eighty-eight it was, or maybe eighty-nine. I was in my twenties then. He told me he'd arrived from India, spent six months down in England and then found himself here, of all places. He came as a locum, just like you. Was never going to stay long. I mean, you cannae blame him. People were less … open to outsiders back then.'

'So what made him stay? How'd he win them round?'

Maggie took a breath.

'He didn't, not really. It was actually all down to Jess. She was a nursery-school teacher. Born and raised right here. One of the few who didn't just up and leave at eighteen. She must have been about twenty-five at the time. I'm not sure how they met, but it certainly put the cat among the pigeons: a local lass going out with an Indian feller. But once they got to know him, most folks were fine about it, even Jess's dad.

'They got engaged about a year later; married soon after. A big thing it was. Everyone in the village invited.

Lots of his family came over too. And then another wedding in India, a Hindu ceremony. A few folk from here even went over. Quite the party, apparently.'

'What happened to her?'

Maggie looked away.

'She died. Drowned in the Torrance burn. Not long after they were married. Poor Adi – Aditya, that is, Dr Chakraborty – he took it badly. Went off the rails for a while. Got signed off sick and went back to India. We all thought that was it, he wouldn't come back, but he did. Returned with his head shaved and all religious. I suppose he took comfort from his faith. Twice a month, he'd go out into the hills and say prayers for her.'

'Into the hills?'

'Aye. He said that's what they did in his religion. No graves, you see, Hindus are cremated. Ashes scattered. Not that Jess was cremated. She's buried in the churchyard next to her folks. Adi said he preferred going out into the hills. That he felt closer to her out there.' She checked her watch. 'I'm afraid I've got to go. Callum's got football practice.'

'Sure,' he said, 'on ye go. I didn't mean to keep you.'

*

As he locked up, he looked to the street where the woman had been standing the previous evening. There was no reason she should be standing there tonight, but still, he looked. Maybe it was as shallow as base lust. It wasn't immoral, he told himself, just hormonal. In the end, the matter was moot. She wasn't standing there, or anywhere else that he could see, and part of him felt relieved.

He hurried home. The snow lay thick now, a carpet draped over the village's streets and trees and rooftops. Lights shone behind curtained windows, but not at the cottage. It was dark when he got there, the car missing from the driveway. A momentary shiver passed through him before he remembered. Mel had an interview at a school in Granton. She'd probably stopped off at the supermarket there on her way home.

Inside he turned on the lights, almost tripping over a pile of paintings in the process. They clattered to the floor and he recognised them as the ones from the living-room walls. Mel must have taken them down after he forgot to do it this morning. He really should take them and Chakraborty's boxes out to the garage, but his feet were frozen and the path was treacherous. If he did it now, in the dark, he might slip and fall and break his neck, and surely that would be worse for Mel than another day of this stuff cluttering up the hallway.

He went through to the kitchen, made himself a cup of tea, then headed back into the hall. The masking tape at the top of one of the boxes had come loose. Curiosity got the better of him. He lifted the flap. Inside, books were piled one upon another. The topmost had a hand-drawn illustration on the cover, strange geometric shapes inked out in black. Beneath it, text in a language he didn't recognise, a plethora of characters, some sharp and angular, others soft and rounded. An Indian language, he assumed. Hindi or something. Whatever it was, it looked rather beautiful.

He picked it up and wandered through to the lounge. The book itself felt old and cheap. A creased, waxy cover and flimsy pages. He flicked through it. More of the strange text, small neat letters, the type set close together as though space were at a premium. The paper was tissue-thin, the print almost showing through from the other side of the leaf. Here and there were short handwritten notes, some in the same script, others in English. He tried to decipher some of the latter. Many were words he'd never heard before: *Vāmācāra; Tantra; Shakti; Daini.*

Daini. That word again.

He took out his phone and typed it into the search bar.

Daini (ডাইনী): a Bengali term, often referring to a witch or malevolent female spirit. Dainis appear in Bengali mythology and folklore and are linked to the darker tantric practices.

What the hell were tantric practices?

He placed the book back in the box and went upstairs to change. He walked to the window to close the curtains and an arc of headlights swept past, illuminating the falling flecks of snow, and then something else caught his eye, a momentary flash of red on the pavement. He turned to look, to focus on the spot, but saw nothing, just the garden wall and lamppost and the falling snow.

Mel came home an hour later. He heard the key turning in the lock, the door shutting behind her. The sound of her voice.

'These boxes, Steven. You said you were going to put them in the garage?'

He wandered through to the hall.

'I'll deal with them tomorrow. How'd it go in Granton?'

'Terrible.'

That came as a shock. Mel was a great teacher. Kids loved her.

'What happened?'

She shook her head.

'I don't know. I didn't sleep last night, I was knackered, then I was late 'cos of roadworks. It went downhill from there.'

'I'm sure it wasn't that bad,' he said, which hardly conveyed what he really wanted to say, but he knew her moods. At times like this, when she was being hard on herself, she didn't want to hear how wonderful and capable he thought she was. She would dismiss it as him being disingenuous and that would lead to them spiralling into an argument.

*

He woke up sweating. The same dream. The same ending. The woman without a face, the man lying there in the crevasse. There was a difference though. This time he'd felt the presence of something evil. He woke suddenly and with a heartfelt conviction: the man's death hadn't been an accident, and it hadn't been suicide. He sat up. Beside him, Mel let out a scream. His heart leaped. Still asleep, she wrenched her head off the pillow and cried out. He held her as she woke, sobbing.

'It's okay,' he said. 'It's just a nightmare.'

For a moment she cried into his chest. Then she looked at him. 'But it felt real – a voice telling me to kill myself.'

Wednesday

'It's not normal, Steve,' she said as he brought her coffee to the bedroom. 'The same nightmare, again and again.'

He passed her the mug, sat on the bed and listened as she retold the story. As she spoke, he realised he knew the details, or some of them: the summer's day at the start; the blackening of the sky; the faceless woman and the walk from the clearing to the trees and then the crevasse. The only difference from his own dream was that when Mel looked down, she didn't see a dead man. When she looked down, she heard a voice telling her to jump.

He should let her know about his own dreams. But what would that accomplish? It would only freak her out further. She'd insist they leave, go back to Glasgow, maybe that very day.

And then, unbidden, the image of the woman in the red T-shirt came into his mind. No, they couldn't go, not just like that. He couldn't leave his patients in the lurch.

'It's only a dream,' he told her. 'The move up here, it's stressful. Maybe it's this cottage. Let's find somewhere else to rent.'

'It's not just the cottage. It's everything,' she said. 'The mountain, the one in my dreams ... It's the one from the paintings. It's the one just outside the village.'

As she said it, he realised she was right. Why hadn't he seen it? That made sense, he supposed. They'd seen that damn mountain so many times on the walls that it had transferred itself to their subconscious. Yet the same dream? Both of them?

'Can you not take the day off?' she asked. 'It's just ... I'm a bit freaked out by it all.'

'I'll go in a bit later,' he said. 'How about that?'

*

Under a grey sky, snow blanketed everything. It was the sort of scene that city people paid good money to see. The first time he'd been outside in daylight since arriving, he realised. Maybe that was it? Maybe it was the lack of light, doing something to his brain chemistry. Seasonal affective disorder, they called it, SAD. Was that what they called nominative determinism or just black humour?

He walked to the end of the path, then turned into the street. Ahead of him, in the distance, was Ben Torrance, the mountain in the paintings, its tree-covered lower slopes washing up against the edge of the village. He was about to turn and head for the surgery when he saw it, a little way up the slope, the clearing that appeared at the start of his and Mel's dreams. It wouldn't take long to get up there. Ten minutes in the car and then twenty on foot.

He called Maggie. Told her he needed a few hours this morning and to reschedule his appointments. She met the request with silence. That was fine.

He went back for the car, then headed for the bridge across the Torrance burn, following the road as far as he could up the mountain, parking up on the verge level with the clearing and then setting off through the forest on foot. The snow was deeper up here, the ground uneven. Once or twice he lost his footing, his boot catching on something, but he kept going. He had no choice. Reaching the clearing was what mattered. His breath crystallised in front of him. His fingers turned raw and red. Around him was perfect silence, broken only by the sound of his own breathing.

It took longer than he'd expected. The incline, the conditions, the sheer numbing pain of the cold, they all conspired against him, but he pushed on. He had to. And then finally the tree cover broke and he was standing there, in the clearing, almost exactly as he'd dreamed it. A pocket of open ground several hundred metres across, and in the vale below, the village of Glentorrance. He stared at it for long seconds, his introspection ended by the howling of an animal. He spun round but saw nothing, except ... there, to the right. It was the spot where the woman in his dream had stood and beckoned to him.

He staggered uphill towards it, then, as if by instinct, continued into the trees. He knew where he had to go. He walked on. The ravine would not be much further, and then, before he realised it, he was on top of it. The man had stood here. On the edge of a sheer drop. A shiver ran through him, a feeling of dread, or fearful anticipation. He turned, but all around was trees and snow and wilderness. He took a step forward, closer to the edge, then stopped. He didn't want to look over; felt that if he did, he might not be able to stop himself from tumbling – but he had to look. *He. Had. To.*

He reached for the branch of a tree, holding onto it and slowly inching forward. Little steps. Knuckles white. Peered over. Below him, at the foot of the ravine, the outline of a body; a fist jutting out of the snow, clutching at the air.

*

The police and paramedics took their time. An hour of standing there, shivering in the middle of nowhere, with only a dead man and the crows for company. Once he'd found the body, the fear had left him. In its place was curiosity. The woman in the red T-shirt. In his mind now, he called her Red. She'd insisted Dr Chakraborty hadn't left. It seemed she was right. Some part of him – the irrational part – had even expected to see her here, but obviously there was no sign of her.

The paramedics checked him out and took him home and told him to stay indoors and keep warm. Mel brought him tea and put him to bed. He stayed there most of the day. She looked at him as though he were half-mad.

'Why did you go up there?' she asked. 'Why didn't you tell me you were going?'

And he had no good answer to give her.

Maggie called from the surgery to see how he was, and in between sobs, confirmed what he already knew in his bones: that the man in the ravine was – had been – Dr Aditya Chakraborty.

'How did you know he was there?' Mel asked.

He gave a shrug.

'I can't explain it.'

She took his hand.

'We can't stay here, Steven. There's something evil going on. The paintings, the dreams – and everywhere I go, I keep seeing the same woman.'

His entrails turned to ice.

'What woman?'

'Some nutter. Standing around in the snow, in a thin T-shirt.'

It was all he could do to keep quiet.

'I want to go home,' she said. 'Back to Glasgow.'

As she spoke, something screamed inside his head. A shrill, piercing scream that set his teeth on edge. He dug his fingernails into his palms. He needed it to stop.

'We can't,' he told her. 'Not yet.'

The screaming ebbed.

She looked at him as though he'd taken leave of his senses, and maybe she was right.

'Why not?'

'Dr Chakraborty. He needs to be cremated. And he needs the right prayers said.'

She shook her head.

'What business is that of yours? Cremation? Prayers? What do you even know about Muslim funeral rites?'

'Hindu,' he said, more firmly than he'd expected. 'The man was Hindu, and I don't know anything about it. But I'll find someone who does.'

Tears glistened in her eyes.

'I haven't slept. I keep dreaming about killing myself. You find a dead body. Those freakish paintings. I can't take this anymore, Steven. I really can't.' She wiped a tear from her cheek, expecting him to relent.

'Fine,' she said eventually. 'Knock yourself out. Give this corpse whatever you think it needs, but I'm going. I can't stay. And you should come with me.'

Thursday

He found someone. Scoured the internet and located a brahmin not far away. A surgeon in a hospital on the Black Isle of all places. The man's name was Bhattacharya. He even claimed to have known Chakraborty. He knew the funeral rites. He'd say the prayers that would allow the old doctor to pass over into his next life.

'Any next of kin?'

A call to Maggie threw up a brother somewhere, with whom Chakraborty had cut off all contact decades earlier.

'The rites should be held as soon as possible,' Bhattacharya had said. 'Immediately after the post-mortem is completed.'

THE DOCTOR'S WIFE

*

The new doctor went into work, finding Maggie at her post, red-eyed and dressed in black. He held her hand and uttered his condolences. Patients came and went; flowers were left at the surgery door. The call came that afternoon. The post-mortem results. Death by misadventure. The body of Dr Chakraborty would be released in the morning.

The daylight faded. The scheduled appointments ended and the walk-ins began. He found himself watching the door, waiting for her: Red. Somewhere in his soul, he knew she would know they had found Chakraborty, just like she had known he had never left. The thought should have been troubling.

The minutes ticked by, the walk-ins stopped knocking on his door. He called through to Maggie.

'Is there anyone waiting?'

'No, doctor. Quiet one tonight.'

He stared at the clock on the wall, the minute hand making its slow circumnavigation. Six o'clock. Six-fifteen. Six-thirty. She wasn't coming, and for some reason the thought upset him. He shook it from his mind. He needed to get a grip. Maybe Mel was right. Maybe they should leave and never look back. But that would look bad on his CV and it was hard to find a practice like this. Anyway, that was a matter for another time. Right now, he had to contact Mr Bhattacharya and ask him to come through to Glentorrance and administer the funeral rites at the cremation.

*

Mel met him at the front door.

'She was here.'

'Who?'

'The woman. The one following me about everywhere. The one in the red T-shirt. She was outside.'

His stomach turned, his entrails twisting in a knot. He needed to see her. He left Mel standing there, ran out into the street, scanned the horizon for any sign of Red, but there was nothing. No doubt Mel had scared her off. He trudged back, his head spinning with dark, incomprehensible thoughts.

He came inside, closed the door. Mel looked up at him.

'Who the hell is she, Steven?'

'I don't know,' he said, 'but I think she's got some connection to the old doctor. She's been into the surgery a couple of times looking for him.'

If his hope was to placate her, he failed miserably.

'So why is she following *me* around? No, this is just too weird. We have to leave.'

'It's nearly over,' he told her. 'Chakraborty's body's been released for cremation. The priest is coming tomorrow.'

He reached for her hand and she pulled it away, folding her arms tight.

'Why is this any of your business? You never even met the man!'

'I know,' he said, and part of him realised that she was right, and part of him knew that he wasn't going anywhere, not until he'd figured this whole thing out. 'I've an obligation to the patients here, at least until they can find a replacement locum.'

'Fine,' she said. 'Do what you want. Sort out what you need to – or don't – I don't care. I can't stay here any longer. I'm leaving tomorrow.'

Friday

He'd slept in the spare room, left the curtains open and the light off, getting up more than once to look out of the window at the street below, searching for the woman but finding nothing. At times, the fever of obsession broke and he told himself this was madness, a ridiculous infatuation, but then, moments later, all rationality would leave and he was thinking about her again.

The morning couldn't come soon enough.

He met Mel in the hallway.

'Stay for the service,' he said.

And, to his surprise, she agreed.

*

Mr Bhattacharya arrived on the stroke of eleven.

Steven didn't know what he'd been expecting – a white-haired old man in saffron robes, maybe – but it wasn't this.

The guy looked late thirties, wore jeans, thin-rimmed glasses and a thick Aran sweater. He must have read Steven's mind.

'Do not worry,' he smiled, 'I'm a priest. I'll be changing for the ceremony.'

Steven led him past Mel's suitcase and Chakraborty's boxes through to the kitchen and plied him with tea.

'Did you know Dr Chakraborty well?'

Bhattacharya shrugged. 'Not really, he was older than me, but we both hailed from Bengal, we spoke the same language, shared the same culture, and so, like every Bengali within a hundred-mile radius, we met now and again at festivals and functions. He was always rather cool towards the rest of us. Some people quipped that he had gone native. Others said the opposite – that following the death of his wife, he had withdrawn from the world and become religious. Still, it came as a surprise when you told me he'd been planning to go home.'

'That's what they told me. At the surgery, I mean. I never met Dr Chakraborty myself.' No, that didn't feel right. He thought of the dreams he'd had. But how was he to explain that to this man?

He nursed his tea as Bhattacharya began explaining the funeral rites, the mantras involved, the prayers to be offered to the gods.

'Ideally, we would have a record of his paternal line: his father's name, his grandfather's name and so on, going back seven generations. Of course, you would not have any of that information, so I will amend things.'

'There're boxes of his things in the hall, by the way,' Steven ventured. 'I opened a couple. There's some religious-type stuff in there. I couldn't make out much of it, but it might be useful.'

Bhattacharya gave him a nod. 'I'll take a look.'

He sipped tea while the priest rifled through the boxes in the hall, before returning with two or three texts. His expression had changed, his lips thin, his eyes somehow darker.

'Is everything all right?'

The other man seemed not to hear him.

'Mr Bhattacharya?'

'Sorry?'

'Is everything okay?'

'I ... These books,' he held them up, 'they are not standard religious texts. They are ...' His voice trailed off.

'They're what?'

The man took a deep breath.

'These are the *Agamas*, and these, the *Kaulas*. They are tantric texts.'

The man seemed to be in fear of the books in his hand.

'I don't understand.'

'Tantrism,' Bhattacharya said, 'is a powerful, mystical practice. It seeks liberation through direct experience, rather than faith. Tantrics, those who practise it, view the universe as a constant battle between two forces: *Shakti*, which is feminine energy, characterised by restlessness and raw power, the churning of creation; and *Shiva*: masculine consciousness and stillness — a form of pure awareness. Tantrics believe that it is only through the union of these two forces, *Shakti* and *Shiva* — the merging of their energies — that one achieves true spiritual awakening. Most Tantrics follow what is called *Dakṣiṇācāra* — the Right-Hand Path. They chant the orthodox mantras and focus on pure devotion and meditation. But others ...' His voice trailed off for a moment, then he seemed to find the courage to continue. 'A handful of souls take the Left-Hand Path, the *Vāmācāra*. They break the spiritual and moral proscriptions, delve into the dark arts in order to transcend duality. The mantras they chant ... they are powerful and taboo. Some say they summon the spirits of the dead and demons such as the *Daini*, or that they commune with Kali, and Chinnamastā, and—'

'*Daini*?' Steven couldn't help but interrupt. 'That word. Chakraborty wrote it under some pictures.'

He got up and led the priest back to the hall, to where Mel had left the paintings.

'There. See?'

Bhattacharya's face became ashen. 'These are terrible things. You say Chakraborty drew them?'

'I think so.'

'They should be destroyed. Burned.'

But Steven didn't want to burn them.

'I'll do it after the funeral,' he said.

Bhattacharya was insistent.

'You should do it at once.'

Steven gave him a smile.

'Come on, now. You're a doctor yourself. A man of science. You don't believe all that stuff, do you?'

Bhattacharya seemed to take stock.

'Fine, it can wait till after the funeral, but you must do it. The Left-Hand Path is formidable. It is *kalaa jadu*, black magic. Few have the ability to master it. And they say that if it cannot be mastered, then …'

'Then what?'

The priest looked unnerved. 'The Left-Hand Path involves the invocation of powerful spirits to do one's bidding. One misstep and the servant becomes the master. One slip and they will enslave you.'

*

The service took place at midday at the crematorium in Nairn. Only a few made the trip: Maggie, three or four of Chakraborty's old patients, the priest, Mel and Steven. Bhattacharya stood next to a photograph of Chakraborty and his wife, Jess, taken on their wedding day, he in Indian costume, she in a red sari. A pang of jealousy passed through Steven. Jess was Red; Red was Chakraborty's wife. It was impossible, but that didn't seem to matter to Steven anymore. What mattered were his own feelings for her.

The priest recited his prayers as the casket went into the furnace, and within an hour it was all over.

Steven said his goodbyes to the priest, promising to burn the pictures of the *Daini* and bury those books of Chakraborty's, then stood outside in the snow with Mel.

'You're going then,' he said.

'You know I can't stay,' she told him.

She came over and held him tight.

'Get things sorted with the surgery,' she said. 'Then come back home as soon as you can.'

He said he would. Said all the things she wanted to hear, and part of him meant it too. And yet, another part, perhaps the greater part, thought only of Red, of seeing her, of being with her ... Those books, the ones he'd promised to bury. Maybe there was something in them? Some incantation? He would learn the language, decipher the texts, he'd—

The car door slammed. He stood and watched as Mel drove off. The light was already fading. It would be dark by the time she made it to Glasgow. Maggie walked over.

'You want a lift back, doctor?'

'Aye,' he said. 'And we should open the surgery. There's been too much disruption already.'

*

Six o'clock saw the last of the walk-in patients. He didn't worry; he knew she'd come. The door opened, as he knew it would. He looked up. Red. He felt something flutter in his stomach. The auburn hair, the dapple of freckles on her cheeks, just as he had seen her in that photograph taken on the day of her wedding. Only her eyes seemed different. Brighter, a piercing emerald.

She spoke before he had a chance to finish the thought.

'He has gone now.'

'Yes,' he said.

Her face crumpled. 'He has left me here, abandoned me.' For a moment he thought she might break down, but only a solitary tear rolled down one cheek. The sight was intoxicating to him.

'Please,' he said, 'maybe I can help you? I'm the new doctor.'

She looked at him as though seeing him for the first time. 'The *new* doctor?'

'That's right. And you are Jess, right? You drowned. Your husband managed to find a way to bring you back. And now he's gone and you're left here.'

Red looked at him and laughed.

Before he could say anything more, she had turned for the door.

'Wait!' he called out, but she didn't look back; just walked out and closed it behind her.

He got up from his chair and lunged after her, reaching the door, turning the handle. It was stuck. He struggled with it for long seconds until finally it moved. He yanked the door open and ran into the hallway. It was empty, the light above his head blinking intermittently. He made for the reception area. No sign of the woman, and no sign of Maggie.

She couldn't have gone far. Once more he ran, this time for the front door, emerging into the frostbitten night. Wind and sleet blinded him. Where was she? He scanned the path. Footprints in the snow, heading forward, merging with others, disappearing into the darkness.

The door slammed shut behind him. He had no coat but it didn't matter. He kept going, following the tracks out into the road. He should be able to see her by now, but there was no sign. He stopped, turning first one way and then the other, gazing past parked cars and vans.

He heard her voice in his head.

In the distance, a flash of red. Maybe two hundred metres away, making for the bridge over the Torrance burn, her back to him, auburn hair flying in the wind. How could she move so fast? Once more he broke into a run, doing all he could to close the distance. She did not appear to be running, but no matter how fast he went, the gap between them remained constant.

She was on the other side of the burn now, into the old part of town, turning and moving parallel to the stream. In front of her, Ben Torrance loomed like a tombstone. He raced on, reaching the bridge, crossing it, the dark waters flowing beneath. Suddenly he remembered his Burns. The tale of Tam O'Shanter. Witches couldn't cross running water. Well, that was something, at least.

There she was, still a few hundred metres ahead, passing the last few houses before the village ran out and the trees beckoned.

'Wait!' he shouted. She turned and looked straight at him, then, once more she was moving, along the road and into the forest. She wanted him to follow her. He knew that. He felt it, like he felt his own heart beating in his chest, and, more than that, he *wanted* to follow her, as though she was lodestone and he iron.

The houses ended, the streetlights died away, and yet he could still see her clearly up ahead. She moved now with a grace, a serenity, that was intoxicating. What was she? It didn't matter. All he knew was that he needed to be in her presence.

The snow lay deeper here and he stumbled through it. She had to be aware of his travails, for she seemed to slow too, never moving any further ahead of him. He did not know for how long he followed her. Time lost all meaning, his body became detached, his mind no longer registering pain or cold or fatigue. He barely had any sensation of movement, and then, finally, she stopped and turned back to face him.

The ravine was close by, he knew it but couldn't see it. He staggered forward and collapsed to his knees in front of her. There was, he realised, no snow here. He was on stony ground, surrounded by geometric shapes cut into the rock, the same as those on the cover of that flimsy book of Chakraborty's. There was no light, but he could see her clearly, and then he realised that the light was coming from her.

He looked up and she put a hand to his cheek.

'You know who I am?'

'You're Jess,' he said. 'You're the wife of the old doctor. You died. He brought you back.'

She looked down at him and smiled, and if he could have spent eternity in that moment of bliss, he would have.

'I am not Jess. I never was. And I never wished to be. Your predecessor didn't bring me *back*, he *summoned* me.' Her expression darkened. 'To this barren place, this rock and ice and wind. He prayed to me, chanted the mantras, made the offerings, all in the hope that I would do his bidding. *His* bidding!' She gave a shriek. '*Dainis* do not serve just any man. Rather the opposite. He realised this and tried to send me back. To banish me! If I had known then of the solitude, the loneliness, the darkness of this place, I might have let him. But I didn't.

'It was a mistake and we both paid for it. I took his wife, and finally I took him. But first I offered him solace. He would come here, to this place, to me, upon the half-moon. He became my consort and my vessel, and I became the doctor's wife.'

She looked at Steven. 'There is no going back now. I shall always be the doctor's wife. Yet no longer will I stay on this forsaken mountainside, but there instead, in that village, with you. I will make it my kingdom, and you shall be my consort.'

He shook his head. That was wrong. He had a wife. She was driving back to Glasgow even now, through the darkness and the snow. As he thought it, the woman in front of him smiled, knowingly, and then her features seemed to change, and suddenly standing before him was Mel, but the eyes were different. The eyes were green. Suddenly he couldn't recall the colour of Mel's eyes. And then he was convinced. They were green. They'd always been green. This was his wife. This was the doctor's wife.

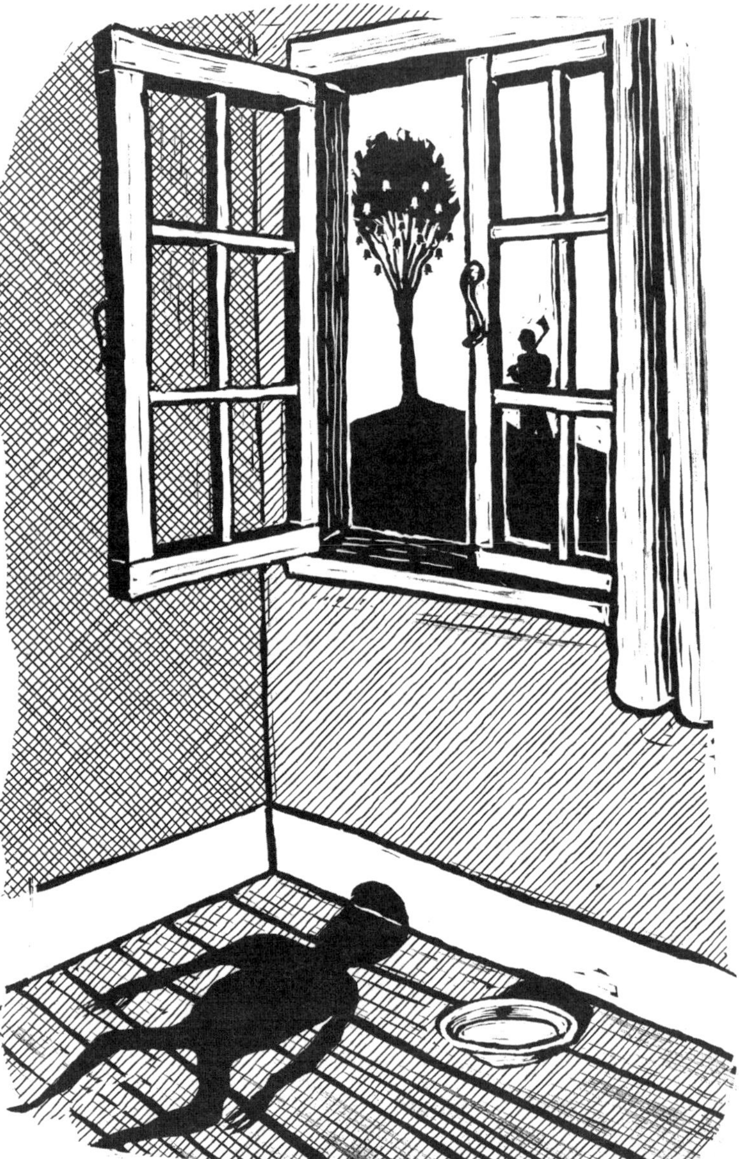

Mr Mischief

REBECCA NETLEY

The cart rattles into the yard of Rowan's Garth. It is the turn of the day and the autumn sun is folding into pink cloud. Midway up the valley, where gorse and heather shrink against the onslaughts of wind, the house squats on a patch of stone and meagre scrub. Even in the glory of the sunset, there is something malign in the oddly shaped rocks, the stunted trees and a gill that cuts through the belly of the valley like a wound. The house itself is watchful and silent; the only sounds are those coming from the stables, where dogs bark furiously in their kennels.

'We have dogs?' Bessie says.

'Of course we do. But they're working dogs, not pets, mind.'

Bessie steps down and glances at her uncle to gauge whether he feels what she does – an uncanny stillness that weaves below the surface of the wind and a faint menace cast by shadows that circle the barn and house. But Kit is whistling, a sure sign he senses nothing untoward.

The horses skitter nervously on the drive and tug at their traces. The driver puts down the final trunk, jumps onto the box seat and turns the cart away with barely a farewell.

Bessie counts exactly twelve paces to the front door. Inside, she lights a candle and begins to explore. The rooms are thick with the sour smell of mires and bogs and Bessie feels as if the house might only be pretending to be a house and is, in fact, an uneasy dream conjured by the moor itself.

Kit comes up behind her and places a hand on her shoulder. His eyes run with covetous pleasure over the smoke-stained walls and littered shelves. He opens and closes the range door, exclaims at the parlour and the tiny hall with hooks for coats and a crooked print of horses on the wall. He caresses the banisters as if he were the one who had turned the wood.

After they have carried in the luggage, set the range and put water on to boil, he slaps his hands together and declares it will do extremely well. 'Much better than you thought, eh?' His glance slips sideways to Bessie, a note of challenge in his eye.

Bessie finds cold meat and bread in the pantry and they eat it in front of the range while rain drips from the gutters and she tries not to think too much of the home she left.

'If he says you go, you go,' Granny had said. 'You know what he's like. And if you don't cook, he won't eat, and he won't clean neither, and you'll be overrun with rats. It's not my choice, Bessie, but you're a big enough lass now.'

Kit tears his bread hungrily and talks of how he will be the finest gamekeeper this piece of moor has ever seen and earn the praise of folk at the Hall.

Suddenly, the dogs begin to bark and whine from the stables and the sound of bells flutters through the air. They both look up. Once, on Christmas Eve in the years before her parents died, they had taken a trip to town, to the smell of roasting chestnuts, shops garlanded with holly and fern. Everywhere had rung with festive jollity. A tree in the marketplace had glittered with bells whose ringing conjured an air of cheer and expectation. But these resound hollowly, shaking drops of something unsettling into the night. Kit gets up and opens the door.

'Where are they coming from?' Bessie asks.

Kit shouts to the dogs to shut up. 'I don't know but they could get on a man's nerves.'

'But what are they?'

'We'll find out soon enough. Now eat up. There's a good lass.'

After supper they venture into the narrow yard and a blast of wind that funnels up from the moor, setting the bells and the dogs off again. They follow the sound to the stables and to the well, beyond which a copse of hazel, oak and mountain ash shivers in the moonlight.

'They're here,' Bessie says.

Kit holds up a lamp. Standing a little apart from its neighbours is a great rowan crowned in berries the colour of blood. Bessie gazes up the ancient trunk with knots and whorls like the skin of an aged hand, where high up, between the berries, tiny bells are strung on pieces of wire. Lower down, the bark is studded with heather.

Kit pulls at it with an exclamation of disgust. 'I hope you know we're not going to hold with this sort of nonsense, not in my house, whatever your grandma said to you afore we came. Do you understand?'

Her uncle's beliefs are well known to her. She recalls the day Kit had come back from the Hall, smelling of ale and bonhomie.

'You got the job then?' Granny had said.

'Aye. Start in a few weeks. The land is crying out for a decent gamekeeper. The fella afore me lost control of the moor a long time ago.'

'That's grand, Kit. Did the squire himself show you round?'

'One of his groundsmen did. You've no idea how backward folk are round there, Ma. They were talking about Mr Mischief living out there and all that household spirit nonsense. I ask you!'

'Now then, Kit. There's strong beliefs everywhere you go and you'll win no favours trampling over them. And don't be so quick to dismiss them neither. I've seen many a thing in my time that would make you think I was half-daft if I told you.'

'Just like you, Ma. Women's rubbish.'

'That's not true and well you know it. Bess, off you go and see if there's more eggs in the henhouse.' But Bessie had leaned against the wall, close enough to catch their words. 'You're the fool, Kit, if you ignore what you're told. There's more on heaven and earth than you or I could ever know. And it's not as if Mr Mischief isn't well enough known hereabouts.'

'Oh, do shut up – and don't you dare put ideas in Bessie's head. She's simple enough already.'

'Kit!'

Later, Bessie had lain in bed and scoured her memory for stories of Mr Mischief: the bowl of milk left for him to sup and the household tasks undertaken in return. In her mind she has always imagined something catlike, with soft paws and an arching back, but perhaps, she ponders, this is because of the milk. She liked the idea of a cat and some help in the house; she'd just have to hide it from Kit.

And as the bells continue to chime, Bessie perceives in their sound the glimmer of something magical, and in her head she sends a silent welcome to their visitor and vows to replace the heather.

Kit stands before the rowan with an expression of contempt but Bessie sees that he is listening hard to the bells and for a moment a part of him seems to drift away. When he eventually turns back to her, it is clear he has forgotten she is there at all.

'Off you go,' he says. 'And leave me be. I want to look round.'

Bessie grips the pail of newly drawn water and paces the forty-five steps back to the house. In the kitchen she clears away, washes pots, wipes down the table and leaves cloths in a bucket to soak. Then she takes a bowl from the pantry and fills it carefully with milk and hides it under the sink where Kit will never find it.

'For you, Mr Mischief,' she says, with a breath of nervous expectation.

Later, when she is in bed, hooves and voices sound outside. Peering out of the window, she sees four men, wrapped warm against the cold, and then there are cheery voices and the slapping of bottles on the kitchen table. The odd word floats up and she knows what it means and turns on her side with a sense of foreboding.

*

'Bessie.' Kit's call comes before dawn and Bessie climbs from the narrow bed, hurrying into her clothes before making her way into the kitchen. Twenty-three steps, although she falters on the eighth and has to start again.

The kitchen reeks of stale smoke and ale. A pack of cards and counters lies in a litter of tobacco crumbs. Kit is cleaning his gun but his lips are drawn tight and Bessie's gut tenses. The money that had been on the dresser for meat and dairy is gone but he dares her to notice and she keeps her eyes averted. Click, click, goes the chamber. One, two, Bessie counts. The smells of grease and black powder mingle with the heat that rises from the stove.

As she makes tea and cuts bread, Bessie checks the kitchen for signs of Mr Mischief's help, but as far as she can tell nothing is altered from the night before.

Kit claps the barrel shut and runs a palm lovingly along its length, then hitches the game bag onto his back and shoulders the rifle.

Bessie follows him into the yard where the dogs are waiting, lifting eager noses to the wind. It is not raining yet, but grey clouds mob the tops and mist lies heavy along the ravine. The dogs come up to her, wagging their tails, and she buries her fingers in Lady's wet fur.

'You'll spoil them,' Kit says, and she tucks her hand away quickly.

It is only when he has gone that Bessie realises how twisted her gut has been, how much she's needed to squash her feelings into the right shape well enough to hide them. She thinks of Granny who will be up by now, pottering in the kitchen with her blue cap and apron waiting for the kettle to whistle on the fire. If Granny were here, she'd say something about the cards. He was banned at home. The thought of Granny makes her throat thicken.

Once Kit is out of sight, Bessie peeps under the sink and finds the bowl empty. A shiver of strange pleasure passes through her but then she thinks of rats and vermin which come in the night and is less certain.

After refixing heather to the rowan, Bessie makes a full exploration of the cottage. One, two, three. She counts each stride meticulously from room to room, pausing to examine the hunting calendar and to finger some pewter mugs. She opens drawers, disturbing tacks, candle stubs and fishing flies, which roll about in layers of dust.

And all the while, the house watches back, contemplative and uncomfortable.

Sometime mid-morning, as Bessie is laying fires, the door rattles followed by a cheery hello. The woman who enters has a soft face like a peach just on the turn.

'I'm Hannah,' she announces. 'The estate sent me to help until you settle in.'

She lays a basket on the table. 'Cook sent down some more things for the pantry. Your name's Bessie, right? I didn't know you'd be such a young lass. How old are you?'

'Ten,' Bessie says.

'And it's your uncle you live with?'

Bessie nods.

'Nobody else?' Her eyebrows shoot up.

'Nay,' Bessie says.

'Where's tha parents, then?'

'They died.'

'At least you have your uncle, else it could have been the workhouse. Where did you live afore?'

'I lived with Granny. Over in Scarsholt.'

'Aye, well.' Hannah pauses before she says carefully, 'What do you think of Rowan's Garth?'

Bessie wants to tell her she wishes she were back home but that would be rude. So she says: 'I like the dogs.'

For the next hour, Hannah and she unpack trunks and put things away and then they chop vegetables and meat for stew.

'So, Bessie,' Hannah says, 'did anyone tell you about some of our special ways here afore you came?'

'I know about Mr Mischief.'

'That's a relief.'

'Is he really here, then?'

'Aye, he is that. Did they tell you what to do?'

'I leave out a bowl of milk.'

'Good lass. See you treat him well and he'll repay in kind. Mind, you'll never see him. He'll only come in the night or if you're out of the house and elsewhere.'

Bessie considers this and thinks, all in all, she's pleased that his tasks will be accomplished without the need to meet him. She does not want to picture him as anything other than the catlike figure she first conceived.

'Come with me,' Hannah says.

In the yard Hannah shows her sprigs of heather lashed above the doors of the house and barn. 'See this?' she says. 'It's sign of respect. He doesn't like to be ignored, does Mr Mischief. You could call it a sort of invitation but he'll come and go as he pleases.' Hannah pauses and searches the moorland blurred with rain, and Bessie looks too and thinks for all its beauty there is also something unsettling about the fells and rocky falls.

'Last night my uncle took the heather on the rowan down but I put it back up.'

'Good lass. Well, hopefully no harm done.'

'But what are the bells for?' They are not ringing now, and only wind and the spattering of rain on the barn roof break the silence.

'The rowan is special and so are the bells. They're a sort of charm, see. Both have been here long afore the house.' Hannah's expression is solemn and Bessie recalls the sound as it fluted through the wind and a shivery feeling crawls across her skin.

Back inside, Hannah says: 'Why don't you tell your uncle what I've said? Everyone at Rowan's Garth needs to respect Mr Mischief.'

'He won't listen.'

She lifts her eyes. 'Aye, most men don't listen to what we have to say. He's like that too, then?'

A flush creeps up Bessie's neck and burns her cheeks. If not listening were the only problem she had to contend with. She thinks of *those* times: how they can slither in and out of Kit without rhyme or reason.

'Well, none of my business anyway.' Hannah pauses. 'Try not to fret, won't you?' She touches Bessie's cheek lightly with her finger. Granny used to do that and Bessie swallows down a sudden, unbearable ache.

*

By late afternoon, Bessie has mapped the entire house in paces. One, two, three, her boots go – up and down stairs, from kitchen to hall and hall to parlour. From the sink to pantry there are six. From sink to table two. On the seventh step of the stairs going up, the riser creaks, and there is a snapping sound on the ninth. From her room to the kitchen there are twenty-three and all the while she ponders what Hannah has said about Mr Mischief. She imagines him at the kitchen table, cupping the milk bowl between round paws, and standing beneath the rowan showered by the sound of bells.

Dusk falls fast and the wind picks up, chattering at the window frames and whistling through the barn with its banging shutter. From time to time, Bessie leaves the house and walks to the edge of the moor to look for Kit's return. And as she stands, dark cloud swamping the valley and shadows prowling the ravine, she senses, as she does inside the house, things unseen but seeing.

Kit is still not back. Forty-five paces to the well where the trees stand sentinel in the twilight. As she lowers the bucket, a jangle of bells comes fluttering through the air before being wicked away by the wind, leaving silence. She tugs the bucket up. Eight pulls of the rope.

The bells sound again but now there is something else in the night, something that is breaking twigs in the thicket, moving stealthily towards her. Her heart jolts and she steps away to search the trees, seeing only patches of spreading darkness.

Another crunch in the undergrowth and the bells chime urgently, as if shaken by a hand other than the wind's. Bessie turns fast, tripping on a root and jarring her palms as she falls. If she does not run now, she may find out exactly who or what Mr Mischief is and she no longer wants to know. At the well, the bucket is gone. She searches frantically, thinking of Kit and how the loss of such an object will anger him. It is not there. But now there are eyes on her back, eyes belonging to something standing among the trees, and panic has her racing back to the house – one, two, three, her boots crack on stone. She loses count.

'Sorry, Mr Mischief,' she chants, one, two, three. Her breath hoarse in her throat.

Once the door is bolted and her senses recovered, Bessie finds the pail sitting atop the kitchen table full to the brim with water. She stops still in surprise. It is true then. Actually true. She makes a shaky bow of thanks. Her thoughts are interrupted by barking and the dogs come panting into the yard followed by her uncle.

Kit's cheeks are purple with cold; the smells of bogs and earths hang about him. 'It's hungry work out there and damnably cold.' He slaps the sack across the table, stained with blood and grease. Bessie's belly crawls but she turns away and stirs the pot.

'Hardly a rabbit out there – must be hordes of foxes. I nearly got one at Hobb's Bluff, scat everywhere. The damned things are having a party and all the traps empty and sprung.'

In spite of the poor hunting, he's bagged four rabbits.

*

At some point Bessie wakes to the sound of bells. Kneeling up, she wipes ice from the window. Kit is standing by the copse, a lantern swinging from his hand. He is gazing up at the rowan while shadows creep and skulk about the barn and a yellow moon hangs low in the sky.

*

The first weeks pass. Bessie learns that Rowan's Garth is a place of strange silences that linger in the empty rooms – empty and yet not quite empty. The men come again, leaving Kit sour and angry, directing the blame at her as if it was she not he who lost a shilling on a poor hand. The food money dwindles and she tries her best with the oats and bread and whatever thin, undernourished animal the estate allows Kit to keep from the moor.

Mr Mischief comes each day and Bessie finds a cleaned fireplace or a jug of milk magically refilled. Each time she makes a bow and thanks him, tries to save some extra treat from the table for his bowl of scraps, and all the while she senses Mr Mischief is drawing a little closer to her. When she is out in the yard, he is in the raft of cold that crouches in the shadow, watching and waiting, and he is in the skies, which should be full of geese and ravens yet remain strangely empty.

Kit's mood darkens although his job fills him with glee, and every trapped fox or rabbit sets up a hunger for more.

When she is in bed, the door below opens and closes and Kit stands at the rowan, gazing up with a strange beguilement that belies his continued irritation with the bells. And often now, when Bessie catches his eye and he smiles, there is a coldness behind it, which conveys the opposite of its intention. And she wonders if, as well as his magic, Mr Mischief also brings a sort of sickness.

*

Bessie wakes suddenly, her heart banging. Mr Mischief has been in her room. May be here still. Before her eyes adjust to the semi-darkness, her nose wrinkles on a scent of rottenness and damp earth. She sits up and with a trembling hand holds out the candle. Climbing from the bed, she takes four shaky steps to the chest and to what is now lying there. She gazes down with disbelief and disgust. Laid carefully on the dresser top is a bird, long-dead and frozen cold with the cloudiness of unseeing eyes, and beside it a rowan twig with a blood spatter of berries.

As Bessie stares down at this horror, the shimmering of bells weaves upon the night and somewhere behind her in the room, in some place she cannot see, eyes rake her skin. All that she has conjured about Mr Mischief, whatever fancy, falters and splinters. What sort of creature would leave such an abomination and why?

Terror sucks into her and she longs to fold in upon herself, to run to Kit for help, despite the threat that would ignite. She does not know how she can bear being here in this room with the dead thing and with Mr Mischief crouched in the darkness, watching.

So she stands shivering, as whatever he is continues to gaze at her – no, not at her but into her – right to her middle where all the secrets she has ever held are tucked away, some even from herself. She thinks of the bowls of milk and her hands on the trunk of the rowan, pressing heather to the nail, the respectful bows and grateful thank yous. Was it not enough? What has she done wrong that means he is here now, bringing this for her to witness? She feels him waiting for her to speak but her lips won't move, her voice is trapped too deep inside.

Then from the shadows he speaks her name in a voice like steel scraping rust from the air. A voice that seems to hang between familiar and imaginary worlds; Bessie is not even sure if she hears it on the outside of herself or if it is on the inside only. But it is both an acknowledgement and a question. What question?

Time passes, minutes or hours, she cannot tell, and then the bells cease and she is left frozen on the icy floorboards. And through the window it is finally growing light.

'Bessie.' Kit's voice is gargled with sleep and the dislike of waking to the cold world that makes his joints ache and mouth dry. At the table, his face is rough with tiredness. 'Those damned bells. I'll rip them down. What would you say to that, eh?'

'No.' The word leaves her before she can lock it away. Her hand quivers as she fills the kettle, and all the while her uncle taps his fingers on the table, one two, one two, and his cold gaze drills into the back of her head.

*

'What's this?' Hannah asks, turning over Bessie's wrist and pushing up her sleeve.

'I banged it.'

'Did you bang anywhere else?'

Bessie clamps her mouth shut before she says more.

'I hear your uncle's a bit of a gambling man,' Hannah says. 'I hear too he's had a run of bad luck.'

Bessie nods.

'How is Rowan's Garth? And Mr Mischief?' She studies the kitchen as if it could offer an answer to such a question and Bessie recognises now Hannah's uneasiness following mention of him.

'Who is Mr Mischief, really?'

'Have tha seen him?'

Bessie shakes her head.

Hannah takes her time answering. 'Very well. There's more than one name for Mr Mischief, but round here, folk calls him a boggart.'

'A boggart? Is it a monster?'

Hannah gives a mirthless smile and the shadows deepen about her eyes. 'I don't rightly know what I'd call it.' She turns to the window and gazes out bleakly.

'Is there more I should do for him than what you said?' Bessie asks.

'Nay, no more than that.'

Is it her then? Is it something she has done that has aggravated him – she angers Kit without meaning to, and as she thinks of him, she says: 'What happens if the bells come down?'

Hannah turns swiftly back to face her, eyes wide with alarm. 'Tell me that's not happened, has it?'

'Nay,' Bessie says.

'Good. I don't know what would happen but I wouldn't test it.'

'If he doesn't come from this world, where is he from?'

'Oh, I think you already know that too.' She puts her mouth to Bessie's ear and hisses, 'Mr Mischief is the devil, Bessie. Don't go forgetting it. Mr Mischief is the devil himself.'

*

Although Bessie prays every night, kneeling at her bedside just as Granny taught her, Mr Mischief comes anyway as if she has left her door swinging wide just for him. Up he climbs, creaking on the seventh step as she huddles under the covers, biting the skin about her nails till they sting with pain. Each time he leaves some tiny creature, half-skeletal, plucked from a hidden grave on the moor.

In the pantry the rabbits hang, bloodied and stinking, and the whole house smells of death. Every dusk, Kit lays his kills on an oilskin, looking for Bessie's praise, and it comes to her, one day, that Mr Mischief is not leaving his offerings to frighten her but that, just like Kit, he considers them treasures, and Mr Mischief intends them as gifts — macabre and unwelcome, but gifts all the same. Why Mr Mischief would do these things for her, she does not know, but later, as wind knifes through the night and the bells chime, she feels a cold sort of comfort that has been absent since their arrival, and all the tears left unshed come loose – hot and bitter and wrung with pain.

She buries her head in the mattress to smother her grief. Silently, the bed beside her sinks and a deathly chill sweeps her skin. Bessie stops crying and lies rigid, preparing herself for a terror that does not fully come, and all the while Mr Mischief's gaping soul empties across the sheets.

The room is icy, yet, somehow, Mr Mischief is warm.

*

October turns to November and the temperature falls quite suddenly, bringing flurries of snow that whirl across the surface of the moor. When Bessie lowers the pail at the well, the thickening water resists its weight. She dreads the sound of hooves at night and voices below.

Upstairs, the windows crust with ice. And as the cold creeps into the bones of the house and the unforgiving moor, it sidles further into other things – into her uncle's aching joints and then his icy gaze, which comes to rest on her whenever she is there. In the past, his moods would peak with a slap or a kick to her shins, and then they would pass. But now the coldness in him grows and spreads, and whatever of Kit there was when they first arrived has been replaced by something meaner. She thinks of Mr Mischief creeping through the house with his offerings of death and disquieting comfort, bestowing both hope and despair. Does he stop in Kit's room to watch him sleeping? Does he gaze into him as he does her? She wishes she could be back home, back with Granny in the house whose shadows hid only spiders and fish moths. When she climbs the stairs to bed now, it is Mr Mischief who waits in the dark spaces, his latest offering sitting rank and decaying on her dresser.

*

Wind is howling outside and the kitchen is cold in spite of the stove.

'I can't eat this.' Kit throws the bowl of stew to the floor where it shatters and the thin liquid spills across the flags. 'A man needs meat and potato. What happened to the hare I bagged?'

'It's eaten and we've run out of potatoes.'

'I provide you with enough for a decent supper. Are you keeping the best for yourself? I don't know why I bothered bringing you with me.'

She presses her fists hard into her belly to quell a mounting panic.

Then the bells begin their nightly toll and they both look out into the blackness. After a moment, Kit's gaze returns with a sneer.

'You like the bells, don't you?' he says. 'Do you think they'll bring *you* good luck?' He grins and his knuckles whiten.

Bessie stares down at the table.

'Look at me and answer when I speak to you.'

'I don't like them,' she says.

'They bring only misfortune.' He pulls out his purse and turns it out. 'Empty, see.' She meets his eyes and catches a sudden shocking glimpse of what is inside him – something rotted-down and diseased, something imbibed from Rowan's Garth and what lies within its walls and in the moor outside. The coils of her gut rim with ice. She thinks frantically of escape but there will be no escape. And Hannah, when she comes occasionally to bring food, now never enters the house but leaves it at the door as if she too senses the coming of an end.

Then Bessie thinks of Mr Mischief and the tiny birds, voles and shrews, fur and feathers stiff with death. He wouldn't let Kit hurt her, would he?

*

It has been snowing all day but now it comes heavier, falling through the night like stars. Downstairs, Kit circles the floor over and over, pumping pipe smoke through the house. Bessie cringes into her skin. The dogs begin to whine in their kennel and wind saws about the house, agitating the barn's loose shutter. Bang, bang, bang – one, two, three. One, two, three. The sound of bells hurtling through the air. The slam of the door.

Bessie wipes frost from the bedroom window and looks down to where Kit has placed a lamp in the copse. It catches the gleam of the axe blade as it rises and falls, rises and falls, the faint lustre of bells in the moonlight. The dogs' whines rising to howls of anguish and the crash of the rowan as it falls.

As the rowan plummets, something splits across the night, something vast and blazing. Without the bells, the sound of the gale screaming across the moor is a dreadful thing. There is a tremor within Rowan's Garth, and something adjusts deep, deep down, in the pit of the tainted earth, and the plaster of the wall cracks and little fissures spider across the surface.

Bessie whimpers beneath the covers, waiting, waiting. She thinks of the monstrous gifts bestowed by Mr Mischief and wonders what a creature who considers such things a kindness might do in the face of Kit's violent affront. She waits for Mr Mischief's fearsome tread on the stair but none comes – only a terrible silence. And all the while the night rips further open and all the badness at Rowan's Garth streams out.

There is a ghastly dawn, snow crusted to the sills and an emptiness to the house as if its heart had been ripped clean from its chest. Her uncle is asleep across the kitchen table, fingernails rimmed with blood. When he wakes, eyes shot with red, his rage is still snuffling around his dreams, not fully woken, not yet, but Bessie knows it is coming.

A little later, his gaze slides over her and when he smiles, Bessie knows that he sees her no longer. He sees only what she would look like if he took his hunting knife to her gut and spilled her out as he does the foxes and rabbits. Slowly he rises, cupping his gun, shouldering his game bag, and steps out into the snowy yard.

At the copse, Bessie gazes down to where the broken rowan spills its bright, dreadful berries across the snow and she gathers the bells desperately in her hands. She tries to hang them on a sapling oak further within the woods but they hang loose and forlorn like the necks of dead game her uncle strings in the pantry, and in the bite of cold and the brittle light that stuns the landscape, she feels Mr Mischief's uncontained rage.

Mr Mischief does not come. Wherever he is, it is not here, but he is in the wind that is rising, snatching her skirts and hair and building into fury.

Bessie finds a nest in the corner of the barn: a huddle of mice, locked together for warmth, now hard and lifeless as stone. Carrying it in her palms, she places it beside the rowan. 'For you, Mr Mischief,' she says. But her voice is snatched away before it makes even a dent upon the air.

By the time her uncle returns, a gale is tearing across the moors. The dogs slink to the kennels and the cottage rattles and groans. Hail hurls itself at the roof and spits down the chimneys and Kit has something new in his veins, as if whatever sickness has been growing inside him has escaped to run hotter and hungrier. His eyes fix on her and remain and Bessie almost welcomes the idea of no longer having to carry the weight of fear.

In bed she listens, her heart beating hard in her chest. The candle flame sputters and dips, and shadows crawl and twitch across the walls. Below, her uncle paces. Occasionally, he stops and she imagines him looking up to where she lies, the chains and bonds of his rage reaching out and tightening about her. She thinks of Granny. Granny, and the chickens that run unsteadily in the yard, heads bobbing to get their food. And Mrs Hainsworth who comes once a week to take tea and how Granny uses the best china from the dresser and lets Bessie hold the sugar bowl and trace the flowers on its surface, if she is very, very careful.

Kneeling on the mattress, she pushes at the window, throwing it open. 'Mr Mischief.' Her scream of desperation is lost in the whirling of wind and yet she trusts it finds its way through the storm and back to him.

So Bessie waits at the sill, cold stinging her cheeks, until gradually the gale eases and clouds shift, bathing the valley in moonlight. And moving up across the new-laid snow is a shadow, heavy and purposeful, too dark to discern more than a shape, stunted but upright and not like a cat at all. Mr Mischief walks on two bent legs and as he nears, his eyes fix upon her and the sound of bells swings through the air, catching up strings and wreaths of horror.

One, two, three, her uncle paces. The sound of his knife on the grindstone, scrape, scrape. The creak of stairs, a tightening and swaddling of air, and Mr Mischief is there beside her on the bed again. This time Bessie does not shy from him but turns and meets him fully: he has eyes that seem to stare up from the pit of a grave and a smile that gouts darkness. She slips her icy hand into his.

Scrape, scrape, from below. His hunger hums through the house.

'Bessie,' Kit growls.

Her name swinging on the end of a noose.

'Please,' she says, and Mr Mischief searches her insides – all her thoughts, her love for Granny, her fear of Kit. He knows what he must do. What she wants him to do.

When Mr Mischief peels away from the bed, it is with a sound like the wet suck of skin being tugged from a carcass.

Scrape … one more slice of the knife. The dogs howling and crying from the kennels. Bessie counts Mischief's steps – one, two, three. She wants to cover her ears for what is to come but on she listens.

Eight, nine.

Down below her uncle is waiting.

Twenty-two, twenty-three.

The bells cease.

Mr Mischief is outside the kitchen door. A dreadful hush.

'Come in, Bessie,' her uncle says. 'Don't be afraid.'

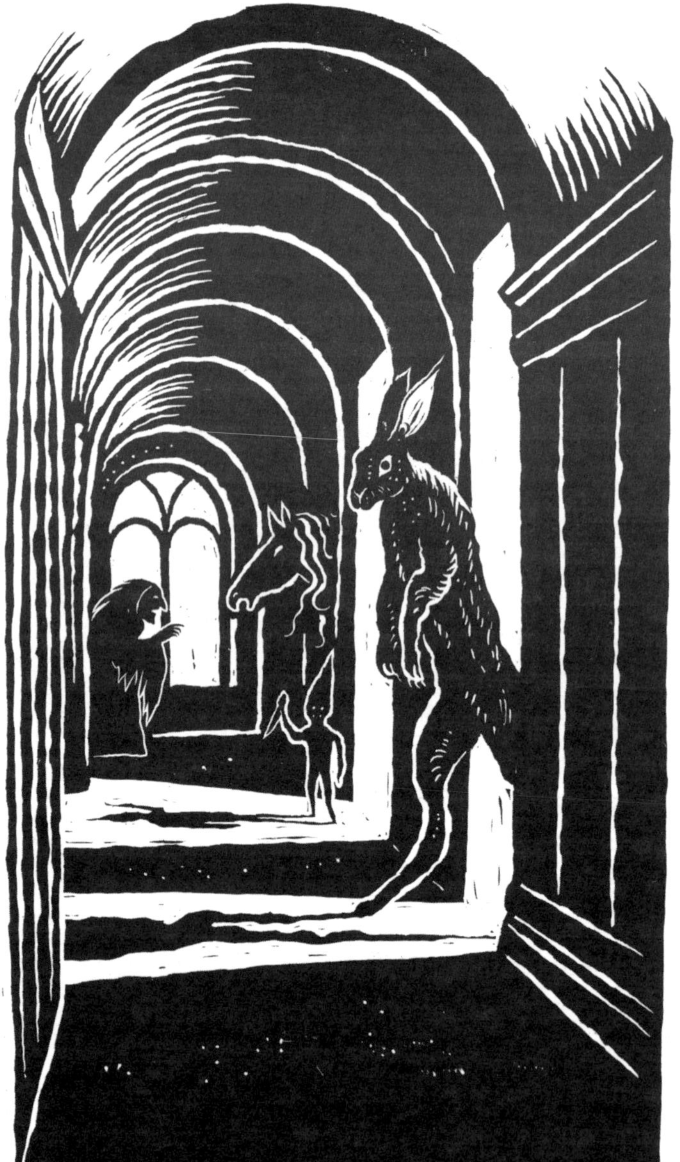

Deaths in the Family

STUART TURTON

'So you think I'm over-reacting?' I ask, wringing my hands together.

Kaley is sitting on the futon opposite, leaning across the gap between us, her face close to mine. Her green eyes are bright in the firelight, her cheeks flushed by heat and the third gin and tonic she's just finished off.

She stares at me sympathetically, rattling the ice in her glass. She's half-smiling – indulging my worry – but enjoying indulging me.

'Ella's six,' she replies. 'She'll get over it.'

'She's stubborn.'

'She's six, Ben.'

I nod, unconvinced. Ella's my only daughter, and my heart didn't start beating until she was born. Being her dad has always been easy. She's good-natured, clever and kind. She asks for things, and I give them to her.

Lately, though, she's started playing up. My mum found a one-word definition of this condition in her big book of parenting clichés. Apparently, she's 'spoiled'.

I took my first steps towards rectifying that tonight by sending Ella to bed after she was rude to her uncle Rob. She called him a 'stupid mango head', which is a pretty good description of Rob as they go, but Ella wouldn't apologise, putting me in the unfortunate position of having to punish the little girl I adore to protect the feelings of the stupid mango head I despise.

'Be firm,' says Kaley softly. 'She'll learn.'

Her fingers brush mine, a spark of longing searing my veins. I meet her eyes, seeing the same longing reflected back. God, I'd tear her clothes off right here except—

I flash a guilty glance towards my brother Rob. Kaley's husband. He's up on the mezzanine, jabbing a finger towards Dad. I'm not sure what's got them so het up, but it must be important. They've been arguing for the last ten minutes, which is nine minutes longer than Dad usually argues about anything.

'You two are just *so* cute,' interrupts my sister Lizzie, playful in the way that somebody juggling shards of glass is playful.

Kaley snaps her hand back, her cheeks flushing.

Everybody else dressed for tonight's party in festive combat chic – Kevlar vests under Christmas jumpers, army boots and antlers. Lizzie never got the hang of survival wear, arguing that surviving isn't the same as dying last. She turned up in a flapper dress, pearls, heels and a lacy headdress. There's a glass of something in her hand, and a lot of something else in her blood.

My sister's every inch the London socialite. She doesn't believe it's a party unless she's floating three feet above it.

My doctor brain automatically summons up the sobriety lecture I give to my patients. The numbers she should call. The people who could help. Then I remember what she asked the hare for and I let it go. She's already got all the help she needs.

A yelp cuts through our awkwardness.

Our heads swivel, trying to work out where it came from. The library we're sitting in is huge, with a teardrop-shaped fireplace and long metal flume at its centre. Bookshelves have been used to subdivide the room into reading nooks, each housing an esoteric assortment of couches, chairs, tables and carefully arranged objets d'art. The Christmas tree is in front of the enormous window, and it's so large that Ella's presents look ridiculously small underneath it.

'Was that one of you?' asks Dad, coming down the spiral staircase from the mezzanine. He wants somebody to say they stubbed their toe or got overexcited by Pictionary. Tonight isn't a good night for anything unexpected.

'I think it came from the kitchen,' replies Lizzie nervously.

I spring up, walking briskly towards the door, which swooshes open automatically. The design of this house is modernist: a lot of wooden cubes connected by glass corridors, surrounded by manicured patches of garden.

My parents had it built when the first of my mum's enormous residual cheques arrived. Five cheques later, it was finished. In five more, it may even be comfortable. They like geometry more than they like cushions.

The blackness of the corridor stretches out ahead of me, cold air kissing my skin. Ceiling lights are supposed to flick on when the door opens but it remains stubbornly dark, aside from a tangle of colourful fairy lights twinkling on the floor further up the passage. When we locked up the house an hour ago, these lights were strung over one of the trees outside.

My heart thumps in my chest, the hairs on my neck prickling.

I fumble in a pocket for my phone, listening to rain patter against the glass walls and roof. Lightning forks down into the distant forest, momentarily blinding us.

Strong fingers grab my arm.

'There's something out there,' says Lizzie, her voice tight.

'I know,' I say, through gritted teeth. 'That's why we're all in here.'

Retrieving my phone, I thumb on the torch as Rob and Dad arrive behind us. I sweep the beam around until it lands on Mum. Or what's left of her.

She's dead, ripped open like a Christmas present. The fairy lights are draped over her remains. One of the bulbs is resting on her left eye, winking at us.

'Oh, god,' cries Lizzie, covering her mouth.

I turn my head away, my vision swimming. Somebody is vomiting behind me.

'No, no, no,' cries Dad, shoving me out of the way to crumple to the floor at Mum's side.

Lightning forks down again, illuminating a huge brown hare with matted fur and burning eyes. It's watching us through the glass, rain running off its coat.

'We need to get back to the library,' I say shakily.

Another light punches a hole in the darkness. It's the torch on Rob's phone. He's kneeling, picking something out of the viscera with his thumb and forefinger. It's a chipped dagger, about the length of my hand.

'Redcaps,' hisses Kaley from behind me. 'They're inside the house.'

'They can't be,' protests Rob. 'I double-checked the defences myself. We did everything right.'

Light footsteps patter further down the corridor. Rob flashes his torch towards them, finding only puddles of muddy rainwater.

'Then what the fuck is that?' insists Kaley.

'We'll figure it out in the library,' I say, grabbing hold of Dad's shoulder.

He's clutching Mum's limp hand, sobbing apologies for his infidelities and years of disregard. He's acting like she didn't have exactly the same faults, like she was a victim of his avarice rather than a fellow practitioner. Their marriage worked because neither of them could love anything more than they loved themself. Vice was their Velcro.

'We have to go, Dad,' I say, trying to tug him away. He ignores me. 'Dad,' I insist, pulling a little harder.

He swings one arm violently, knocking me aside.

'This was your fault,' he says, staring at me with glistening eyes. 'She'd still be alive if not for you and that fucking hare.'

The breath goes out of me, as if I've been hit. I've never heard such vitriol from him. I've never even heard him raise his voice.

Mum was always the shouter in our family, prone to dramatic rages straight out of the Oscar-bait movies she starred in. I was never close to her, none of us were.

Dad is different. He was a failed writer who suddenly unfailed, then kept unfailing all the way to a series of huge bestsellers. As kids, his was the hand we'd reach for when we were unsure, or the lap we'd sit on while he read us *Wuthering Heights* or Jekyll and Hyde. Always the classics. His 'muses', as he pretentiously called them.

He enjoys reciting bits of Shakespeare and drinking Old Fashioneds in places where people can see him drinking Old Fashioneds. He's warm and fun, and he's looking at me now like he'd happily run me over with a car.

Strange jagged shapes are emerging out of the darkness. Kaley lowers her mouth to my ear.

'We have to go,' she says, terrified.

'I can't leave Dad.'

'And he can't leave her,' she says, jerking her chin towards Mum's body. 'Save him or save Ella. You can't do both.'

The shock of hearing my daughter's name jolts me to my feet. She's sleeping upstairs, all alone.

Kaley's fingers slip into mine, pulling me towards the square of light pouring through the open library door where Rob and Lizzie are standing, screaming at us to hurry.

Lightning forks down beyond the windows.

Chancing a look behind me, I see dozens of twisted little creatures in red caps swarming towards Dad, their daggers shining like rows of jagged teeth.

His agonised screams chase us inside the library as Rob hammers the green button that locks the door. Kaley is already dragging a drinks cabinet over to barricade it with.

'It won't hold them,' he says breathlessly. 'We need the blood.'

He gestures to the small ink pot by the fireplace, which Lizzie scoops up. For a second, I worry she might drop it. She's half-blind with tears, pale with shock. Her hands are shaking violently.

Obviously worrying about the same thing, Kaley plucks the ink pot off her and delivers it to Rob.

'I was doing it,' says Lizzie defensively.

Kaley's glance at her is kindly but doubtful. Lizzie throws her arms in the air and stalks away. The problem with being the party girl in the family is that nobody trusts you to be anything else.

Rob withdraws a calligraphy brush covered in blood and swiftly paints an occult symbol on the door we just ran through.

'What about the window?' says Lizzie, trying to save face.

'Bombproof glass,' he replies curtly. 'They test it by firing tank shells at it. The redcaps would have more luck burrowing through the concrete.'

As Rob finishes the last symbol, a sickly red shimmer seeps out of it, covering the door, floor and some of the wall to either side. Any redcap that touches this shimmer will burn.

Satisfied, he runs to the opposite side of the room, obviously planning to seal that door up, too.

Every Christmas, our family gathers here and we paint these symbols on all the ways into the house. Once it's done, we turn the music up, dance, drink and eat, and try to pretend we can't hear the things outside scrambling to get in.

Come dawn, we go back to our lives, like nothing happened.

This routine has kept us safe for the last six years, so why isn't it working tonight?

I glance at Rob, seeing my doubt playing on his face. Everybody helps to draw the symbols, but it's always Rob who checks them over for mistakes. Did he miss something?

I doubt it.

We gave him the job because he's the most diligent of us, the only person we all trust not to half-arse it after a couple of cocktails, which begs the question: what if this wasn't the result of a mistake? It's these fears that carry me to the weapons cupboard to the right of the window. It has a pin lock on it, to which I can't quite remember the code.

I frantically start jabbing in our birthdays.

For years, Dad's been collecting armaments in case the worst should happen, but guns proved hard to come by, so it's mostly lethal bric-a-brac.

The lock clicks. Lizzie's birthday. Figures.

I tug the doors open. At the centre of the collection is a solitary shotgun, which Dad bought from a farmer along with a half-empty box of shells. It's dusty and has never been fired. Not something I'm going to trust my life to when a redcap's bearing down on me.

There are a couple of Japanese swords, which are deadly-looking, but almost impossible to wield without cutting your arms off. I should know, A&E is full of teenagers who found things like these in an attic and started swinging.

There are also several cricket bats, a hunting crossbow and a machete. Mum sarcastically called this cupboard the arse-nil. Looking at it now, I can see why. Nothing in here will help us hold back what's coming.

I lift a machete off the rack and swing it experimentally on my way to the door Rob's painting.

'You can't go out there,' he says, blocking it off.

'I have to get Ella,' I say.

'No, I'm saying you *can't* go out there,' he repeats firmly. 'Both doors are sealed and there are no other ways into this library. All we have to do is sit tight until dawn.'

'Your niece is asleep upstairs,' I say incredulously.

'And if I could do something about that, I would,' he replies.

I try to sidestep him, but it's no use. He's a big brute, engorged by years of private trainers, workouts and protein shakes. He's wearing a tight shirt and tighter waistcoat to show off his muscles, which are so large they almost disguise the crippling lack of self-confidence beneath.

'We don't know what's behind that door,' he says levelly. 'We can't risk letting them in.'

I search his face, unable to believe he could be so callous. This is a child we're talking about. Helpless and alone. How is his conscience not eating him alive?

My eyes go to the faces of Kaley and Lizzie, searching for support.

Lizzie has checked out. She's on the floor, cradling her knees, muttering Dad's name over and over again.

Kaley is watching us blankly. She does this when she's overwhelmed. She packs herself away in some corner of her own mind, like a keepsake wrapped in newspaper. Tomorrow – assuming there is a tomorrow – she'll spend the day in bed, sobbing.

'You're an arsehole,' I say to my brother.

Suddenly, every light goes out, plunging us into darkness.

'They must have cut the power,' says Rob. A second later the backup generators kick in, powering the emergency spotlights.

For a second, the hare's mangled shadow is splashed across the wall behind Rob. Hearing me gasp, he turns to look for himself.

Seeing my chance, I knee him in the balls, sending him crashing to the floor.

He writhes, screaming after me as I unlock the door and sprint into the corridor.

This time the lights flick on, their glare reflecting off the glass walls and making it impossible to see outside. That's a mercy. There are worse things than redcaps out tonight.

I arrive in the entrance hall, which is a square box with glass walls, a floating metal staircase and passages leading to the study and workshops. A modern chandelier dangles precipitously overhead, made up of shards of glass, metal, mirrors and gems.

Kaley designed this for Mum, who immediately took to calling it the 'junkelier'.

It was jealousy. In a family of artists, Kaley was always the most talented of us. The deal with the hare just meant more people saw it. I know that still bugs her. She would have preferred to earn her success rather than have it gifted to her.

Three knocks boom against the front doors, rattling the chandelier. There's a pause, then they come again. Each one hits me like a body blow, rousing some deep, primal terror.

I grip the machete tight then run up the stairs two at a time, charging down a passageway lined with doors. It's decorated with Mum's acting awards and favourable reviews of Dad's books, each framed and uplit.

I avert my gaze. God knows when I'll be able to look at those covers again without crying.

My foot catches on something, sending me sprawling to the ground, the machete skittering away into the darkness.

Glancing back, I realise a tripwire's been strung along the corridor. Steps pelt towards me, and pain explodes in my right palm.

I instinctively try to pull my injured hand closer, but a dagger's pinning it to the floorboards. A redcap is hopping up and down, clapping giddily at its work. It's about the height of a garden gnome and is wearing a saggy human face, ineptly stitched to its head. Two red pupils stare out through the eye holes and lank hair is dangling down from beneath a Santa hat dunked in blood. It's barefoot, wearing what looks like a filthy blue cardigan, probably taken from a child.

Another redcap emerges from the darkness. The two of them point and grunt, arguing between themselves, waving their daggers in my direction.

I slowly slide my left hand along my body, hoping to free my right while they're distracted.

A huge weight lands on my chest, knocking the wind from me.

It's another redcap. Bigger than the others, carrying a staff embedded with razor blades. This one's wearing my dad's severed face.

I howl in grief, bringing scratchy laughter from the creature.

'Daddy.' Ella's opened her door a crack and is peering down the corridor at me, rubbing her tired eyes.

The redcaps stop dead, pointing excitedly towards her.

'Get back inside, love,' I scream desperately. 'Barricade the door.'

The big redcap that was on my chest leaps down, making for my daughter.

I rip the dagger out of my palm and snatch hold of the creature by the leg, swinging it at the wall as hard as I can, splattering its head across the brickwork.

The remaining two charge me, but I kick one of them back down the passage. The other leaps out of the way, slashing my shin as it does.

Wincing in pain, I club it with the dead redcap I'm holding, then stamp on its back, grinding its fragile bones underfoot.

'Daddy?' calls Ella, frightened. 'What's happening?'

'Nothing,' I say, dropping the tiny dagger. 'Stay there, I'm coming to get you.'

I'm swaying, the pain from my injuries starting to overcome the adrenaline that's propping me up. I'm almost to my daughter's door when a dozen more redcaps emerge silently from the shadows, cutting me off.

They've been watching this entire time, letting me think I've won.

The machete I lost earlier is a little to my right. It won't be enough, but I pick it up anyway, trying not to pass out as a wave of agony shoots up my arm.

'Come on then, you pricks,' I say weakly, feigning bravado.

They exchange nervous looks, the tenor of their chittering changing to something recognisably fearful. A few of them scurry away, then a few more, until the whole lot of them scatter and flee.

Astonished by my victory, I open my mouth to jeer, only to notice the incredibly long, razor-sharp talons that are curling over my right shoulder.

Something cold and wet presses itself against my back. It reeks of old bodies on a slab. Dirty hair falls across my cheek, dripping rainwater onto my jumper.

I stand perfectly still, too scared to move. Even if I could, those talons are digging into my shoulder, piercing my skin.

It sniffs me. Then again.

'Old,' it hisses disappointedly. 'Tough. Bitter ... corrupt.'

No sooner has it passed judgement than it withdraws with a vast rustling.

I wait until the corridor's silent then glance around nervously. Whatever it was, it's vanished.

I could sob with relief, but I don't have time. I don't know how far the redcaps have run, or when they'll be back.

On heavy legs I stumble into Ella's bedroom, the glow of her nightlight illuminating her Christmas stocking and ruffled unicorn covers. Her bed is empty.

Panic fogs my brain, but before it can settle, my daughter barrels straight into me. I scoop her warm little body into my arms, hugging her tight. She smells like soap and sleep.

'Daddy, what happened to you?' she asks, her arms around my shoulders, her cheek against mine.

'I fell over,' I say.

'You're bleeding.'

'I fell over *a lot*,' I say, forcing a smile.

'Can you doctor it?'

'Of course I can, I can doctor anything,' I say, peeking outside, checking for danger.

The creature I encountered earlier is upside down on the ceiling, clinging to the rafters. It's vaguely human-shaped, though with talons instead of hands and long, spindly limbs. Its face is blue and has the texture of bark. It's wearing a tattered dress that's dangling down like a frayed cobweb. I have the sense things won't go well for anybody who gets caught in it.

Thankfully, it's not blocking our route to the staircase, and it doesn't appear to have noticed us. It might even be asleep.

'What the hell is that?' I mutter under my breath.

'That's Black Annis,' replies my daughter, apparently unperturbed by the bird woman that's taken residence among the rafters. 'I read about her in Grandfather's books. She's a witch. She eats children.'

That's why she didn't kill me earlier, I realise. I'm old meat. It's Ella she's after.

Still holding my little girl, I creep into the corridor very slowly and start walking towards the staircase.

I'm barely breathing, for fear of making any sound.

We're nearly at the end of the corridor when I hear Kaley's tremulous voice calling up to us from the bottom of the staircase.

'Ben, are you okay?'

Black Annis's head whips towards us. Her ravenous gaze passes over me, narrowing on Ella. Shrieking in triumph, the witch lopes along the ceiling, her sharp talons shredding the beams into splinters.

I turn and run, flying down the staircase. Redcaps are swarming into the lobby from the direction of the workshops. They must have followed Kaley's voice.

My only option is to charge through them. Clutching Ella, I brace myself for a collision, only to watch a redcap come arcing through the air in front of me, leaving a ribbon of blood in its wake. Another follows. Then two more, bouncing off the far walls.

Lizzie, Rob and Kaley have emerged from the library and are thwacking the little bastards with cricket bats from the arse-nil.

'This way,' Lizzie screams, carving a path towards us.

Hearing us on the stairs, Rob glances in our direction – his eyes going wide when he sees what's chasing us.

'Holy shit!' he cries out.

I leap the last few stairs with Ella in my arms, landing awkwardly but making precious strides towards the safety of the library. A few more steps and—

There's a rush of air as Black Annis bounds over our heads, landing heavily in front of us, blocking our escape. She's monstrous, a head taller than me, her skin covered in welts and lesions.

Rob and Lizzie are being pinned back by the redcaps, who have learned to keep their distance. There's no way past this monster. No way to reach the library.

Black Annis unfurls a long, sharp talon towards Ella. 'Give,' she hisses.

I shake my head, clinging tight to the only thing I've ever loved. I consider bolting back up the stairs, or trying to dart around, but there's no use in trying. The witch is too fast, and I'm spent. Every breath is a struggle.

I press Ella's face against my chest, so she can't see what's coming, then turn my back on Black Annis. My body is the only shield I have.

'Close your eyes, my love,' I whisper, dread creeping up my spine.

There's a whistling sound, then an almighty crash, followed by a howl of rage and pain. I gingerly open my eyes, then even more gingerly look behind me. The chandelier has fallen, shards of metal, glass and stone impaling the witch, who's writhing in pain.

Her terrible eyes fix on Ella. A long arm stretches out then drops lifeless to the ground.

I look at Kaley in astonishment. She's holding the pulley rope that had previously kept the chandelier suspended.

'Your mum was right,' she says darkly. 'The room looks better without it.'

Kaley helps me limp into the library, while Lizzie puts her arm around Ella, who's chattering in shock, words tripping over themselves as she tells her aunt everything that happened upstairs.

The two of them have always been close, despite my best efforts to keep them apart. Lizzie's lifestyle isn't exactly aspirational and my hopes for Ella stretch well beyond knowing which uppers and downers work best together.

As soon as we're inside, Kaley locks the door and Rob snatches up the ink pot, painting the protective symbols once more.

I slump to the ground in exhaustion. Through the window, I see the hare watching me through those burning eyes, its mangled ears twitching. I have the sense it's amused.

I close my eyes, remembering the first time we met.

It was seven years ago. I was hiking in the forest when I spotted it on the trail. It was bigger than any hare I'd seen before. More watchful. More terrifying.

I knew straight away that it had been waiting for me.

I don't remember quite what it said, or how it happened, only that it could see inside of me, to the thing I wanted most in the entire world. It said I could have it, for a price.

After I agreed, it visited the rest of my family. One at a time, and always with the same offer. Anything they wanted in life, for a price in death.

Nobody took much convincing.

Lizzie chose eternal youth and a life of hedonistic freedom without consequence. Rob – stammering, shy Rob – craved admiration and respect, and ended up marketing misogyny to right-wing nut jobs on social media. Kaley kept it simple, opting actually to make money from her art, while Mum and Dad breathed life into long-dead careers.

What we didn't realise until later was that the hare wasn't willing to hang around waiting for our souls. The first Christmas after we signed the deal, it sent the redcaps. Only a handful, and only for me at first.

They slaughtered my best friend and my girlfriend, along with dozens of innocent passersby, and chased me and Ella halfway across London. They had us cornered when dawn came, forcing them to scatter underground.

That was when I learned the rules.

Exhausted, bloody and terrified, I called a family meeting to warn everybody that we had to prepare ourselves for whatever the hare threw at us the next year.

Somehow Dad managed to trace another family who'd made a deal like ours. Most of them were dead, but the few who'd survived had learned how to protect themselves. They gave him an old book of occult stuff and that's when our Christmas parties started.

'How the fuck do they keep getting in?' demands Rob, as he finishes drawing the last symbol.

Fearful glances are exchanged, everybody suspecting the same thing.

'Come on,' scoffs Kaley. 'We don't really think this is sabotage, do we?'

'What else could it be?' replies Lizzie, who's hugging Ella tight against her body.

Kaley shoots a look at Rob. 'Maybe one of the symbols was smudged—'

'I checked them,' he interrupts firmly.

'That's all it would take,' she carries on helplessly. 'If one of those things got in—'

'I checked the fucking symbols, Kaley,' he snarls. 'They were fine. This wasn't an accident. Somebody's done this to us.'

There's another round of nervous glances, interrupted by Lizzie, who's taken a few steps closer to the window.

'Can anybody else hear that?' she asks, cocking her head.

In the hush that follows, I faintly hear a strange drumming sound outside. 'Now you mention it …'

The window explodes inwards, jagged shards of glass flying across the room as a black horse leaps through, snorting and stamping its hooves.

My eyes find Ella, who's ducked out of sight behind an overturned couch.

Rob's hit the floor beside me, while Kaley is backed against the far wall. Lizzie is staring in stunned befuddlement at the whinnying horse. It's black as midnight, with seaweed for a mane and tail, and a coat that ripples like the surface of a lake.

The horse prances sideways, bumping into her with its hindquarters. Instead of bouncing off it, her left arm and shoulder sink into its body, as though she'd plunged them into a bath.

'Help me!' she screams, struggling to free herself.

I stand up, intending to grab her arm, but Ella's panicked voice holds me in place. 'Daddy, don't!' she screams from behind the couch. 'It's a kelpie. If you touch it, you'll get stuck.'

I stare at my sister, my heart tearing in half.

A rough hand grabs my arm, twisting it up behind my back.

Before I can react, I'm pushed towards the horse, my flailing forearm sticking fast to the kelpie's shoulder.

Screams of outrage erupt from my family.

Ella's trying to get to me, but Kaley is holding her tight. In contrast, Rob is backing away with a look of horror on his face. I suddenly realise that he was the one who pushed me.

The kelpie whinnies in triumph, rearing up on its hind legs before leaping out of the window with me and Lizzie still attached to it.

Bouncing violently against the muddy earth, I'm dragged along by my trapped arm as pounding hooves spray turf.

It's raining hard but the ground is riddled with glowing cracks, spitting embers and soot. Through them I can see the world below, the one forgotten and scorned. There are thousands of redcaps down there, along with monsters without a name, wreathed in fire. I see many-headed giants and twisted witches, hobs and sprites, creatures so old they tormented the first men.

That's what's coming for us.

The redcaps and Black Annis. The kelpie. They were a warm-up. Every foul thing under the earth is waiting its turn to claim us.

The house is receding behind me, the brown hare sitting patiently on its hind legs in front of the broken window. A soul is due and it's come to collect.

I need to get free. I need to get back to Ella.

'Ben,' says Lizzie weakly. Her speech is slurred with pain. She's struggling to stay conscious. 'My ... my leg.'

I glance at it. She's got a jagged fragment of glass sticking out of her thigh. It must have hit her when the window exploded.

'Cut yourself ... free ... for ... for Ella.'

I stare at the glass, realising what Lizzie is getting at. My arm is the only part of my body stuck to the kelpie, which means I can free myself by hacking it off.

I gag at the thought, my subconscious delivering excuses not to do it. I'd pass out from the pain. I'd die of blood loss. I don't have tourniquets or bandages to patch myself up with.

It's insane.

'It's the only way,' I mutter to myself.

Dozens of monsters are climbing out of the cracks in the earth, to join the ones already shambling, slithering, crawling and swooping towards the broken library window. I imagine Ella, surrounded by teeth and claws and terror, screaming for me to protect her.

One arm to save the only thing I've ever really loved. It's a small price to pay.

I reach across, wrenching the shard of glass from my sister's thigh. That's when I realise I'm wearing a thick Christmas jumper. Mum gave them to me and Rob as presents.

I'm not stuck. The sleeve of my jumper is.

My heart soars. I check Lizzie, hoping for a similar miracle, but half her body is submerged in the kelpie. There's no way to free her.

'I'm sorry, Liz,' I say, wriggling my way out of my sweater and splatting onto the muddy earth.

Rolling onto my stomach, I watch the kelpie run straight into the lake near the forest, diving under the water with my baby sister still attached to it.

I get weakly to my feet, the world bouncing up and down.

There is a sea of monsters between me and the house, and no obvious way around them, unless ...

I check left, taking off at a sprint towards the garage. Dad was an avid collector of cars that cost a fortune to insure, but he never actually drove. I'm not even sure he liked driving. It was their beauty he paid for.

I slip through the side door into the garage, collecting the keys for his armour-plated Land Rover. Apparently, it once belonged to some sheikh, who sold it because he wanted it in gold rather than silver.

My hand's trembling and I almost drop the keys. My imagination keeps showing me movies of Ella being ripped apart by Black Annis.

Manoeuvring past the Ferraris and Aston Martins, I unlock the car and slide inside, covering the expensive leather in mud and blood. The control for the garage's roller door is on the steering wheel. I hit the button and it ascends with teeth-grinding stateliness.

It gets halfway up when I decide that's good enough.

I slam the car into gear, hit the accelerator and wheel-spin out of the garage, tearing through the bottom of the roller door as I speed towards the library.

Alerted by the roaring engine, redcaps turn and disintegrate as the Land Rover ploughs through them.

I mow dozens of them down, their blood and innards smearing the windscreen. Unable to see where I'm going, I flick the wipers, then the spray, trying to clear it. I must nearly be at the—

The car smashes into the house, the airbag exploding in my face.

Gasping, I open the door and stumble out. My ears are ringing and I'm seeing double, but I need to get into the library before they regroup. Wobbling forward, I half-climb, half-fall over the shattered library window.

Most of the bookshelves have been knocked over and there's a pool of water on the floor, where the rain is swirling inside.

Ingeniously, Rob and Kaley have drawn protective symbols on the broken window frame, creating a dead zone the creatures can't cross.

It won't last long. Every drop of rain smears the symbols a little more. In a few minutes, they'll be washed away completely.

Hobbling forward, I see Kaley cradling a sobbing Ella on the same futons where we sat earlier in the evening. They turn their heads as I approach, Ella immediately disentangling herself to run straight into my arms.

'You survived,' blurts out Kaley.

'What happened to Aunt Lizzie?' asks Ella, her face pressed against my stomach.

'She's gone, love,' I say, wishing I could think of something more reassuring. I've never been good at comforting bereaved families. Even my own, it turns out.

Rob emerges from behind one of the stacks, doing up his zip. He hesitates, then hangs his head.

'Fuck,' he says, upon seeing me.

'You tried to kill me!' I yell, jabbing a finger at him.

'Yes, I did,' he confirms, without any hint of remorse.

'Why?' I demand.

'You know why,' he growls.

I flash a glance at Kaley, whose face has flooded with guilt. 'Nothing happened between us,' she stammers.

'It didn't,' I confirm. 'I just really wanted it to.'

Rob's eyes narrow in confusion, then out of nowhere, he starts laughing. It's a strange, awful sound, amidst all this death and fear. 'I didn't ... Christ, you really think ... me and Kaley have been over for years.' He shakes his head, catching his breath. 'You're my brother, Ben. I'd never – not for *that*.'

'Then why did you do it?' I demand, wrong-footed.

'If one of us kills somebody we love, the contract we signed with the hare is nullified. It's a loophole or something. Dad found out about it from that other family, the ones who taught him the symbols. That's what we were arguing about earlier. He wanted to sacrifice you.

Fucking rat poison in your drink. I was trying to talk him out of it.'

My mouth hangs open in disbelief. 'Dad wanted to—' I can't even finish. 'Why?'

'Do you remember what we were like before the hare? You, me, Lizzie and Dad? We were so close, Ben. Not rich, or famous, but happy. Then you brought that fucking thing into our lives. One by one, you lured us out into the woods to meet it.'

'That was part of the deal,' I say hollowly. 'It wanted me to – it wanted to meet all of you.' My voice rises an octave in guilt. 'You didn't have to accept what it was offering.'

'But you knew we would, didn't you? You'd heard its voice, felt it wriggle around inside your mind. You knew how convincing it was.'

'How long did *you* object for, Rob?' interjects Kaley. 'How long did any of us? It's not like Ben forced us to—'

'It doesn't matter,' he interrupts firmly. 'The only way this ends is with a sacrifice. One of us has to kill—'

Kaley moves so quickly it takes me a second to realise what she's done. One minute my brother's talking, the next he's reeling back clutching his throat, blood seeping between his fingers.

Backing away in disgust, Kaley flings a shard of the broken window to the ground. She'd used it to slit his throat.

'What have you done?' I scream as my brother drops to his knees.

I go down with him, but it's too late. He gurgles his last breath then falls sideways. I stare up at Kaley angrily.

She's trembling, pale with shock. 'Did it work?'

I glance at the window. The brown hare is sitting on its hind legs, watching us through those pitiless yellow eyes. Behind it, hundreds of redcaps are climbing out of those glowing cracks in the earth. Kelpies are emerging from the lake, shaking water off their seaweed manes. The sky is filled with dark shadows, while rotting wolves come growling out of the forest.

'No,' I say.

'Because I don't love him,' she whimpers, frantically wiping his blood from her hands. 'I thought maybe there was something left. A bit of what we'd had before … before he became—' She gestures at his body. 'That.'

My heart thumping, I look at Rob. I remember Mum and Dad butchered in the corridor and Lizzie drowned in the lake. And then I imagine Ella among them. Caught in that horse's skin. A redcap wearing her face.

Every part of me feels like it's trying to scream.

An idea sleets through my brain, my blood freezing over. Something dreadful, and possible. A chance. Maybe our only chance.

'We need to find the contract,' I say, trying to keep my voice from breaking. I can already feel a sob rising in my chest.

'What contract?' asks Kaley.

'The one we all signed with the hare seven years ago. If we destroy it, there's no deal.' I glance back at the monsters swarming towards the house. 'This will all be over.'

Hope shines in Kaley's eyes. 'Do you know where it is?'

'More than likely it's in Dad's study, on the other side of the kitchen.' I point at the far door, the one with Mum and Dad's bodies behind it.

Kaley instinctively flicks a look in the direction I'm pointing. The second she does, I leap forward, scooping a glass shard off the ground and driving it into her back. It's the cleanest, quickest death I can give her.

She exhales heavily, then slumps into my arms.

Howling in grief, I withdraw the shard from her body, then stab her again.

'I'm sorry,' I whisper into her ear, lowering her to the ground. 'I'm so sorry. I have to save Ella.'

'Ella ...' She coughs blood. 'Ella's not ...' She swallows, her eyes finding my face. 'Who was ... her mother?'

I open my mouth, then shut it again. It was Denise, wasn't it? My last girlfriend. She gave birth to Ella, then the redcaps got her. No ... no, it can't have been Denise. She couldn't ... or I couldn't. That's why we – all those doctors. All those meaningless words and shakes of the head.

I strain for the rest of it, trying to remember. Why can't I remember?

'Why ... why are there ... no ... no ... pictures ... as a baby?' Kaley licks her lips, struggling to breathe. 'What was ... your ... your ... heart's desire, Ben?'

I glance at Ella. The hare has come inside and is sitting calmly in front of her with its head bowed. My daughter's kneeling down, staring into those terrible eyes. A second later, she reaches out a hand in benediction.

'Ella sabotaged … us …' Kaley sighs, then goes limp in my arms.

A huge sob rolls out of me as I check her pulse. Her neck is warm, but there's no life left in it. Everything she could have been, I've taken from her. Everything we could have had, I've tossed away. I'll never forgive myself.

I lower Kaley's body gently to the ground.

'The hare says it's over now,' says Ella with a peculiar calmness. 'He says he's proud of you. He had to know if you were worthy. If you could protect me.'

She smiles happily. 'You passed the test, Daddy. He says we're going to do great things together.'

The hare has vanished and the cracks that riddled the garden are closed. There's nothing outside now except rain, darkness and whatever future I've just bought us. Questions skid through my mind – *Who was her mother? Why are there no pictures of her as a baby?* – but Ella nuzzles against me and they all go away. Whatever price I paid for this, I'd pay it again. That's what being a father is.

Sacrifice.

I hobble over to Ella and scoop her up. For a second, her skin feels like fur.

A NOTE ON THE AUTHORS

ROSIE ANDREWS was born in Liverpool. Her first novel, *The Leviathan*, was an instant *Sunday Times* bestseller and was shortlisted for the HWA Debut Crown and the Goldsboro Books Glass Bell award. She teaches English and lives in Hertfordshire with her husband, her daughter and their dog.

JENN ASHWORTH is a novelist and memoirist. Her latest book, a memoir of walking in the north, is *The Parallel Path*, published by Sceptre. She is a Fellow of the Royal Society of Literature and a Professor of Writing at Lancaster University.

SUNYI DEAN is a multi-award-losing author who was born in Texas, grew up in Hong Kong, and now resides in North England. She writes speculative fiction with a dark slant, and her debut novel, *The Book Eaters*, was an instant *Sunday Times* bestseller.

JANICE HALLETT is the author of five best-selling novels. Her debut, *The Appeal*, won the CWA New Dagger Award 2022. Her second, *The Twyford Code*, won Crime & Thriller Book of the Year in the British Book Awards 2023. Her first murder mystery for children, *A Box Full of Murders*, was published in 2025 by Puffin.

JANE JOHNSON is a Cornish writer and publisher. She works as Fiction Publishing Director for HarperCollins, where her authors include George RR Martin, Robin Hobb, Raymond Feist and Dean Koontz. She is the author of twenty novels for children and adults, including *The Sea Gate*, *The White Hare* and *Secrets of the Bees*.

DAN JONES is a historian, broadcaster, and award-winning journalist whose books have sold over two million copies worldwide. His non-fiction includes *The Plantagenets*, *Powers and Thrones*, and *Henry V*. His fiction includes the Essex Dogs trilogy. He has created numerous TV series, and writes and hosts the podcast This Is History. He is a Fellow of the Royal Historical Society and a Trustee of Historic Royal Palaces.

ABIR MUKHERJEE is the bestselling author of historical and modern day crime thrillers. His books have sold over half a million copies in the UK and won numerous awards including the Theakston Old Peculier Crime Novel of the Year, and the British Book Awards Crime & Thriller Novel of the Year.

REBECCA NETLEY is a writer of long and short fiction; her debut novel, *The Whistling*, published by Penguin in 2022, won the Exeter Novel Prize and was longlisted for the Michael Ondaatje Prize. *The Whistling* has been adapted for stage. It was followed by *The Black Feathers* which was published by Michael Joseph in 2023.

STUART TURTON is the author of *The Seven Deaths of Evelyn Hardcastle*, *The Devil and the Dark Water* and *Sunday Times* bestseller *The Last Murder at the End of the World*. He very much hopes you like them, but your mileage may vary.